DEATH IN A
Gilded Frame

CECELIA TICHI

Death in a Gilded Frame

Copyright © 2023 by Cecelia Tichi

ISBNs:
979-8-9851216-8-1 (paperback)
979-8-9851216-9-8 (eBook)

The Val and Roddy DeVere Gilded Age Series

A Gilded Death
Murder, Murder, Murder in Gilded Central Park
A Fatal Gilded High Note
A Deadly Gilded Free Fall
A Gilded Drowning Pool
Death in a Gilded Frame

Chapter One

Newport, July 1, 1899

SHARP SEA AIR AND tattered clouds greeted my husband and me when the carriage pulled up at the front entrance of our oceanside cottage, Drumcliffe. Our butler opened the front door, the footmen bowed, the housekeeper curtsied, and a maid took our dog, Velvet, for her feeding. Days earlier, a network of ferries, railroads, and teamsters delivered trunks and crates to the rear entrance, and our household staff wove a spell of flawless expectation. Every room was readied for the new summer season, a marvel of fine-tuned precision.

Awed and grateful, I was aware that our household staff knew Drumcliffe better than I, the lady of the house who was heading into a fourth summer by the Atlantic Ocean in Newport, Rhode Island. My husband had spent a good many youthful summers here with his parents and knew the floorplan by heart. I ought to know the twenty-room cottage—or was it thirty?—just as I ought to be well versed in the conduct required of a Lady in Society. Raised in Rocky Mountain mining camps, I graduated in due course from the Fourth Ward School in Virginia City, Nevada. Manners were second nature, but I had married into a cosmos demanding etiquette. My husband overlooked countless blunders in good humor while a good friend tutored me in silver service, French furniture, and other details I ought to know as Mrs. Roderick Windham DeVere of New York City.

Again this summer, my *oughts* would accrue, most in the shallows, but one to sink deep into the abyss of homicide. It was no secret that I, Valentine Mackle DeVere, together with my lawyer husband, Roddy, were thought to have a taste for murders. In the past year, a shocking number of violent deaths had swerved at us, and our sleuthing became a safeguard from legal troubles and personal peril. At times, the killers we exposed surprised the police, but our narrow escapes stirred rumors. Fair to say, our reputation preceded us, as did Society's suspicions that our marriage was utterly bizarre.

Murder was not yet in mind at this moment as Roddy requested afternoon tea for two in the Lafayette drawing room, which proved my point about the Drumcliffe layout. Doffing a cloak, I heard his persuasive tenor voice, "This way, dear" as he turned us down a hallway into a wing of the cottage we had rarely occupied. On this afternoon of our arrival, the room named for the Marquis De Lafayette was Roddy's choice for a talk about a large painting of a brooding man counting gold coins near a mud hut. *The Counting House* was a DeVere family ancestral portrait purchased in the Netherlands years ago by Roddy's parents. It was supposedly in the "School of Rembrandt."

I loathed the dark, dismal painting on sight and wanted it permanently hung in a remote drawing room. The painting had sparked a marital tiff early this spring with the redecoration of our *Empire* room in the Upper East Side chateau that was now my permanent home in the city. My decorator, the spirited Elsie De Wolfe, brought new light and air to the drab room, and she suggested an out-of-the-way hall for the painting she termed "misbegotten." On her advice, the brooding man henceforth counted his coins in a back hallway beside the wall-mounted telephone box.

Offended, Roddy determined to have an evaluation once and for all without delay, so we had *The Counting House* crated and packed for Newport, where a renowned art dealer was about to open a gallery for the season.

I also hoped that my husband had forgotten another portrait idea that recently gripped him. My blue-eyed, broad-shouldered Roddy, a fifth-generation Knickerbocker New Yorker, imagined that a likeness of me on canvas in oil paints and set inside a frame would grace his study on the second floor of our house at 620 Fifth Avenue. He hinted that I might sit for a portrait this summer in Newport.

I tried to joke my way out of the picture. Last week, sipping one of Roddy's special cocktails in our favorite green velvet Bergere chairs in an upstairs drawing room in New York, I quipped about a title. How about *"Daughter of Irish Immigrant Silver King Comes to Gotham."* Our French bulldog Velvet bounded into the drawing room, and Roddy added, "...'with French Bulldog on Lap.'"

We laughed and continued joking. "Roddy, I would feel framed."

"A lovely Rococo frame to complement your eyes, my dear." He winked and sipped.

"Eyes to follow you around the room," I said. "You won't have a minute to yourself with me staring out from your study wall."

"While I toil on upcoming court cases," he replied, "your lovely gaze will inspire me."

"Blarney," I said with the Irish dismissal favored by my papa. We had laughed, finished our drinks, and said no more about my sitting for a portrait as we readied to depart for the summer.

Here in Drumcliffe's Lafayette room on the first day of July, I looked past the spindly furniture at walls of massed paintings in frames large and small. "Roddy," I said, "where could we put *The Counting House*? There must be fifty pictures on each of these walls."

For the moment, my husband looked distracted. "Mother went mad for pictures, Val, and dealers spotted her a mile away. Each time my parents went abroad, Mother rushed to the galleries and never said no...that is, until a few years ago."

I could supply the date when Rufus and Eleanor DeVere abruptly halted their world travels, stunned to find themselves nearly bankrupt. They promptly journeyed to the West in a futile attempt to recover the family fortune in the wake of Rufus's disastrous Wall Street investments, not to mention the misguided notion that their law school student son, Roddy, needed to dry out from alcohol.

Little did the senior DeVeres guess they would be rescued from insolvency by their son's hobby of newfangled cocktails. They could date their recovery from the evening when they dined at Nevada's Virginia City hotel where Papa and I were having dinner at a nearby table. The couple's blue-eyed son caught my attention when he took over the hotel bar for the dazzling demonstration of a flaming Blue Blazer Cocktail, which set my heart racing and launched the love affair that led to our wedding. To this day, the DeVeres were loath to admit they owed their recovery to Roddy's Blue Blazer—and to the dirt-like ores that made my late papa a rich Silver King.

A slight "a-hem" just then signaled our footman Chalmers's arrival with a tea tray, while a second footman, Bronson, stood inside the doorframe. I recalled an etiquette stricture about two servants necessary for the proper serving of tea.

"Thank you, Chalmers and Bronson," I said, "but I will pour the tea myself."

The footmen bowed out, and I poured tea into two eggshell-thin cups my mother-in-law insisted were perfect for Drumcliffe. A matching plate held ginger cookies and silver tongs. I would not pick a bone over bone china, but I could pour tea and reach for a cookie. Etiquette had limits.

"Roddy, so many paintings on these walls...like a crazy quilt."

My husband stirred sugar into his tea and flashed a sly smile. "Look at the portraits, Val. Look at the poses."

I gazed at ruff-collared Elizabethan nobleman peering into the distance and a fresh-faced peasant girl toting wood buckets down a path, followed by a swordsman on guard with a flashing saber. The portraits ranged from busts to full figures posing head-to-toe, a Doge in Venice beside a woman with hair so high she must be Madame Pompadour.

"Val, I thought we could get ideas about dimensions for your portrait...and possible poses."

"Oh, Roddy, not that again...." So, he had not forgotten my portrait. If I joked, could we laugh it off? I held out my cup. "*Woman in Newport Holds Fragile Tea Cup*?"

"No more jokes...please, Val." My husband's gaze hovered at frustration. He wanted to come to terms, while I would postpone the notion forever.

"Roddy..." I said, "in the West, if you had only seen the snow-slashed peaks, or the blue mountain lakes of the Rocky Mountains...if you watched the cobalt blue turn to amber in the setting sun." I looked closely into my husband's eyes. "How could a frame compete?"

My foolish comparison of portraits and landscapes brought a predictable frown to my husband's handsome face. Admittedly, the pictures in the house my papa built for the two of us in Nevada fell far short of art with a capital A. Papa made sure that our Queen Anne Revival house had up-to-date furniture and the latest plumbing and steam heat. The art on the walls, however, was mass produced Currier & Ives lithographs of different seasons titled *Home, Sweet Home.*

If my mama had lived, our household art might have gone beyond prints sold by the thousands, and Mama would surely have frowned at the life-sized nudes on the walls of saloons where Papa and I often enjoyed a meal. For "taste," however, I relied on instinct and advice from those who knew better, including Roddy and my friend Cassie who was already at her mansion-sized summer cottage, Seabright.

Roddy took two cookies. "Val," he said, "let's talk about portraits that we both have seen here in Newport, portraits of ladies and gentlemen too."

I took a cookie and sipped my tea. Ladies and business titans kept portrait painters busy these days, and artists found their way to Newport in the summer season and reaped commissions, especially when lubricated by cocktails at cottages such as Mrs. Harry Pratt's Arleigh or the Vanderbilts' Breakers. The drinks were sometimes devised by my husband on request, though Roddy's mixological expertise was a closely kept secret, as he wished.

I suspected that rubbing shoulders with portrait artists gave my husband this idea of a painting of his wife. Roddy was no soft touch, but I had seen him taken aside at a reception by Benjamin Curtis Porter, whose portrait of Alva Belmont had caused what Society termed "a stir" when it was unveiled at the Belmonts' Newport cottage, Belcourt.

Alva's portrait by Benjamin Porter was the example on Roddy's mind. "I believe Porter would be available this season for you, Val. His striking rendition of Alva—"

"—absolutely not, Roddy. The rope of pearls across her chest looks like a gun belt, and that fixture in her hair looks like devil's horns." I bit my cookie with a snap. "And you needn't bring up Boldini. His portraits remind me of nude ladies on the walls of Virginia City saloons...bar nudes dressed in couturier gowns. And forget John Sawyer Sargent."

"...*Singer* Sargent, Val. It's John Singer Sargent."

"Singer," I corrected myself. "He would want me to come to London or Paris or Italy. When we travel, I want to see the sights, not be stuck posing for days in an artist's studio, not moving a muscle.

"Then, Val, I think we might have a solution. Cuveen's gallery is sponsoring a distinguished portrait painter. We will have *The Counting House* appraised and see about having you painted this summer by André Cole."

"Cole..." I said, with neither a *no* nor *yes*. The artist's name was vaguely familiar from social chitchat in the city about a new portrait painter said to mix his colors from rare minerals and employ techniques in homage to artists from the Renaissance to the present day.

Fact and fancy had circulated about André Cole for the past several months, but neither I nor Roddy paid much attention when a death involving a reported plunge down a staircase took us to Chicago. Before that, a series of murders in Central Park and a homicide last winter at the opera—it all kept us busy. As for André Cole, I could not recall seeing the man's work, so I had no basis for refusal or rebuttal. Roddy's earnestness, however, was not to be dismissed. He had said my portrait would be a cherished gift to him and suggested we would visit the Cuveen gallery and see about it.

"See about" was Roddy's term. Neither of us guessed we would soon see about a murder—and about the suspicion that we, ourselves, were involved.

Chapter Two

THE NEWPORT SEASON BEGAN with registration at the Casino, a recreational center on Bellevue Avenue where members signed in to announce they had arrived at their various cottages. An inked signature in the membership book proclaimed the beginning of luncheons, dinners, parties, balls, and sports from croquet to yacht regattas. The Casino registry was Newport's social megaphone.

While Roddy registered us, I bicycled to Seabright in hopes of seeing my friend Cassie who was here with her children. I had not cycled here since last summer when a bad fall sent me to the sofa with a sprained ankle. As it turned out, my bicycle had been sabotaged, and the repercussions were dire. I tried not to recall it while pedaling past the cliff where my mishap occurred. My new bicycle suit of cotton twill fit well, and gaiters kept my skirt clear of the spokes. New this season, my "bike" boasted red-and-white fenders, a wicker basket over the handlebars, and a loud bell to announce a fresh start.

Seabright, my friend's cottage, stood behind ornate iron gates and a circular driveway. Its inlaid oak doors with a bell pull summoned the Forsters' butler, Hayes, who smiled and summoned a footman to take charge of my bicycle, then stood back to usher me inside.

"Mrs. Forster will see you in the morning room, ma'am."

The morning room in the mid-afternoon? Was something wrong? I followed the butler through a familiar hallway to the bright wallpapered room where my friend pored over business papers on the table in front of her. She looked up as the butler announced, "Mrs. DeVere for you, ma'am."

"Thank you, Hayes."

My friend sprang up, took my hand, and drew me to the closest chair. "Val, I so hoped you and Roderick had arrived at Drumcliffe. I told Hayes to show you in immediately if you chanced to come by. Would you like tea? Mineral water?"

I accepted the Apollinaris water, which a footman promptly set before me in a crystal glass.

Cassie pointed to the papers on the table. "In a day or so, I'll need a word of advice about an important decision."

"At your service, Mrs. Forster," I said. My mock salute brought a smile to a face so refined that Cassie was sometimes mistaken for a Gibson Girl, a likeness she often dismissed with a tiny frown between her perfectly arched eyebrows. The well-meant link to the illustrator Charles

Dana Gibson struck my friend as intrusive. It was a sensitive point since she, too, suffered repercussions from last summer's turmoil that included my bicycle accident.

Cassie brushed at a wisp of her lush auburn hair and pushed aside the papers. Her warm brown eyes twinkled as she said, "Are we ready for the season?"

She meant, was I braced for the trials of etiquette. "With your assistance, Mrs. Forster," I said. "I have not mistaken the finger bowl for the consommé for over a year."

Cassie smiled. Two years ago when I bicycled on a Newport pathway, this very lady needed help with a blown tire on her "mechanical horse." Recognizing her as the stranger who had recently rescued me from a nasty incident, I offered to help. In a public tearoom a few days earlier, my fierce French tutor, Madame Dureau, had berated me for misusing a verb. In turn, the tutor found herself rebuked in an elegant stream of French by the very lady now before me with the downed bicycle. On the pathway, I introduced myself as the tearoom student who was at her wit's end over verbs, nouns, and most everything beyond *bonjour* and *au revoir.* We struck up a conversation on the pathway and became friends. I learned that Cassandra Van Schylar Fox Forster traced her lineage to the Old New York Knickerbockers and that Roddy had known her from childhood dancing lessons.

Roddy and I were now the "courtesy" aunt and uncle of the Forsters' young son and daughter, Charles and Beatrice. "Are the children at the beach with their nanny?" I asked.

Cassie shook her head. "At the moment, they are in the garden in their South Sea playhouse. Bea is wearing her grass skirt and Charlie his lava-lava loin cloth. They asked me to wear my muu-muu, but I said, not today."

I laughed, picturing my friend's hourglass figure disappearing into billowing tropical garb as she joined her children inside the grass hut their scientist father had built upon his return from an expedition.

"What's the latest from the Pacific?" I asked.

"Dudley's last letter said he should soon reach Fiji…an island rich in fossils, he hopes."

Cassie's husband, Dudley Forster, sought the secrets of earth's origins in prehistoric fossils on Pacific Islands. My friend hung maps that showed his whereabouts, and she carefully pronounced the names of the islands. The ordeal of her husband's months-long absences was offset by the couple's wedding vows that sealed their enduring commitment to one another and to their children.

"The hut's thatched roof needs repair," she said, "and I haven't a clue who can do it."

"Dudley will fix it when he returns," I said.

"But not this summer," my friend replied wistfully. As the mistress of Seabright, Cassie oversaw the cottage, the stable, and the household staff. What's more, my friend had inherited a great deal of money and property in the last year, including another cottage here on Ocean Drive, a cottage with a dark recent history. The new responsibilities weighed on her. An ashtray with a stubbed cigarette signaled her worries.

I pointed to the papers on the table. "The Stone Point cottage affair?" I asked.

"Affair, for sure." Cassie crossed her arms and made a sour face. "Stone Point needs to be rented, Val. The lawyers fear a suit filed against me if the cottage is vacant and the nearby properties decline in value. Or if someone breaks in and causes damage...the La Farge stained glass window. Or a roof leaks, a pipe bursts in the saltwater bath."

"Stone Point has piped-in sea water?"

"Saltwater and fresh too, depending on preference...or whim. Evidently, it was the two waters that persuaded the latest prospective tenant to offer twice the sum than others offered...all of whom I refused this entire spring. I fended them off, every single one."

My friend bit her lip. "Or if there's a fire. You've heard about the fires?"

"What fires?" In fact, Roddy and I had very recently escaped a terrible fire. "Not fires in Newport," I said.

Cassie's sharp laugh was unlike her. "You haven't heard? The Gill Street houses from colonial times, cedar shingles and clapboards. Three of them burned to the ground in the past month...fires of 'undetermined origin.'"

"Perhaps chimney fires?" I remembered chimney fires in Virginia City. Houses gone in a wink.

Cassie seemed not to listen. "Hayes has ordered extinguishers for Seabright," she said. "Ugly cannisters, but Roderick ought to see about them. I wish Seabright was like the Breakers."

She saw my puzzled look. "You didn't know? The original Breakers burned to the ground. When Vanderbilt bought the property, he built with concrete and steel. The Breakers is fireproof."

I did not know what to say. I patted Cassie's hand across the table.

"And the financial advisers heckle me," she continued, "baffled that I would not sign the lease when a tidy sum awaits my signature." She pointed a beautifully manicured finger at the papers. "Now, here come the Rickers…Ezra and Geneva Ricker. He's the 'king' of oleomargarine. A substitute for butter, isn't it, Val?"

"Cheap and profitable," I said. "In Virginia City, the International Hotel tried to sneak it into the dining room ingredients, and the chef was fired."

"Rightly so," Cassie said. "But if I sign the lease and something unpleasant comes up with the Rickers…suppose a water pipe bursts and spoils the saltwater bath and leaks to the floor below and damages the *cartouche*?" She saw my face and said, "It's the plasterwork you see on ceilings, Val…fruit and birds and flowers fashioned with plaster."

"Oh, that…of course." Now the fancy plaster had a name.

"If a pipe bursts and ruins the *cartouche*, what then? The ceiling was just redone by a young Italian man, Marco. He worked day and night sculpting wet plaster with clever knives. I watched him work…marvelous. He is fierce, almost frightening. His scowls made me wish Dudley were here. But if a pipe bursts and ruins the *cartouche*, I wouldn't know where to find him."

"Cassie, surely Newport has plasterers."

"Not like Marco. If you see his work, you'll notice the difference right away. I hate to take the chance...one burst water pipe...."

"You will deal with it at the time, Cassie, but oleo is legal, and if the 'king' of margarine wants to rent Stone Point for the summer, why not?"

I gave a *why-not* shrug and brought up an issue we had discussed weeks ago. Cassie and I decided to devote some of our Newport time to issues beyond social gatherings. "If you proceed with the rental," I said, "you can give your attention to your new idea...about the birds."

"Feathers," my friend murmured. "Bird protection."

Cassie had learned that flocks of birds were sacrificed for the plumes and wings on ladies' hats. She attended a meeting in New York, and the name of John James Audubon came up. My friend felt she must somehow begin to organize ladies in this Newport season when ostrich plumes waved like banners on sun hats.

"Dudley will love it," I said.

Cassie's eyes glowed in that moment. Her Dudley had long denounced the wild animal hunts that put tiger skins and polar bear rugs on fashionable floors. No such rugs were permitted at Seabright or the Forsters' house on Madison Avenue. (Nor at Drumcliffe or our New York chateau because I had faced grizzlies up close in the Rocky Mountains and wanted no reminders when I walked on floors of waxed hardwood, tile, or wool carpet.)

"So," I continued, "with Stone Point rented, you'll see about the 'feathered friends' this summer, and Roddy and I will pursue our own interests. My lawyer husband wants to purchase an orange grove in Florida."

Cassie fanned her shapely fingers. "For his cocktail bitters, isn't it? Will the labels say, '*Roderick DeVere Orange Bitters*?'"

She knew better, and we laughed. The bitters bottles would never bear the DeVere name, though Roddy was in high demand for signature cocktails for clubs, resorts, steamship lines, special events, and so on. Those clamoring for his mixological magic were sworn to secrecy, which my husband required. The master bartenders got the credit, which suited Roddy just fine, especially since his courtroom clients were the cafés, taverns, and barrooms besieged by Temperance zealots determined to shutter all alcoholic oases. In city court, my husband joked that he worked both sides of the bar.

"And you, Val?" Cassie asked. "You will again join me on the Newport bridle paths?"

"With pleasure! I also want to take sailing lessons this summer," I said. "And I plan to acquire a property for a children's summer camp in the Hudson Valley." I sipped my water. "Something good for needy youngsters."

"Unfortunate children," Cassie said. "'Blessed are the poor.'"

"Not unless we do the blessing," I said a bit tartly. "Anyway, I will move ahead to buy the property."

My friend's eyes narrowed. "It's the aftermath of your last month's trouble at the Hudson Valley country house isn't it, Val? It's about Ulster County?"

I nodded, hesitating to delve into the full account of last month's agonizing venture at a country house in the Hudson Valley. It was rumored that we DeVeres repeatedly invited trouble, but trouble chased us up the Hudson River when a body was found on property owned by Roddy's parents. We spiraled into a serious situation and looked forward to this calm Newport summer.

I felt it, you know." Cassie leaned close and said, "You know that I felt it."

I lowered my eyes and acknowledged Cassie's words with a murmured, "yes." My friend had warned me with her premonitions, which proved to be true—and not for the first time since I had known her. Roddy remembered Cassandra's dreaminess from childhood when she seemed called to faraway sights invisible to others. The child's "spells" embarrassed and angered her cold-hearted mother, who blamed these episodes on a nanny from the Islands who loved the infant and who, in time, introduced the child to faraway worlds unseen by others. Saffira of the Islands was sent away, but Cassie already had the "Sixth Sense" that enriched her life even as it caused confusion and sometimes anguish. She once told me of a dance instructor whose face and hands seemed to melt like candle wax, a terrifying vision made more so when the man died within days. Cassie's Sixth Sense baffled her scientist husband, whose bemusement turned to concern for their children's welfare. For her family's sake, Cassie had promised to "tame" her Sixth Sense. So far, the effort caused more stress when the visions came unbidden and caught her off guard.

The light was shifting, and I should return to Drumcliffe. I pointed to the papers on the table. "If that's the lease," I said, "Roddy can look over the agreement, and if it passes his lawyerly inspection, then let the oleomargarine people have Stone Point for the summer. We'll plan to see the children very soon, and their South Seas outfits sound like fun for all."

I buttoned my bicycle suit jacket. "And perhaps you can do me a favor, Cassie?"

She arose to walk me to her front door. "Anything," she said. "What is it?"

"Will you please come to the opening reception at the Cuveen Gallery? We're scheduling a painting for appraisal, and there's a portrait painter that Cuveen is sponsoring for the summer. Roddy wants to engage him to paint my portrait. His name is André...."

At his name, I broke off as my friend began to slightly sway and gripped the edge of the table. Her gaze had the faraway look that I knew too well.

"André Cole," she said. Cassie seemed to bite back the words on her lips. Her breathing became halting as the butler appeared and ordered a footman to bring my bicycle. "André Cole," she said in a slurred voice. "But I'll be there, Val. You know you can count on me."

Chapter Three

THE TRAVERS BLOCK ON Bellevue Avenue enticed summer colonists from early July through August. Among its boutiques, Tiffany offered jewels, lamps, and other curios, while the House of Worth sent silks and salesladies from New York to promote the latest fashions. Gentlemen's haberdashery and neckties were by Brooks Brothers, while Black, Starr & Frost purveyed cufflinks and the slimmest gold watches. All this opulence was nestled in the rustic, shingle-styled block with half-timbering, gables, and mansard roofs on the most exclusive avenue in Newport.

The Cuveen Gallery invitation announced its opening reception to take place on Thursday, July the sixth, at seven o'clock p.m. in the Bellevue Avenue location on the Travers Block. Printed on a creamy card and delivered by messenger last evening, the invitation stated that Cuveen Brothers Antiques would no longer occupy the gallery.

"Under new management, Roddy?"

We lingered with coffee, tea, and toast in the Drumcliffe breakfast room on a bright Sunday morning, July 2, on our first full day in Newport. Our French bulldog, Velvet, lounged on a floor cushion, having licked every morsel from her breakfast bowl and noisily lapped her water after a short walk outdoors. Like the two of us, our dog reacquainted herself with the cottage last evening and early this morning.

She went on my tour with our housekeeper, Mrs. Thwaite, which felt more like a march in double-time for me and our dog who cast doleful glances at the housekeeper. With iron-gray hair lashed to a tight bun and dark eyes pinpointing disorder, Mrs. Thwaite walked us through drawing rooms and reception rooms with pride in their museum-like perfection. She announced each chandelier crystal had been polished by hand and the marble floors scrubbed by housemaids on hands and knees (despite my rule against such backbreaking toil).

Before I could pause to object, Mrs. Thwaite hastened us into the music room where the harp and piano had been tuned and pursed her lips when I fingered an ivory key. My fond hope that the housekeeper might resign had faded under suspicion she was a pipeline to my mother-in-law and reported every misstep of the Wild West "gal" who had lassoed the DeVere son-and-heir. (Mrs. Thwaite disapproved equally of me and the dog Roddy and I adopted when her troubled owner abandoned her. Named for her velvety black fur, she was a charming pet and dear companion to all except the housekeeper.)

Roddy's rounds with the butler had started pleasantly when Sands first showed off the newly installed green felt on the billiard table, then proudly displayed the fully stocked liquor cabinet and barware ready for new cocktails Roddy would mix in the library. My husband rearranged a few bottles, and his summer "libation foundation" was ready to go.

Sands then took Roddy aside to suggest the immediate purchase of fire extinguishers. The Drumcliffe servants had learned that other cottages were equipping their butlers and footmen with extinguishers. The Gill Street fires were mentioned, together with a church fire put out by a sexton wielding an extinguisher. The servants did not know which church had caught fire, but the footmen hoped Mr. Sands would have a word with Mr. DeVere about acquiring the new equipment.

I told Roddy about the recent Newport fires and Cassie's fear that her rental cottage might be at risk. "Hayes has ordered extinguishers for Seabright," I said. "Shouldn't we have them too? Cassie called them 'ugly cannisters.' What's in them?"

Roddy paused, then said, "I think it's water under pressure...expelled when sodium bicarbonate mixes with sulphuric acid."

"Sounds fierce."

"Fire is fierce...which we know too well." Roddy signaled the footman for a refill of tea. "Tell you what, Val, I'll send

Sands to the fire station to ask about extinguishers, and we'll go from there. I would not involve Mrs. Thwaite."

"Certainly not." Eager to move past sulphuric acid and the housekeeper, I said, "The invitation says 'Mister Joseph Cuveen will present premier works of art.' And the gallery will offer 'private consultations and appraisals by appointment.'"

"Because Joseph Cuveen has taken over from his father and uncle." Roddy squeezed lemon into his tea. "The gold standard in antiques has been Cuveen Brothers, with artworks a sideline." Roddy took a sip. "From now on, Joseph will give his undivided attention to a career in fine art."

"That's good for us, isn't it? *The Counting House* will be...." I almost said "counted" but stopped before annoying my husband. Antiques were a mainstay of Society, and my mother-in-law drilled me in the furnishings of French Louis kings and assorted English Georges, not to mention this era of Queen Victoria. Proper décor, she said, could supplement family heirlooms with pieces acquired with discernment.

Not that I disliked historic furniture, but my mother-in-law's choices were not mine, and the replacement of dreary DeVere interiors would be slow-and-steady, lest Roddy feel uprooted.

"The Cuveen invitation," I said, "also promises an introduction to 'Monsieur André Cole, Artist-in-Residence and celebrated portraitist...winner of the *Paume de Lisbon.*'"

Roddy shrugged his broad shoulders. "I never heard of it, but we can inquire at the reception."

"More than inquire, Roddy. We must see his actual work."

"Of course."

Roddy's gaze was calming. During dinner last evening, he told me whose names were already entered in the Casino membership book, and I told him about Cassie's quandary over the Stone Point rental. Roddy promised to review the lease, and we discussed my portrait over a Chantilly whipped cream dessert.

"The invitation also names a director of the gallery," I said, still holding the invitation. "Guests are invited to meet Mister Warren T. Eccles, Curator and Executive Director." I sipped my coffee. "Roddy, is that a fancy title for the accountant?"

My husband smiled and shook his head. "Not likely. My guess is…Eccles, is it?"

I spelled the name.

"He will operate the gallery for the season, Val, but Joseph Cuveen will not linger long in Newport. He will be off to Europe and his London headquarters, buying and selling on commission, just as Cuveen Brothers did for years. While in Newport, he will agree to consultations at the cottages, but very few."

"Principle of scarcity?"

"Exactly."

"So, Mr. Eccles will mind the store and speak as though he knows what his boss would say to customers."

"Clients."

"Clients," A robin perched on a limb outside the diamond pane window. "The invitation also says Warren Eccles is 'late of Florence and London.'"

"It means he has been active in centers of the art world," Roddy said.

"But 'Late of,'" I said, "makes him sound dead."

Roddy did not reply. I would think about this morning in days to come when "Late of" gained the double meaning that started as a joke.

❧

The gallery reception slipped to the back of my mind as Independence Day festivities took hold in Newport. Patriotic bunting draped the Market Square Police Station under Chief Ronald Cherry's orders, and the fire station hung banners as well. Flags flew on Long Wharf where Roddy and I inquired about buying a small sailboat. My husband approved the lease for the Stone Point rental, and Cassie's signature let the oleomargarine people move into the cottage. We briefly saw our friend's children who were going to Bailey's Beach with their nanny Cara and made plans to see the Independence Day parade together.

"Can we watch it in front of the bakery again?" asked an excited Bea, who would soon turn five years old. "Oh, can we?"

"*May* we?" her seven-year-old brother Charlie retorted. "It's '*may*' we," but desire quashed grammar as he begged, "Can we get chocolate doughnuts too? Can we eat them on the sidewalk?" Flustered Cassie said she would see about that, which meant we would all gather to watch the parade in front of Libby's Bakery off Broadway on Market Square.

Which we did, waving little flags while brass bands played John Philip Sousa marches and colorful floats were pulled by horses combed and brushed, every hoof polished a shiny black. A photographer behind a tripod-mounted camera captured the scene for *The Newport Daily News*. The day ended with oohs and aahs when fireworks bloomed in the night sky.

Early in this Independence Day week, I scheduled my first tennis lesson at the Casino with instructor Richard (Dick) Thatford and arranged to have my racket restrung. I also strolled the Travers Block where shops were open for business, though the Cuveen windows were soaped and the front door shut tight. No notice of its schedule was posted to the public. Those with invitations knew when to arrive—by carriage.

Our brougham lined up behind a half-dozen carriages on July 6 at 7:20 p.m. and inched toward the gallery entrance. Our coachman Noland decided the high-stepping black Hackneys, Atlas and Apollo, ought to be reacquainted with Newport. Others apparently felt a similar need to hitch teams, and in front of us loomed a grand parade coupé drawn by four enormous snorting and stamping Percherons.

"Roddy," I whispered, "is that who I think—?"

"—shhh, Val. Yes, it's Mr. and Mrs. Oliver Perry Belmont."

"Alva," I said. "It's Alva Belmont. Look...."

We watched two grooms assist Mrs. Belmont onto the carpet laid across the sidewalk. Her husband took her arm, and the couple started toward the entrance. "Her hair, Roddy...look at the fixture in Alva's hair. It's like the portrait...devil's horns."

Roddy took my arm as grooms approached to assist me from our carriage. "Not a word about devil's horns or 'gun belt' pearls, Val," he said. "And it's likely that Elizabeth and Harry Lehr will be here, so please do not hint that her portrait reminds you of bar nudes in Nevada saloons."

"Oh, Roddy...."

"Oh, Val...."

We crossed the carpeted sidewalk where a tuxedoed guard verified the guest list and gestured us toward the interior that glowed with candlelight and sparkled with jewels as the space filled with gowned ladies and gentlemen in evening dress. We were greeted by a lithe man whose slicked hair and scraping bow reminded me of a stage actor in the role of a courtier.

He swiveled at the waist and seemed ready to kiss my fingers, unfazed when I made a fist. "If I may introduce myself," he said with a servile smile, "I am Mister Warren Eccles, Curator and Executive Director of the Cuveen Gallery at Newport. I welcome you on behalf of Mr. Joseph Cuveen." His smile glistened at Roddy. "And I understand that the name DeVere signifies an ardent commitment to the fine arts."

"My parents, Mr. Eccles," Roddy replied drily, "who now summer in Bar Harbor."

"You surely sustain a fine family tradition, sir." Eccles's sloe-eyed gaze implied that he would like nothing better than to escort us personally to the gallery's exquisite art that was exhibited expressly for our collection. "Mr. and Mrs. DeVere, please do enjoy our paintings in the company of your friends, and I will seek you out for a special word with Mr. Cuveen. In the meantime, feel free to call upon my assistant." He gestured to an extremely pale young man at the door with the guest list. "Asa will be happy to assist."

To my eye, Eccles's pallid assistant looked busy checking names against arrivals. Events like this drew imposters and newspaper reporters eager to publicize the flagrant idle rich.

"And you will also wish to meet our artist-in-residence, Monsieur André Cole."

"And see his work," I said, but Eccles had turned his lacquered smile to the couple just arriving. With champagne, we made our way to a wall of paintings in elaborate frames, all for sale, none with a price.

"Here's *French Artillery in Snowy Winter*," I said, scanning a scene with cannon, horses, and soldiers lying dead in the snow. "And this with cows on a hill...also French... *Dans les Dunes....*" Sand dunes?

Cassie would know, but I did not see her amid the ladies whose dresses were accented with downy feathers. My friend would have a hard task this summer if she pursued bird protection. She had promised to be here tonight but had not arrived. I turned back to the pictures.

"All this reminds me of the Lafayette room, Roddy. I do not see one painting signed by André Cole on this wall."

"Cole...did I hear Cole?"

We turned to see acquaintances, Madeline and Edwin Glendorick whose point of pride was their daughter's recent marriage into a British royal family.

"Good evening, Valentine...Roderick." The affable Madeline eyed my dress as I scanned her mauve crepe with velvet at the shoulders. At my maid Calista's urging, I had chosen a cerise satin evening dress with appliquéd stars, bias panels, and silver-thread embroidery edged with brilliants.

"Good to be back to Newport," I said. "I hope the countess plans to visit this season?"

The Glendoricks' daughter Emily became a countess when Edwin's profitable ships let the financially hobbled House of Cleave replenish its coffers. Last winter, the young bride was newly titled among a number of others who were slurred by gossips nowadays as "Dollar Princesses."

"A summer visit, most certainly," Madeline said. "Countess Emily will be with us in Newport for several weeks."

"Long enough to get her painted," Edwin said. "We're looking for a top-notch painter, maybe this new fellow, Cole. We want her done up in full length."

"Edwin is disappointed in a recent portrait," Madeline said. "And I agree justice was not done to our daughter's lovely eyes."

"We want life-size, head-to-toe," her husband said, "with that little crown."

"Coronet," his wife said, "an entitlement of her rank."

"Emily..." I said.

"The Countess of Cleave," trumpeted her father. "Step over there with me. Let's have a look at the man's wares."

The shipping titan led us across the room as if he were the prow of a vessel. Everyone parted to make way as Roddy and I followed toward the opposite side of the gallery, where a slender man with brooding eyes and a mane of curly dark hair presided over three portraits mounted on easels and lighted by candles and wall sconces. With an upturned moustache, André Cole appeared stylishly European, especially in his velvet jacket, ruffled shirt, and an outsized silk bowtie appearing carelessly knotted. With arms folded across his chest, he stood before three portraits of women and moved deftly from side to side to allow onlookers a full view of his work. Dark paint edged his fingernails.

"Take a look, Roderick," Edwin said. "Valentine, if you were to judge, what's the grade?"

We nudged in beside the Glendoricks to see portraits of three women at different stages in life: on the left, a young woman barely past girlhood, and in the center a lady in full matronly authority, while an elderly grandmother or great aunt was shown on the far right. Silently, we looked from one to the other, comparing features and coloring. Whether the eyes were blue or brown, the hair blonde or raven black, the cheekbones high or a nose somewhat sharp, all three shared one quality across their ages. Their skin tones shone with extraordinary luminescence. The facial features, the necklines, the gowns...all were detailed but subordinated to complexions brought the figures to their fullest life. They seemed to glow from within.

"Extraordinary," Madeline murmured.

"I hear his secret is the paint," Edwin said in a lowered voice. "Mixes it himself, nobody the wiser." He stepped closer toward the portrait of the older woman with a rose in one hand. "The chap better get to work on the fingers," he whispered. "The woman's thumb looks downright crooked."

I did not comment. Nor did Roddy, for at that moment Warren Eccles beckoned us to a recessed area where a gentleman in evening dress shook hands with Roddy, bowed to me, and welcomed us in a voice of London, England, at its most charming.

"Mrs. DeVere," he said, "splendid to meet you at long last. Word of Roderick's nuptials reached me in London, but business has kept me bound to the rock, so to speak."

Joseph Cuveen's receding hairline gave him the profile of a diplomat, and his eyebrows seemed ready to arch in amazement or knit together in regret or censure. I was reminded that he was just a year or so older than thirty, almost Roddy's age.

"I am barely up for air in your seaside Newport," he said. "The gallery has consumed me day and night. Be assured, the evening's reward is renewing acquaintance with connoisseurs of art and antiques whom we first met across the pond."

We all smiled at the catchphrase for the Atlantic Ocean.

With a puckish wink, he said, "Mrs. DeVere, has Roderick told you of our London days as boys? And what's that phrase...'little shavers?'"

"'Shavers' at Cuveen Brothers antique galleries," Roddy replied. "I was ordered to be 'invisible' while my parents dealt with furniture."

"Accessioned antique pieces, sir." Cuveen winked again, whether in ironic agreement or reproach, I could not decide.

"Roderick, surely you recall the piece my Uncle Henry found for your mother."

"The Lafayette table," Roddy replied. "As a boy, I saw nothing but a dark wood table with burn marks on the legs."

"With the underside inscribed, *'Marquis de L.'*" Cuveen added, pronouncing the French as naturally as would Cassie.

"An acquired taste," I said, trying out the term but puzzled that Roddy had not already told me why the Drumcliffe drawing room was named for Lafayette. Or showed me the table.

"Joseph, may I bring up a point...." Roddy said. "We are interested in Mrs. DeVere sitting for a portrait this summer. Perhaps Mr. Cole...."

Joseph Cuveen's eyebrows arched. "Roderick," he said, "you cannot improve on Cole. I put him in league with Sargent and Carolus-Duran, and he is already besieged...a virtual cannonade of commissions await the man. Be assured, however, if you wish Cole to execute a portrait of your lovely bride in the weeks ahead, I will have Eccles see to the scheduling."

It did not escape my notice that the two men had omitted me from their bargaining. "Mr. Cuveen," I said, "if we might ask another favor.... We have brought a certain painting to Newport in the hope you might settle questions about its history and value. We would appreciate your judgment."

At this, the gallery owner looked truly distressed. He closed his eyes and slowly shook his head. "I would like nothing better," he said, "but my departure date has been moved up. I will spare you the details, but I am due in London. Eccles will see to it, Mrs. DeVere. You will be in good hands. Newport is fortunate to have him for the season...and so am I. Establishing galleries across Europe in a year's time has been...may I say, somewhat daunting. Warren Eccles came at the very last moment. I nearly despaired, but fortune has favored Newport's Cuveen Gallery this year... favored with Eccles, to be precise. He has a young assistant to manage clerical details, a pale fellow who ought to free him for more important work." He paused. "Perhaps you know the Eccles folio on greyhounds?"

"Dogs?" I said.

He winced as if I said "cur" or "mutt."

"A breed long beloved by the nobility, Mrs. DeVere. Greyhounds appear on family crests, tapestries, paintings, and sculptures as well. Mr. Eccles will enlighten you. And be assured, he will schedule your portraiture with Monsieur Cole and undertake the authentication of the painting in question. I give you my word."

At that, our interview concluded. I glimpsed Eccles nearby, signaling the moment for others' private audiences with Joseph Cuveen. Roddy and I stepped away, accepted another glass of wine, and approached a group suddenly laughing at one of Harry Lehr's jokes. Just then, Madeline Glendorick crossed my path.

"Edwin and I are to meet Cuveen," she said. "And I am sorry your friend became ill and left so early."

"My friend?"

"Cassandra...Cassandra Forster."

"Cassie...? She was here?"

"One of the first carriages, just behind us. I believe she came with the minister...Father Rewers, the one from Trinity Church. She barely said hello and looked about before calling for her carriage. She looked rather...dazed. Yes, dazed. I hope it's nothing serious. I thought you knew."

Chapter Four

I TIPTOED DOWNSTAIRS AFTER a fitful night's sleep, anxious to learn whether Cassie had been taken ill or otherworldly visions beset her at the reception. I wrote her a note, dispatched a footman to Seabright and requested that he await a reply.

Footman Chalmers prepared to set the table, but I asked that our dog be brought to the loggia where I would like a cup of black coffee.

"Coffee on the loggia, ma'am? Outdoors?" The footman raised an eyebrow at the wayward notion of a Newport sunrise in the open air.

Drumcliffe's loggia was a feature that Roddy and I neglected on previous summers but could enjoy this year on fresh mornings. The mist was lifting to reveal calm seas in hues from azure to turquoise, and the click-click of our French bulldog's paws on the tiles cheered me as

Velvet ran to lick my cheeks and wriggle her soft furry self. "Girl," I told her, "you are an armful, all twenty-three pounds of you."

Lifted to my lap, the dog sat up to face the ocean like an Egyptian deity at the Nile. We both peered out while the footman Chalmers brought a small table and tray with a pot of coffee, a cup and saucer, and two little crackers that were shaped like bones. He poured my coffee and said, "Ma'am, the kitchen baked a dozen of these. We call them dog biscuits."

Velvet bit the treat from my fingers, and I sipped coffee as the dog jumped down, her pointy ears darting higher at the sound of footsteps.

"Roddy...."

"My dear...an early morning."

"For both of us."

He kissed my cheek, ran a hand through his wavy light brown hair, and rubbed Velvet's head. Roddy had already dressed for the morning in trousers, a linen shirt and a tie, and a sport jacket.

"Breakfast here in the loggia, Val...outdoors?"

"Roddy," I said, "do not forget that mining camps were my 'Morning Rooms' for years... strong black coffee and sour-dough biscuits at the break of day in the Colorado Rockies."

My husband pulled a second wicker chair close, signaled for tea, and sat down. "Your Rocky Mountains are about to become most sharply memorable, my dear."

I knew what he meant. "Theo," I said. "Our friend is due back from Yellowstone. And Roddy, if Theo's name is in the Casino membership book, let's invite him for dinner. We can tell him the news that I will now announce to you after a fretful night of sleep...."

"Which is...?"

I raised my hand in a little salute. "I hereby volunteer to have my portrait painted by André Cole to decorate your study in New York."

"My dearest Val...."

"Your choice, Roddy...full length in a rippled satin gown, or close-up to the shoulders.

My husband beamed, took my hand and gently fingered my wedding band. He softly said, "'I never knew before what such a love as you have made me feel.'"

"Oh, Roddy...."

The poet said it, Val, to you from me."

"At dawn."

"Our dawn, always."

Time stopped for that moment. We would later reflect on its truth and its trials. For now, we held hands and gazed seaward until small paws tickled our legs.

"Velvet," Roddy said to the dog, "have you had break-fast?" He rubbed her furry head. "And what is this, shaped like a...bone?" The biscuit was close to her muzzle, and we listened to Velvet's crunching and munching. Roddy laughed, as did I.

The loggia at sunrise proved to be the day's indelible blessing. By this evening, a troubling tale from our friend over cocktails and dinner would darken the Newport glow like a candleflame smothered in a gust of wind.

After breakfast, Roddy went to our stable to make certain coachman Noland and the grooms were fully equipped and the horses and turn-outs ready for the season. Few gentlemen visited their Coggeshall Avenue stables, but my husband insisted on inspection and consultation. He would order Justice saddled for a ride to the Casino to arrange a croquet match and to look at the membership book for the name, Theodore B. Bulkeley. He also stopped at the Cuveen Gallery to notify Mr. Eccles that Mrs. DeVere would wish to arrange for her portrait by André Cole.

After dressing in a blue-and-white shirtwaist and navy skirt, I reviewed the dinner menu, a daily task when the butler presented the menu for approval by the lady of the house. I nodded at a terrapin soup, a salad, beef *rôti*, and three French dishes that defied translation.

Footman Bronson returned from Seabright with Cassie's note saying that her day was claimed by the children and an afternoon call at Stone Point, meaning my polite friend would visit her tenant, Mrs. Oleo Margarine. Cassie omitted any mention of illness at the Cuveen reception. Her elegant penmanship implied wellbeing.

So I thought at the time.

A quick bite, and I took a carriage to the Redwood Library for information on outdoor recreation for children. The librarian agreed to look further when articles on "Hill Climbing" and "The Walking Rink" seemed as useless as the book, *Tips for Tricyclists.*

Roddy came home in the afternoon with good news. "Theo's in Newport and will be delighted to dine. He has leased the old colonial Bannister place, so we'll hear about living in the mid-1770s...and touring Yellowstone Park. So, it's cocktails and dinner with Theo this evening."

The butler's 6 p.m. announcement, "Mr. Theodore Bulkcley," brought Roddy to his feet in a Drumcliffe reception room, while etiquette kept me seated to offer the gentleman my hand. "Theo, it seems like ages," I said, "and we look forward to a 'Yellowstone' evening."

"Doubtful, dear friend," he said with a twinkle in his pale blue eyes and a little shrug of his narrow shoulders in his Saville Row formal coat. "My buckskins are retired, Valentine, and so are the snowshoes that you wisely suggested, but I will have you know that I snowshoed eye to eye with a buffalo...and lived."

"And deserve a cocktail," Roddy said. "Will a gin martini suit you this evening?"

"My favorite, Roderick. And if I may join you on the settee, Valentine ...and admire your gown while the Svengali of cocktails plies his trade." Theo eyed my violet silk gown with flower garlands of silvery thread while Roddy poured

and mixed at the tea wagon-turned-bar cart, every movement by now second nature.

Martini (Dry)

Ingredients:

- 2 ounces gin
- 1 ounce French (dry) vermouth
- Small olive (unpitted, optional)
- Ice

Directions:

- Add ice chunks to mixing glass.
- Add gin and vermouth to mixing glass and stir.
- If desired, add olive to chilled stemware glass.
- Strain mixture into stemware glass and serve.

"A libation for one and all, and here's to the summer,"
Roddy said, serving our guest and me, despite a rule that
cocktails were for men only, a grating custom that must
soon end. Few knew that Roddy often tested his new cocktails on me.

"Imagine this at Yellowstone," Theo said. "A martini
cocktail to sip in time with the geyser."

"Old Faithful...." I murmured.

"Erupting each hour, on the hour," Theo continued, "and
spectators shouting, 'Oh, wonderful...beautiful...splendid...
majestic....'"

"And did they shout?" Roddy asked.

"Ear-splitting every time, with applause." Our friend sipped his drink and said, "Admit it, Roderick, that poetic naturalist John Muir might as well be a travel agent for the Northern Pacific Railroad. He has spun a tangled web for travelers bound for the West to see Old Faithful blow on the hour."

Theo plucked the olive from his drink. "Your *Louisa* private car is a mansion on wheels, but the same geyser effect is on view in the steel mills spewing smoke and steam every hour of the day and night in Andrew Carnegie's steel mills in Pittsburgh, Pennsylvania."

"Theo, you joke," I said.

"Watch me," he replied with a twinkle in his eyes. "All season, I will promote travel to the geysers of Pittsburgh. All Newport will be encouraged to see the Old Faithfuls of the 'Steel City.' Here's to it!"

He sipped and winked at me, and I gave him my comrade-in-arms smile. Theo and I understood one another as Society's outliers. His New England roots traced to the *Mayflower*, but his visits to maiden lady cousins in Boston were reminders that the "city on a hill" was too *yesterday* for this son of Beacon Hill who shocked his family by bolting to Gotham to become a man about town with membership in several clubs and his name on invitation lists for events that mattered. The "shabby genteel" old money Boston would not do for stylish Theo Bulkeley, who knew the latest news before the papers went to press and was embraced by New York Society as a Boston Brahman.

To me, Brahman was a hearty breed of cattle raised in western ranches, but here the term meant elevated class and caste. In New York and Newport, Theo and I were Society's adoptees, with one crucial difference: my bachelor friend was signed, sealed, and delivered as the blueblood of these years that Mark Twain's novel had dubbed the Gilded Age.

As an Irish immigrant's daughter from the Wild West, however, I was suspected of roping the Knickerbocker bachelor who otherwise would have married a proper debutante of the East Coast. In short, Theo was *in*, while I remained in the outskirts on probation.

"So, Theo," Roddy said, "you have taken the old Bannister house this season? Sheltered in the colonial past?"

"Yes, it's the mid-1700s for me." He sipped. "A rental agent urged a lease for Stone Point, but I would not risk it."

"Cassie's cottage?" I said.

"The notorious Stone Point," he replied. "Scandalous… but let us not ruminate on last summer."

"Let us not," Roddy said firmly.

"But for your information," I added, "Stone Point has been rented to a Mr. and Mrs. Ezra Ricker."

"Do we know them? Are they new to Newport?" He frowned. "Unless someone in Society takes them up, the poor things will be castaways."

Theo was right. Newport's strictures were infamous. Wealth was crucial, but never enough. First-timers rented mansion-sized cottages but found themselves marooned and shamed in isolation as parties and balls swirled around them. By the end of July, they were gone.

Roddy said, "So, this season, it's the old Bannister place for you."

"Nowadays fully plumbed," Theo said, "and a cord of birchwood stacked for each fireplace. On chilly nights, a good book and a crackling fire for me."

"The Bannister house is all wood," I said abruptly. "How many fireplaces?"

"Every important room," he said, tilting his head. "Why?"

"Because of the chimneys," I said. "An old house, there could be a chimney fire." Theo looked as though I had gone daft. "House fires can start in chimneys," I said, which did not put our friend at ease.

"I believe my bride has fires in western towns in mind," Roddy said, "and extinguishers too. Recent fires have apparently set Newport households in quest of extinguishers... one per footman, two for every butler."

Theo gave me an indulgent glance. "Valentine, be assured that the Bannister hearths will be swept and the chimneys free of soot. But ease your mind. I plan to hold one of those outdoor picnics that everybody liked years ago when Ward McAllister hosted his *Fêtes du Champagne* at his farm. This year, expect an invitation to an outdoor picnic on the Bannister grounds. I'll find a date. Plan on it."

We finished our drinks as Sands announced dinner and soon sipped terrapin soup and the courses I had approved.

The dining room light softened in the evening hour. Theo asked about our plans for the summer.

"I will find a small boat and take sailing lessons," I said.

"Then, you must race in the catboat regattas," Theo said. "I will cheer you on."

"Also, Val agrees to do me a great favor this summer," Roddy continued. "My bride has agreed to sit for her portrait."

Our friend's lips parted in disbelief. "Do tell."

"Theo, there is nothing to 'tell.' The Cuveen Gallery is sponsoring the portrait artist André Cole, and we admired his work at the reception last Thursday. We plan to have a painting of ours appraised by the gallery and also arrange for my portrait through the new curator who has worked in Italy...in Florence. Perhaps you have met him. His name is Eccles."

"Eccles..." Theo echoed. "Eccles...in Newport."

In the weeks ahead, I was to recall the look on Theo's face at that instant when the footman refilled the *Chateau Lafite* and a slight breeze stirred the flames of the candelabra. The flickering light cast our friend's face as a mask of doubt...no, of alarm.

"Warren Eccles," Roddy said. "Do you know him, Theo? Joseph Cuveen vouches for the man and feels fortunate to have him run the gallery."

"There cannot be two Eccles," Theo murmured.

Roddy and I exchanged a glance. "Theo," Roddy said, "If something ought to be made known to us, please speak up."

Our friend took a slow sip of wine. He seemed unnerved.

"If it is the same fellow...notorious," he began, then put his wine glass down, cleared his throat, and put both wrists on the table edge, the European style that proved no malicious intention by a hidden hand.

"Let's hear it, man," said Roddy.

"Quite simply, Eccles is a forger."

Candle wax dripped on the table with a soft splat. We ignored it.

"Florence every spring..." Theo began, "the people we know gather and renew acquaintance...all unplanned, but reliably present. You understand?"

Roddy said, "You see the same friends each year."

"Some enjoy sketching...or lessons in Italian. And the Uffizi and the *Accademia*...and jewelry and art when negotiations proceed. Some are collectors, and for years, Warren Eccles was relied upon for transactions...and for art."

"He was an art dealer?" I asked.

"Not at first," Theo said. "I knew Eccles as a skilled artist who supported himself producing excellent copies of Florentine paintings. He excelled at fifteenth-century military commanders, especially Niccolò Acciaiuoli. But he was best at famous women, the Cumaean Sibyl and Queen Esther. He made a good living. People were happy to have the copies."

"A copyist," Roddy said softly, "is not a forger."

"Of course not." Theo reached for a sip of water. "It was later on...when those who bought copies were told they could privately view originals that might be available for acquisition...a long-lost Andrea del Castagno or a newly discovered Sebastiano del Piombo...art recovered from private chapels or villas and entrusted to Eccles for sale to connoisseurs."

"And they were forgeries?"

Theo nodded. "Eccles painted well enough in the Florentine style, and he made the surfaces look historic. The sales were hush-hush, supposedly to prevent claims by the Church or the heirs of estates."

"So," I said, "people bought copies, and forgeries too."

"They did, and Eccles made a great deal of money. He took a villa midway between Florence and Siena...vineyards and a winery. Then he overstepped."

"How so?" I asked.

"He claimed to have a long-lost Titian."

"But Titian was not Florentine," Roddy said. "He was Venetian."

"Precisely. That's what tripped up the fraud."

"Oh," I said. "And what happened?"

"Being Italy, nothing official, but money changed hands... settlements were rumored to have been paid. Eccles lost his villa and left Florence. The next thing I knew, he opened a small gallery last winter in New York."

"Where?" Roddy asked.

"Somewhere in the ladies' shopping district."

"The department stores?" I asked.

Theo nodded. "Hired a young assistant he worked to the ground while he played the Lothario, probably thought he could pass off his fakes to ladies...especially older ladies. It did not work. The gallery closed, and then he did something with greyhound dogs in art history, all under the patronage of an important collector of tapestries, as I was told. His reputation was somewhat restored, but I have not seen hide nor hair of him for the last two years."

Theo looked from Roddy to me. "Now he is Cuveen's curator in Newport? And you will deal with him? Valentine and Roderick, take my word...the less you have to do with the man, the better off you will be. Take my word...stay clear of Warren Eccles."

Chapter Five

THE DINNER ENDED IN patchy cheerfulness when Theo apologized for sounding like an Old Testament prophet. We assured him his warning was well taken, and over crème de menthe in the drawing room, we three bantered feebly about the barrage of Newport invitations from competing hostesses. With a "good night," we thankfully closed out the seventh day of July, 1899.

At the oak gate-leg table the next morning, Roddy pushed aside *The Newport Daily News*. If the weather cleared, we would ride Justice and Comet along the trails on the wooded side of Newport. Roddy's Arabian gelding stood in sharp contrast to my western Quarter Horse, but both needed exercise, as did we. Velvet lounged at our feet, her head between her paws as Bronson announced that poached codfish was available this morning. Roddy recalled that his mother started many Newport days with poached codfish.

He nodded yes. I preferred a fried egg and toast. We lifted our cups and sipped. "Here's to the day," Roddy said.

"And to us." I blew him a kiss. The dog raised her head. "An honest earful from Theo last night," I said.

"And a timely warning."

"Otherwise, Roddy, we would know nothing about Eccles."

"Don't be so sure, Val. I'd guess that a good many in our social set might have heard something about him. Tuscany and Venice are a well-trod route for American travelers."

"Where exactly is Tuscany?"

"That's Florence."

"Oh." I tried to recollect the boot-shaped Italy on the pull-down map in the Fourth Ward School in Virginia City but got no further than Rome and Genoa, the birthplace of Christopher Columbus.

"Tuscany," Roddy said softly, "is in the northwest, and Firenze...Florence...is a must for American travelers who migrate there in the springtime. The art market is brisk. As the saying goes, 'Americans have the money, and Europe has the art.'" Roddy squeezed lemon into his tea.

"So," I said, "a good many paintings here at Drumcliffe came from Florence."

"And the Netherlands, but mainly Paris and London...."

"Where Joseph Cuveen now operates," I said. "Do you suppose he knew about Eccles? Hired him anyway?"

"Not sure." Roddy sipped his tea. "To strike into the fine arts business on his own, the man has been nearly overwhelmed, which he admitted to us. His father and uncle probably helped, but the antique market differs from fine arts."

"He sounded relieved to find a curator for Newport," I said. "And Eccles's greyhound folio was apparently impressive. Whatever it is."

The footman appeared with our breakfasts. I fed Velvet a bit of egg white. "Maybe Cuveen is giving Eccles a chance to redeem himself," I said. "But we will not take *The Counting House* for his appraisal."

"Absolutely not." Roddy gave Velvet a codfish flake. "We can leave the painting in the crate for the summer. Better yet, we can have it hung in the cottage."

Too quickly I said, "It is protected in the crate."

Roddy shot me a look. "Val, let us not spoil the morning. We will take *The Counting House* back to the city and have it appraised in the autumn. For the time being, it will stay crated."

Silently I cried, "Hallelujah." A footman refilled our drinks, and Roddy put down his fork, leaned toward me and said, "Arrangements for your portrait will require dealing with Warren Eccles."

"But only for scheduling?"

"Correct. As curator and manager, he will mainly sell the paintings that Cuveen has allocated for the season. Eccles will earn commissions in addition to his salary."

"And commissions on the portraits? André Cole's portraits?"

"Probably," Roddy said.

"Haggling for my portrait? How cheap!" I bit my stone-cold toast.

Slowly my husband said, "All established artists have assistance with their affairs. I will discuss the terms with Eccles. You need only agree about your hours."

"Tied to a chair. Frozen like a statue."

My outburst upset our breakfast. Somehow, *The Counting House* and my portrait played havoc with me, and Roddy's patience was wearing thin. "We'll hear what the artist has to say, Val. Let us take things in stride."

With "stride," we turned attention to Velvet until *stride* took us to the windows where we stared at the fog and guessed about the day's weather but agreed to dress for the saddle, my husband in britches while I donned a long culottes skirt with a shirtwaist and pulled on boots, knotted a scarf at the neck, buttoned a lightweight coat, and carried my hat downstairs, all the while resolving to improve my mood.

In the foyer in his riding clothes, Roddy did not see me as he reached for an envelope Sands handed him on a silver tray and unfolded the letter. I paused, seeing my husband's self-assurance in this simple gesture and suddenly found myself filled with thankfulness. Across three thousand continental miles, two different worlds met and joined together. We found one another, and I must never take us for granted.

Roddy turned, saw me gazing and softly asked, "Are you all right, Val? You look...starstruck."

"I am."

The butler had withdrawn. I leaned toward Roddy and said, "Kiss." We kissed. I said, "Let's ride."

"Oh, we will ride, my dear Val...count on it." Roddy touched my chin. "But for now, Justice and Comet have been brought round and await us." He opened the letter in his hand. "Meanwhile, this from the Gallery...from Mr. Eccles. Let me see what it says."

Roddy frowned. "It seems that Mr. André Cole requires photographs of his subjects, and Eccles requests that he come to Drumcliffe."

"André Cole here with a camera?"

"No. On the artist's behalf, Eccles wishes to call at Drumcliffe with a photographer from *The Newport Daily News*...at our earliest convenience."

I started to blurt, "Why on earth?" but asked why Eccles and a newspaper photographer needed to call here.

Roddy replied that the sooner the photographs could be taken, the sooner my portrait could be scheduled.

I agreed to be agreeable, and we settled on available hours for the next day, then passed the mid-day hours at a walk, a trot, and briefly at a canter on the wooded trails before we returned to the cottage in good spirits but dampened to the skin. The horses were promised cotton blankets by the grooms who admired Roddy's Arabian gelding but were bemused by the "cowboy" Quarter Horse here in Newport. Stable hands were also curious as to why I straddled Comet on an Army saddle while the lady's sidesaddle gathered dust. I told them the sidesaddle was "medieval." Roddy said I was no Lady Guinevere, at which they blinked.

We waited as Saturday's hours slipped away. The French gilt Louis XVI clock chimed the exact hours of my agreement to receive Mr. Warren Eccles and a photographer.

At 1:50 p.m., with ten minutes remaining, Sands announced Mr. Eccles and Mr. Bullard and showed both men into a reception room large enough for the photographer and his tripod. Toting a leather satchel, Eccles bowed with a cringing apology for unavoidable delay and introduced *The Newport Daily News* photographer, Mr. Hugh Bullard, a thickset man who doffed his derby hat, briefly bowed, took the satchel, and busied himself with the camera.

We invited Eccles to take a seat, but he glided across the room in his fashionably wrinkled Irish linen suit, scanning the paintings and stepping close to two of them, pausing to take his time before each one. He could have sent his assistant, but zeal for a first-hand look at Drumcliffe's walls was probably the idea.

Perhaps these photographs were a ruse to gain Eccles admission to every cottage where a portrait commission was undertaken. Casting his curatorial eye on Newport's cottage walls, did the man assess artistic merit? Or monetary value? And for what purpose?

"Has your assistant been given the day off?" I asked. "We would think the young man might accompany Mr. Bullard to help with his equipment and free you for more important work."

"There's nothing more important to the Cuveen gallery than personal attention to a valued client, Mrs. DeVere... and our artworks are overdue for cataloguing. Today, Mr. Durling is busy at that all-important task."

"Mr. Durling?"

"My assistant, Asa Durling. You might have noticed him at the reception...at the door. He proved his worth that night, turned away a charlatan who might have been a jewel thief. We hope not, but isn't prudence the better part of care?"

With a long look at the two paintings, Eccles seated himself at last in a Louis parlor chair, touched his pointed chin and narrowed his eyes. "Rosa Bonheur, I do believe," he said.

"Who?"

He pointed at the two paintings. "*The Highland Shepherd*, by Rosa Bonheur. And there is her *The Monarch of the Herd*. Miss Bonheur's work will rise in value, especially since she passed away this year, as you must know."

I knew nothing about the artist, nor recalled Roddy mentioning her name, but we both lowered our eyes just as the photographer's camera gave a little whoosh.

"Folds out, accordion-like," the photographer said, shoving the tripod legs into the carpet. The camera looked like a wood box with a big glass eye.

"Shall I continue to sit here? Is this the correct distance from the camera, Mr. Bullard?" I perched on a chair with padded arms.

"Few more minutes," he said, pulling a black curtain over his head.

"Mr. Eccles," I asked, "can you tell me the whereabouts of Mr. Cole's studio?"

"Indeed I can. Do you know of Mrs. Muenchinger? Amanda Muenchinger?"

"Her rental cottages?" Roddy asked. "On Catherine Street?"

"And others on Cottage Street," Eccles said. "Mr. Cole has taken two of the six cottages. His studio is on Catherine, and he has leased the Cottage Street cottage for himself and Mrs. Cole...or Miss.... We aren't quite certain."

"Either his wife, or his...lady friend," said Roddy.

"Precisely. Her name is Marianne, and she is lovely... rather bashful. She keeps house on Cottage Street. The Catherine Street cottage is solely in use for the studio. You will sit for your portrait there, Mrs. DeVere."

"Then, why these photographs for the artist who works in oil paint, Mr. Eccles? it seems unusual. It seems abnormal."

Eccles pinched his paisley cravat as if insulted. "Art is abnormal, Mrs. DeVere." He jabbed a finger at the paintings. "Rosa Bonheur's animals leap from the canvas because she did not rest with *beaux arts* schooling but sought the slaughterhouses...*abattoirs* where she wielded boning knives and cleavers. She knew the animals from the inside, Mrs. DeVere. The muscles, the tendons, the blood...."

"Ready when you are, Mrs. DeVere," the photographer bellowed.

Relieved, I faced left, then forward, and finally to the right as he signaled his readiness. The camera shutter snapped, and Mr. Bullard slipped plates out and into his box. He said a muffled "Good" each time from inside his cloth hood.

At last, the awkward afternoon was at an end. Eccles rose and waited for the photographer to fold the "accordion" and the tripod legs. Roddy and I agreed to come to the gallery on Monday at 11:00 a.m. to arrange my first sitting in the cottage on Catherine Street. We all stood, and Sands appeared to show the two men out.

Once again Eccles apologized for the lateness, but the photographer stepped in front of him and spoke up for the first time. Waving Eccles to silence with his derby, he said, "All my doing...assignment earlier today, and you'll see the photo in tomorrow's paper." He wrapped his arms around the cumbersome camera. "Bungalow on Gill Street...unoccupied.... You'll see it on page one. Got a close-up shot of the smoke. Fourth fire already, and summer just got started."

Chapter Six

SURE ENOUGH, A COIL of black smoke swelled over a rooftop on the first page of the morning's *Newport Daily News.* The headline hailed Hose Company Number 6 of the Newport Fire Department for a rapid response that extinguished the fire and prevented its spread. Alert neighbors had first reported seeing smoke, according to the paper, and a telephone call to the fire department proved the importance of Mr. Alexander Graham Bell's invention in today's Newport.

Far down in the account, we learned that a body was found inside the house. A deceased woman of approximately thirty years of age was discovered by fire patrolmen who entered the building after dousing the flames. Fully clothed except for shoes, the deceased apparently succumbed to smoke inhalation. Neighbors reported having seen recent activity in the unoccupied house whose damage was determined to be extensive. An unresolved, years-long property dispute was said to account for the vacancy of the house. Repairs were now pending.

"Mr. Bullard said nothing about a body," I said, holding the newspaper. The warm, clear morning had drawn us to the loggia, where white sails dotted the distance. Velvet napped at Roddy's feet. "Not one word from the photographer about a body."

"Bullard might not have known," Roddy replied. "He probably rushed to the darkroom to develop his picture for the morning edition. A reporter stayed on the scene."

"And the dead body is far down in the account," I said. "The telephone seems more important than the deceased."

"As a summer resort," Roddy reminded me drily, "Newport relies on telephoned news about yacht races and visiting aristocrats. Also, the *News* is not a Hearst scandal sheet."

"Even so...the 'recent activity' indicates people going in and out of the house. Squatters?"

Roddy did not answer. He raised binoculars at the sails in the distance, then turned to me. "These fires make a good case for extinguishers," he said. "Sands tells me Covell's Hardware has temporarily sold out of them. An order is placed for another dozen, and Sands will be notified."

"Why didn't Sands tell me?" But I knew the answer. The master of the house had priority in most matters as this century came to its end. The next years could be different, must be different. Folding the newspaper, I said, "Tomorrow at this time, we will be at the Travers block to schedule my 'sitting' for André Cole. And you will haggle with Eccles over the price. I will be bargained for, like a rug."

"Certainly not."

"There's something distasteful about Eccles," I said, "like a ferret. Or a weasel."

"Val...."

"He enjoyed talking about the artist's butchery, didn't he? His eyes shined. His fingers danced. I had a teacher like that in Virginia City. We dissected mice...but suffocated them first. She rubbed her hands together the whole time, stood over us and smacked her lips. Eccles reminds me of that woman."

Roddy reached for my hand. "Never mind Eccles, Val. For your purpose, he is a clerk. If it eases your mind, know that I plan to estimate the outlay by a visit to the...frankly, the Reading Room."

Roddy's fingers tightened at mention of Newport's exclusive, gentlemen-only club, a two-story house on Bellevue Avenue with spacious porches and schoolboys hired for the summer to fetch drinks for members in comfortable chairs. In our first Newport summer, I had complained that women had no reading room, but Roddy replied that Newport belonged to the women. By now, I knew what he meant.

"And Val, why not talk to ladies who have sat for portraits? Ask them about the experience. Pay a call on Mrs. Chanler. Or Elizabeth Lehr. Better yet, isn't there a ladies' luncheon next week?"

"Next Tuesday at Belcourt," I replied, "the ladies of Newport will be hosted by Mrs. Oliver Belmont…Alva."

"So, never mind Warren Eccles."

"Totally out of mind," I said with a flourish.

Twenty-four hours from now, I would wish it could be true.

&c.

Sunday passed quietly. At Roddy's suggestion, we walked Velvet along the oceanfront Cliff Walk, a stone pathway some forty feet above rearing waves that clawed at the rocks while sojourners gazed from the ocean to the green lawns and cottages set back behind grillwork or stone walls. Arriving for parties and balls on summer evenings, we would approach the cottages at their Bellevue Avenue entrances and never pay heed to the ocean that smashed below.

Roddy pointed out Mrs. Astor's Beechwood behind a vine-covered brick wall and the Goelets' Ochre Court that peeped from the distance. The Breakers was recognizable on sight, as was Marble House, which was owned by Alva Belmont, the hostess of the luncheon I would attend in a few days at her new cottage, Belcourt, said to be based on a hunting lodge at Versailles.

"Roddy," I said, "why visit France, when France is here in Rhode Island?"

My husband said the "crack" did not merit a response. We held hands, and when Velvet overheated and began to pant, Roddy picked her up and carried her back to Drumcliffe. We dined at eight o'clock, deciding to forego a lecture at the Casino on "The Future of Mongolia" by a traveler promising lantern slides on yurts and yaks. In weeks to come, I would yearn for an evening like this one, my husband reading Bancroft's *History* while I dipped into *A Lady's Life in the Rocky Mountains*, a book I had bound in leather last autumn in the city when book binding seemed like a lady's pastime until it drew the fire patrol to my door.

If I thought about the aftermath of that hobby on this Newport night, I might have listened to myself. On the eve of the Cuveen Gallery visit, I might have pondered the impulsiveness that so often hurled trouble at me—and at Roddy. The accumulating *mights* would have served as fair warning, but they went unheeded.

We estimated a thirty-minute drive from Drumcliffe to the Travers Block on Monday, July 10. Accordingly, Roddy and I were seated in a four-wheel trap hitched to Apollo and Atlas, setting forth at 10:30 a.m. in bright sunshine. Driven by our coachman Noland, the high-stepping horses trotted in rhythm, and the harness jingled. Not a soul stirred on Bellevue Avenue, which was not unusual for late-night Newport. The Travers shops ordinarily opened by noon, so the retail clerks were probably inside setting out wares.

When we arrived, Roddy suggested that Noland drive along the avenue to exercise the horses for another half an hour. Assisted from the carriage, I approached the gallery front door one step in front of Roddy, who reached around me for the door latch. The gallery windows were curtained, as was the door glass.

The latch gave way, the door swung open, and I stepped inside, my husband behind me. I later recalled that Roddy doffed his hat and said "Hello" once, and then twice. The opened door let a shaft of light pierce the dim interior, but no one answered Roddy's "Hellos" as I took another step forward, then halted at the sight in front of me. Halfway sitting on a table like a figure from Pompeii, Warren Eccles screamed in silence, his hands like claws that clutched at a gilt frame pulled down over his head and shoulders. Framed...the man was framed. Then the blood, the ripe red that darkened his cream-colored suit coat and shirt, and dribbled to the floor where I saw the knife.

In the next moment's blur, I heard Roddy's "Don't" as I bent to pick it up, a jeweled handle that twinkled in my gloved hand, the bloody curved blade, and my kidskin fingers suddenly sticky, just as familiar voices behind me cried out, "Valentine...is it you, Valentine? Oh, what have we here...? Oh...what have we?"

Chapter Seven

EVERY NEW YORK POLICE station had a stout oak desk, a file cabinet, a telegraph key and wall-mounted telephone with a separate earpiece. Each one featured a brass cuspidor that might or might not have been emptied and cleaned in recent days. And every station had a room where suspects were questioned. Without fail, this room was bare of decoration except for a wall clock. I should know all this because, in the last year, I have been invited to answer a number of questions in police stations in the state of New York. I could now offer the same observation about the Market Square Police Station in Newport, Rhode Island.

"Once again, Mrs. DeVere...you say the knife lay on the floor at the feet of the man you believed to be fatally stabbed...Mr. Eccles."

"...Eccles," I repeated in a hoarse whisper.

"And you picked up the knife in haste."

"I did."

Police Chief Ronald Cherry folded his hands, sucked one cheek, and fixed me with his steady gaze. A barrel-chested man with bright blue eyes, thick white hair and a huge handlebar moustache, the Chief of Police commanded great respect in Newport. Nearing retirement age last year, he was persuaded to extend his term.

"Without thinking," I said, "I reached down and grabbed the knife and picked it up. It was impulsive."

"And the next words you recall hearing were...to the effect of, 'What have we here?'"

"Mrs. Glendorick..." I said. "It was Madeline Glendorick." My mouth felt dry.

"You recognized her voice?"

"I turned around and saw Mrs. Glendorick and her husband."

"And you let go of the knife?"

"That's when I dropped it," I said.

"But before you picked up the knife, your husband warned you?"

"He did, yes. He said, 'Don't.'"

"Just the one word?"

"Yes."

"And you heard Mr. DeVere's warning, but disregarded it?"

"It was...it happened very fast."

"How fast, Mrs. DeVere? Would you say a minute? A few seconds?"

"Right away...I cannot detail how long, Chief Cherry."

Were his eyes kindly? Understanding? The chief had politely requested to continue speaking with me alone, and my husband agreed to wait in the reception area. A young officer in a chair against the wall took notes as I answered these questions. The chief had already interviewed us about our visit to the Cuveen Gallery this morning. Actually, his questions were directed at Roddy, who answered as I sat at his side. He was asked, Was the gallery door unlocked? Did Mr. DeVere recognize the victim? Was he an acquaintance? Did Mr. DeVere see anyone else near the Travers Block? Anyone on Bellevue Avenue?

Roddy's answers were accurate but terse.

"Would you care for a drink of water, Mrs. DeVere?"

The young officer looked ready to spring up, but I said, "No, thank you."

"About the knife, then," the chief said, "it was not familiar to you?"

"I never saw it until...." My fingers splayed as if to release the weapon once again. At the sight of Madeline and Edwin Glendorick, I remembered clasping my hands together and smearing blood on both gloves. The stained kidskin gloves were now in police possession. I had peeled them off and was told they would be locked in a cabinet for "safekeeping."

"And so, Mr. Glendorick advised you to wait in the art gallery," the chief continued, "and not to move while he and Mrs. Glendorick drove here to Market Square for police assistance?"

"Their coach was nearby," I said, "but ours was not."

Did the absence of our coach raise his suspicion? Roddy assured Edwin Glendorick that we would wait. And we did. We stepped outside the gallery and waited on the sidewalk. My husband closed the gallery door, and we waited.

The Travers clerks opened their shop doors and asked if they might help us? Were we here for Tiffany? For Brooks Brothers? Perhaps for Worth, since new samples of satin with a floral appliqué had arrived.

One polite "no" followed another until the sounds of the arriving police wagons drew every saleslady and clerk to the sidewalk to stare and whisper among themselves. When the police rushed inside the gallery, they craned their necks and looked quizzically at Roddy and me, the immobile couple who peered skyward amid the surrounding turmoil. I would remember feeling flushed as minutes passed with no sign of our carriage.

Finally, when our coachman returned to find police wagons crowding the block, he dutifully saw us into our carriage and to Market Square under police escort. Inside the station, we learned that the Glendoricks had returned to their cottage, Owls Roost. They had arrived early at the gallery, they said, to schedule a portrait of their daughter, a countess. The police might request a further interview with them, and the Glendoricks would happily comply.

As would we.

The wall clock hands said 12:45, and Chief Cherry pushed his chair back, a signal that my discussion with him was at an end—for now. I assumed he would thank me and ask that my husband and I be available for further discussions. When he did exactly that, I rejoined Roddy and proceeded to our carriage outdoors on the Square with its fish market, locksmith, and coffee house. Behind us loomed the brick police station that so recently boasted red, white, and blue bunting in honor of Independence Day.

"Roddy...now what?"

"Now lunch."

"I have no appetite."

"Which is precisely why we must eat something."

At Drumcliffe, my husband led us to the inglenook, a feature that seemed like an architect's afterthought. Bench seats on either side of a stone fireplace allowed two persons to fit very snugly across a small table in the center space. Roddy signaled the footman and inquired about the day's soup.

"Tomato, sir...early this season, vine ripe red."

Ripe red like Warren Eccles...splashed...spotted. I fought the gagging in my throat.

"What other soup, Chalmers?"

"Green pea, sir."

My husband loathed it, but he asked for two cups and a plate of sandwiches here at the inglenook. "And ice water," he added.

We held hands across the table. "Horrible," I said. "I feel I can't breathe."

Roddy pressed my fingers. "Shock to us both, Val...and afterward, you by yourself with the chief."

"He wanted to know about the knife, Roddy. If I hadn't stooped for the knife...and then the Glendoricks...so stupid."

"Maybe not. They witnessed—"

"—me with a knife in my hand. That's what they saw. Did you see the look on their faces? Madeline's eyes? The woman is a notorious gossip."

My husband pressed my hand tighter. A clock struck 2:00 p.m., and the footmen brought the soup, water, and sandwiches. Roddy said, "Bronson, please have the tomato slices removed from the sandwiches."

The platter was whisked away, and we sipped the soup and the water. I said, "Roddy, we have never been so close to...." I took a breath. "...so close to what we saw. And no clue that any such thing...I mean, so sudden."

"Completely."

"Do you know anything about Eccles?" I asked.

"Only what Theo told us."

"And our impression when he came here with the photographer," I said. "He did not seem nervous. Prickly, but not anxious. Maybe the newspaper photographer has information...Hugh Bullard. Or else Eccles's assistant...Asa somebody."

"Durling," Roddy said," Asa Durling. I made a note about him and about the artist, Rosa Bonheur. It is true that she passed away this year."

I met Roddy's gaze. He had verified Eccles's facts as a skeptical attorney would do, but Theo's warning also took hold. "To be frank, Val, I had concerns about Eccles's scrutiny of our paintings. Art theft is no joke. Let's say that I wanted to take precautions."

"Now it's a moot point," I said. "Moot."

"Maybe so," Roddy replied.

I did not ask about that *maybe*. "The police will investigate," I said. "And the...remains?"

Roddy sipped his water. "When the investigation concludes, the coroner will...take over. The police will search the gallery again and question the assistant."

"But suppose he's the killer...." I broke off.

"The police will take nothing for granted, Val. They will ask where Eccles has been living, which his assistant probably knows. He will be questioned about his whereabouts and asked whether he and Eccles had a disagreement. He will be asked about next-of-kin."

"So," I said, "the police want information...and an alibi."

"Both."

"And what about Cuveen? Who will reach him?"

Roddy pushed away his soup cup. "If the assistant does not wire him, the police will do so. Or the Travers family that owns the Block. By now, Joseph Cuveen is probably at sea."

"At sea," I said. "That's the feeling."

The sandwich platter arrived with fringes of lettuce. Roddy said, "We will get through this, Val. But in the meantime...Swiss cheese or chicken salad? Your choice."

"Choice," I said. "...choice in Newport? Face this fact, Roddy...the gossip will spread like a prairie fire. I gave the

Glendoricks a new topic just when everyone got their fill of their countess daughter. Madeline will be tireless describing what she saw...with gestures to paint the scene, how I turned around and saw her, and then dropped the murder weapon...and my bloody gloves."

I reached for a sandwich. "A big question is whether Eccles died when he tried to stop a thief. Did he interrupt a robbery when he was so violently...?"

I held the sandwich. "If paintings are reported stolen, maybe no one will believe Madeline Glendorick's story. She will eat her words and apologize. But hear this, Roddy...for now, I will ride up and down Bellevue Avenue and Ocean Drive with a fierce smile on my face. Newport pinned me as a Wild West creature from the minute I got here as your wife, but Society knows nothing about the Rocky Mountains where I learned how to handle myself. I learned lessons in the Rockies, and I will teach Newport what I have learned.

Chapter Eight

I ORDERED OUR PHAETON, left a note for my husband who was busy about a Florida orange grove purchase, and cast one last glance at the invitation:

BELCOURT, BELLEVIEW AVENUE

My dear Mrs. DeVere:

Will you give me the pleasure of your company at luncheon on Tuesday, July the eleventh, at one o'clock.

Sincerely yours,
Alva Belmont

Without fanfare, I set out for Alva Belmont's luncheon, where I would try my best to convince Newport ladies to reject the scene seeded in their minds—that Valentine DeVere was caught red-handed with a bloody dagger in the Cuveen Gallery.

Minutes before 1:00 p.m., the Belmont grooms and footmen assisted me from my carriage to see me into the "cottage" based on a Louis XIII hunting lodge at Versailles. In the receiving room Alva welcomed guests.

"Valentine DeVere...so good of you to join us. And what a lovely frock."

"Alva, so nice...."

With a strong jawline, full lips, rosy cheeks and piercing eyes, Alva Belmont shimmered in royal blue with energy known to strike at targets near and far. She scanned every stitch of the muted silk brocade that Calista selected for me, along with an aigrette instead of a hat and a modest necklace in gold filigree with citrine stones.

"So good of you to host the ladies of Newport," I said, aware that my hostess had been compared to an electrical unit at world's fairs—the dynamo. She was now the mistress of this sixty-room Versailles hunting lodge summer cottage. Briefly shunned for her scandalous divorce from the unfaithful Willie K. Vanderbilt, she had flirted, simmered, cajoled, and connived to smash all barriers to the social heights.

What heights Alva might command if she beamed that energy at worthy works, such as Votes for Women. In this summer of 1899, having bundled her daughter Consuelo in marriage to the Duke of Marlborough, she seemed content to be the mother of a duchess and the wife of a man devoted to prize horses and medieval armor.

I joined the dozen ladies in a reception room ornamented with Chinese porcelains and awash in yellow and white roses. Madeline Glendorick was across the room, her arms waving wide while she chatted with Mamie Fish and Tessie Oelrichs. I started their way, intending to set them straight about yesterday's fiasco.

But a familiar figure in ice blue cut velvet took my arm to pull me to her group. "Valentine DeVere, lovely to see you here. It's been months."

The searchlight-eyed Paulina Bourne briefly served with me on a committee investigating working conditions of retail saleswomen, and we had been guests at a dinner last winter. We were not friends.

"And Valentine, you remember Norma Doolittle and Henrietta Franklin...perhaps from the flower show."

I did not go to the show nor recall meeting the full-figured woman in cream satin with flounces, nor the willowy woman in spinach green silk. Hearing my name, both women cocked their heads and peered with eager interest that bordered on indecency.

"Ages ago," Paulina continued, "that sad committee on shopgirls' woes. Never again to the Lower East Side for that so-called charity. Shopgirls' tribulations are their own affair, are they not, Valentine?"

I started to say that shoppers ought to know the truth of the hard lives behind the counters and work for improvement, but Paulina slid into her topmost topic. "So fortunate to be served by the Newport salesladies and clerks...." She wet her lips. "...on the Travers Block."

The two women's eyes glittered.

I got no further. As if from thin air, Cassie appeared in the instant, touched my wrist and began to speak, over-riding my words as she purred, "Valentine ...and Paulina Bourne...and Norma and Henrietta...a delightful occasion to begin the season."

Behind flashing eyes, Paulina looked deflated, but confusion filled my head to the temples. What was my friend doing? Why did she interrupt me?

"And do we understand that you have tenants at Stone Point, Cassandra?" asked Norma Doolittle.

"I do...indeed, I do," Cassie began. I looked left and right as my friend chatted on about the splendid view from the Stone Point terrace and the outlook for favorable weather for her tenants who had come to Newport for the very first time. She held my wrist tight.

"Very first time?" asked Henrietta Franklin. "Never before on Aquidneck Island? Your tenants have much to learn, do they not?"

I tried to wedge in, but a butler's tinkling bell summoned us to luncheon, and Alva smiled us to a dining room table that was massed with flowers and ivy that outlined each place setting on the damask cloth. Name cards in calligraphy sent us in search of our seats, and *Valentine Mackle DeVere* put me in the middle of a row.

Seated, I eyed sterling utensils that might satisfy a surgeon and a calligraphed menu card with courses looking vaguely familiar once I got past *Oeufs*:

Hors-d'oeuvres
Oeufs Cocotte
Sole grillé Diable
Faison poélé au Céleri
Parfait de fois gras
Salade Rachel
Soufflé Chocolat
Fruits

Cassie was nowhere close. Across from me sat the fearsome Mamie Fish whose neck was encircled by a double choker of large red stones and a matching cuff bracelet. From the egg to the grilled fish, conversations turned to the Casino events and the visiting aristocrats to be honored with dinners. Before the salad, Madeline Glendorick was asked when her daughter would visit and whether the baronet would accompany her to Newport.

Regrettably, Madeline said, duties detained the baronet at his family's own Cleaveleigh Hall, but the countess was due at Owls Roost by midmonth and would remain in residence for several weeks.

"Edwin vows the Countess of Cleave will not sail for England until she sits for her portrait," Madeline said. "He is determined to have her portrait done this season."

"By that young artist, Cole?" asked Henrietta Franklin.

"Mercy, no," Madeline replied. "Not after what happened yester...that is... we have decided on Boldini."

The table went silent as stone for a long, deathly minute. Someone gasped, and a napkin fell to the marble floor. The only movement in the room was a footman offering a fresh napkin and others serving *salade Rachel.* My hands felt cold. The room felt cold.

Every woman stared at her plate of shredded vegetables. Cassie would say *julienne.* I looked around the tables for a glimpse of my friend but could not find her.

At that instant, Mrs. Leeds spoke up, a woman of generous proportions and good cheer. "Anyone who sits for Antonio Boldini," she said brightly, "must know that he likes to perch himself on a stack of *Encyclopedia Britannica* books on his stool. He will require a footman on either side as he paints, for the man is terrified of falling. So, for your daughter's portrait, Madeline, I recommend footmen and two maids to stand by, since I, Nancy Leeds, speak from experience at the Ritz Hotel in Paris where my portrait was done."

The table seemed uncertain whether to laugh or shake their heads, but Alva raised her gleaming salad fork and said, "Excellent advice from Mrs. Leeds, ladies." She lifted her punch cup. "To Nancy Leeds...and to Rachel of the *salade.*" We all raised our cups. At that moment, I thought of my papa's word for a passage leading to all levels of a silver mine, a passage opening the way to every shaft where a miner could work his ore with a pickax in the light of a candle flame. That passage was called the ramp.

Count on Paulina Bourne to block the ramp. Count on my edginess to play into her scheme. And count on the fruit course to send me to a sudden flashback.

We had progressed from the chocolate soufflé to the *Fruits*, which could have been blueberries or honeydew melon. Either would be fine.

As it was, however, the footmen brought red raspberries with cream...cream the color of Warren Eccles's suit. And berries screaming red.

I waved away the footman, but he already set the bowl of raspberries before me. Paulina said, "Cream, Valentine?"

I managed a "No, thank you," but a cream pitcher hovered, and Mamie Fish reached toward me, her bracelet near the cream pitcher.

"Mamie," said Paulina, "such vivid stones. Carnelian, aren't they?"

As if these two were in league, Mamie Fish said, "Choker and bracelet, both bloodstones." She added, "In recognition of Valentine's appearance in the newspaper."

"What appearance?" I asked. "What appearance, Mamie?"

"Why, today's *Newport Daily News*, pet. No false modesty, now. You have surely seen it. You are on the very first page."

Chapter Nine

FROM BELCOURT TO DRUMCLIFFE, I pressed Noland to use the whip, but the carriage crawled past cottages, trees, and snatches of the sea. I stumbled on the front steps, but a footman saw me lurch and took my arm. The butler informed me that Mr. DeVere would be in the library. "Shall I assist you, ma'am?"

"The newspaper," I blurted. "The Newport newspaper?"

The butler's shoulders stiffened, and he blinked his eyes, which meant he had seen the paper.

Which meant the household staff saw it too.

"Ma'am, I believe that you will find Mr. DeVere in possession of...."

He did not finish. In the hallway dash I lost a shoe, my petticoats caught at the knees, and my hair tumbled loose at the library entrance where I cried, "Roddy...."

"Val, dear...." He sprang from an armchair to clasp me in his arms, but comfort was beyond me at this moment.

"Where is the newspaper? Show it to me."

This dark brown room glinted with glass liquor bottles and flavorings, and my glance stopped at the black stone fireplace where two andiron dragons snarled.

"Val..." Roddy said softly, "your shoe." He stepped into the hall, returned with the silk pump, knelt, and slid my foot gently into the shoe. "Now then, let's sit down."

I went to an overstuffed chair and perched on the cushion edge. "Show it to me, Roddy."

As if touching a stick of dynamite, my husband put the newspaper into my hands. I mouthed the headlines before me—

TRAVERS BLOCK SITE OF MURDER

Smaller headlines peppered the front page...**Gallery Manager Fatally Stabbed... Police Search Cuveen Gallery...Robbery Suspected...Travers Clerks Fearful....**

Amid columns of fine print, three photographs were captioned. On the left, beneath the picture of the gallery front door, the caption read, "Cuveen Gallery, Travers Block, Bellevue Avenue." And on the upper right, two inky photographs, one of a man with slicked-back hair identified as "**Mr. Warren T. Eccles**" and to his right, "**Mrs. Roderick DeVere**."

"Roddy, who did this? It's Bullard's photograph of me, isn't it? Taken for the artist. Taken here at Drumcliffe...last Friday. The artist should have the pictures."

"But the photographer can develop additional prints, Val. He has the negatives."

"How could he do such a thing? Why the photograph of Eccles?"

"Probably from early publicity about the gallery this season, probably on file."

The newspaper crinkled in my hands, and the tiny print looked impossible. "What does it say?"

"It says we had an appointment at the gallery and expressed shock at what we saw." Roddy pulled up a chair beside me. "Val, I already marched into *The Daily News* office. I collared the editor-in-chief and nearly came to blows when he muttered about press freedom. He offered to run another story on Mr. and Mrs. Devere at the scene of the murder."

"More publicity...horrible."

"Out of the question. I told him so. Threatened to take him to court."

"Why did they do this? What were they up to?"

"They needed graphics. A new editor thought their photographs of Eccles dead in the frame were too—"

"—graphic?"

"Too much for Newport at the breakfast table. But the police want photographs of the gallery interior to be held for their investigation."

I looked again at my photograph. Of three poses for Bullard, the newspaper printed my face beamed at the camera eye. Did the editor think Mrs. DeVere looked sinister? Did Hugh Bullard?

"What about the Glendoricks?" I asked. "What does the paper say about Madeline and Edwin?"

My husband bit his lip. "They are not mentioned."

"How can that be?"

Roddy did not answer. "When you read the full account, Val, you will find us under '**Clerks Fearful**....' Here, let me...." Roddy took the paper from my hands, folded it back, and read aloud:

> Clerks and saleswomen observed a well-dressed woman and man who lingered on the sidewalk outside the gallery. Appearing to be a couple, the two were taken into police custody, later identified as Mr. and Mrs. Roderick DeVere. According to a salesclerk at The Brooks Brothers, the two forced their way into the Cuveen Gallery and appeared unconcerned when they exited. When offered assistance, they coldly refused.

"'Coldly refused?' Roddy, the clerks took us for customers. The gallery door was unlocked. You lifted the latch, and we went in and.... Don't reporters need verification?"

I knew better. At that moment, the footman entered the library to adjust the draperies in the changing light. A jade mantel clock chimed, and Roddy took my hand. "Val, let's take a breath. How about something to drink? Let's have sherry."

The footman stepped out, and I sat back, more in surrender than ease. In moments, we sipped the amber wine in Waterford crystal, the Irish import my husband chose to soothe me.

"So," I said, "this afternoon while Alva's footmen served us figs and fish at Belcourt, you hurried into town?"

Roddy sipped and put his glass on a table. "My orange grove business took all morning and into the early afternoon. The valet murmured something about today's Newport paper, but I waved him off. By the time I saw the headlines and your photograph, it was too late."

"Too late for what?"

Roddy rubbed his chin. "What I mean is, the household had seen the *News*. I'm sure they have discussed it."

"Whispered, you mean," I said, "the parlor maids... the kitchen. Chalmers closed those drapes a few minutes ago, and—"

"—and we need not name each member of our staff." Roddy folded his hands. "The household must be informed that your photograph was published in violation of policy at *The Newport Daily News* and has no bearing on the crime that occurred in the gallery. The season at Drumcliffe is to proceed normally, which the staff will hear from Sands this evening."

I sipped my wine. Unless a crisis rose to the level of warfare or plague, the butler summoned the household for important communications. Only once in our marriage did Roddy personally address the staff.

"As we know, every cottage subscribes to the newspaper," my husband continued, "but our Drumcliffe assembly will generate its own hearsay among servants from cottage to cottage. We will put every household on notice about the paper's violation and our concern for regular order."

"But the newspaper will not apologize, will it?" I said, "because my photograph is not ...." I paused to sort out slander from libel. "Not libel, is it?"

My husband shook his head. "Val, had I known what was coming, I would have dashed to Church Street and bought up every paper before the first delivery this a.m. No one would have seen your photograph."

My short laugh was brittle. "The newsprint might not matter, Roddy, when Newport has a 'town crier.' Madeline Glendorick wasted no time spreading the word. The luncheon ladies looked askance at me and loosed a few barbs."

"Surely not Cassandra."

"Not Cassie, though she interrupted at a pivotal moment...maybe for my own good. I'll find out."

"And Alva?"

"Our hostess was gracious from beginning to end. Some of the others...." I put my wine glass on a table. "Was it a robbery, do you think?" I asked.

"We don't know. Quite possibly."

"Our best hope, isn't it, Roddy? Selfish to say this after what happened to Eccles, but the gossips will find another target if the police catch a thieving murderer. And Madeline Glendorick will be forced to apologize."

The moment felt promising. I would think back on it in the weeks ahead. Somehow, I recalled the early days in Colorado when Papa first struck silver, only to find hard prospecting ahead and false starts in treacherous terrain.

Chapter Ten

BY DELIBERATE TRICKERY, WE learned Warren Eccles's murder did indeed result from a foiled robbery. First, a card delivered to Drumcliffe sent us to the gallery assistant when Roddy read, "'Arrangements for portraits by Mister André Cole will proceed under the coordination of Mr. Asa Durling in the Muenchinger Hotel at the corner of Bellevue Avenue and Catherine Street.'"

The footman brought tea and coffee refills on this Wednesday morning, July 12, as we sat in the breakfast room with the newspaper. I read every rehashed word under ***"Death of Gallery Manager Probed*** "and ***"Travers Block Gallery Closed."***

"Nothing about a robbery, Val?"

"Not a word."

"Or motive for the murder?"

"Nothing."

Roddy sipped his tea. "The card says we are invited to meet with Mr. Durling in the hotel's newly opened Cuveen Suite in the Muenchinger Hotel, or to schedule an appointment with him at our earliest convenience here at Drumcliffe."

"I don't want that man here," I said. "Bullard and his cursed camera were a mistake. And who is Asa Durling? An overworked assistant to a murdered man. Suppose he is the killer?"

"Val, let us credit the police for the essentials. I'd wager Durling has an airtight alibi. Otherwise, Joseph Cuveen would not entrust him to carry on at the hotel.

But Muenchinger...the same name as the cottages André Cole rented?"

"Same people. Gus and Amanda Muenchinger own the hotel too, a decent lodging house for clerks and salesmen in Newport for the season. Let's make the appointment for your portrait. And let's find out whether the killer stole paintings...the murder a robbery gone horribly wrong."

The Muenchinger Hotel stood at the corner of Bellevue Avenue and Catherine Street, a four-story house with a mansard roof, add-on portico and classical columns. The suite occupied a glassed-in side porch where the late Warren Eccles's assistant sprang up from a walnut desk.

"Asa Durling at your service, sir...Madame."

I was not prepared for a man so unearthly pale. His slate-gray suit set off thick snow-white hair, a ghostly white face, and pale eyes rimmed pink like a white rabbit. He must be an albino, doubtless coping lifelong with rude stares. Was he now in his late twenties? Thirties? His baggy suit coat meant he had lost weight. Or was the coat someone else's to begin with? Theo said Eccles had worked his assistant mercilessly.

We were expected, Asa Durling assured us, because Mr. Cuveen cited our name in recent cables from London. Seated on burgundy brown armchairs, we faced the desk and, behind it, framed paintings of rural scenes mounted on easels, likely retrieved from the Cuveen Gallery and now for sale. Also in sight, the three portraits we had seen at the reception, each signed with a flourish, **A COLE**. No other artworks were visible.

The assistant gave no sign that the couple seated before him had come upon his murdered employer.

"I have taken the liberty of keeping your name at the forefront of my files," Durling said, "with officers of the law and so many papers to sign. Even now, the Gallery documents are helter-skelter."

"Difficult days," Roddy said.

"You cannot imagine, Mr. DeVere. The insurance people give a man no peace."

"A business," my husband said calmly, "that operates in mysterious ways, does it not?"

"Magicians with trunk loads of ill-gotten gains, sir." Durling looked at Roddy as if he feared being brash. With eyelids lowered, he said, "As ship cargo, artwork is fully insured, Mr. DeVere. But everything is muddled now because of the...terrible misfortune...and disappeared paintings."

I did not meet Roddy's gaze when the assistant murmured "disappeared," but the words shouted in my ears. Shouted in Roddy's too. My husband did not miss a beat but mildly remarked that valuable artwork could also go missing when transported by rail. "We once lost a splendid landscape by Corot" he lied. "To this day, Mrs. DeVere is certain it was stolen from a railway car."

"I am certain," I said, taking my cue. "Fully convinced it was stolen."

"But persuading the insurance company was quite another matter," my husband continued in the boldface lie meant to pump information from Asa Durling. "Someone out there has our Corot.... Someone, but the police never found the painting or the thief. We feel the police were out of their depth."

"Over their heads," I said.

"I fear the same in Newport," Asa Durling said. "I am asked to say nothing while they look who might have.... Of course, I will comply, but frankly I have my doubts." He shook his snow-white head.

Roddy also shook his head. So did I, hoping a steel hairpin would not fall out to break the bubble of sorrow.

From the exchange that followed, I decided the man hungered for company. His extreme pallor doubtless isolated him in Newport where he was made to feel lowly and alone as well. For Asa, we appeared at the right time.

Roddy pointed to the rural scenes in paintings behind the desk. "Art retrieved from the gallery, I assume?"

"Fortunate to have those you see," Durling said. "A workman helped me move them out, scowling fellow, one of those foreigners, works on plaster. But I cannot account for three paintings missing since...since Monday, July 10 of this year. You know the artists' names, Millet and Dupré.... And Eduard Detaille."

I had no notion of the names as Asa Durling softly said, "*Les Planteurs de pommes de terre*...Potato Planters. And Jules Dupré, *Cows Crossing a Ford.*"

"These are paintings missing from the Cuveen gallery?" Roddy asked.

Durling nodded. "Also missing is Detaille's *French Artillery in Snowy Winter.*"

"Oh," I said, "I saw it at the reception."

"Of course you did...that is, it was exhibited prominently."

Somehow, the genial mood broke. Durling shuffled papers and said, "Monsieur Cole is prepared to set to work. He is in possession of your photographs, Mrs. DeVere, and he works on Saturdays, though not on July Fourteenth."

Roddy said, "Bastille Day."

"Precisely."

"And Mr. Cole is French?" I asked.

"A devotee of La France," he murmured, looking sideways and running pale fingers down a page of a leatherbound book. "Mrs. DeVere, your consultation with Monsieur Cole can take place at noon, July the fifteenth, at Number Four Catherine Street. Will that suit you, Madame?"

"It will," I said.

Roddy said he would call upon Mr. Durling soon. "And may the paintings be recovered, Mr. Durling, and in your care for safekeeping."

"And may Mr. Eccles's slayer be found, Mr. DeVere." Durling pulled at his lapels and chilled us with a curse from his pale lips. "I pray that he will be hanged, drawn, and quartered, as in days of old."

Gritting my teeth, I would spend the necessary hours posing for the foppish dandy we had seen at the reception. If he unleashed mouthfuls of French while I sat motionless, I would endure it. If paints and solvents gave me headaches, so be it. This was my gift for Roddy. We had agreed on a head-and-shoulders portrait. Still, the prospect of meeting André Cole in the small cottage of a studio recalled visits to a Virginia City dental parlor.

Shortly after 11:00 a.m. on Friday, I stepped into the carriage and opened a sealed envelope just delivered from Seabright cottage. Inside, a note from Cassie read, "*Stone Point crisis as feared. Please help...C.*"

The ink splotch meant my well-mannered friend was distraught. I could order Noland to drive immediately to Seabright, but dealing with Asa Durling once again kept me quiet in the carriage. This consultation should be short. Noland would wait on Catherine Street and drive me straight to Seabright. I would go directly from the artist's cottage to Cassie.

The Catherine Street cottage was a two-story clapboard with a gleaming front window and a huge brass door knocker doubtless added to spruce up the rental. One rap, and the door was opened by the artist himself, taller than I recalled, but the upturned moustache, brooding eyes and curly dark hair were as familiar as the ruffled shirt, the velvet jacket and the silk bowtie so casually knotted. His portraits had spoken for him at the gallery, and his voice streamed French. Or French-ish.

"Madame DeVere, *bonjour*...good day, and welcome to the studio of Monsieur André Cole."

Ushered inside, I sniffed turpentine in the parlor that was well-lighted by windows on two sides, though I understood artists liked north light. A paint-spattered tarpaulin spread like a rug beneath an easel, a stool, canvasses, and a table with brushes, tubes of paint, crocks and tins with indistinct markings. Some six feet from the easel and tarp stood the cushioned chair I would be expected to occupy while Cole painted my portrait. Eyeing the chair's claw-and-ball feet, I stood in place but noticed a table with three chairs under a window in the corner of the studio-parlor. The table was set for a meal. A smaller table nearby held serving pieces that appeared to be silver.

"Madame DeVere," Cole said, "the hour is favorable for *déjeuner*...as you say, lunch."

"Oh, surely a mistake," I said. "I am here to only discuss my portrait."

"*Vraiment*...truly," he said. "First, we will discuss, and then Marianne comes to us. She must know all my subjects, especially the ladies. We are then *confortable*."

"Comfortable," I said. "Nonetheless, it is difficult to be at ease after last Monday when the...." Whatever was French for murder, I cleared my throat and said, "The terrible event in the gallery."

"Dreadful, Madame...terrible." He turned his face away and rubbed his eyes. I stayed silent. Had he heard the rumors about me? That the lady he was to paint was suspected of killing Warren Eccles?

"Madame, we must trust *les gendarmes*, the police. But the world must not intrude upon art. The work of André Cole proceeds, and your portrait, Madame, must fill my thoughts." Cole's voice rose as if addressing a throng.

He drew me to the closest window and once again spoke in the third person. "If you please, Monsieur André must see in the light." Touching a finger at my chin, he turned my head slightly to the left. "Ah yes, a complexion *tres exposé* to the sun," he said. "Madame, do you not veil your face?"

"Only at funerals," I said.

He drew a sharp breath. "No matter, Madame DeVere. Your complexion will be beautified at the hand of Monsieur André." He leaned closer and waved a finger darkened with paint at the cuticle.

Another touch of his finger turned my head to the right as he leaned close to study every feature. "Eyes in proportion," he murmured, "and the chin of a moderate size. The nose with a little rising in the middle, and the lips well turned, fortunately."

This felt like an auction in the West. Every cow, every horse, every mule or donkey was detailed by the auctioneer before bidding began. All this, I told myself, was for Roddy.

"Your neck and shoulders, Madame...? From the graceful neck, the shoulders must gently spread with a soft appearance."

Was he asking that I strip my cotton jacket and high-neck shirtwaist?

He was not. "All to be decided," he said, glancing at the windowpane. "For my Marianne comes to us now from the other cottage...and brings today's *déjeuner.* Non, non, Madame DeVere, you cannot depart."

"I must," I said. "I have another appointment."

"*Ce n'est pas possible,*" he said. "It is impossible." Arms crossed across his chest, he backed away. "Monsieur André cannot proceed. *Fini...*we conclude."

"The portrait...."

"No more."

The defiant artist held his pose while knocking began at the front door. Or rather, a bumping at the door as if a person had hands full.

"Please reconsider, Mr. Cole..." I began. But he did not budge. At Seabright cottage, Cassie was depending on me. What's more, my husband's gift was at stake. Despite the thudding at the door, André Cole did not move. Cassie must wait, and Roddy's portrait meant I would bow to this stubborn painter here and now, whether he was truly French or pretending. Masking disgust, I finally said, "I shall stay for lunch."

Instantly, the parlor studio filled with *"Cherie, ma Cherie...."* as Cole flung open the door to welcome a cloaked, hooded figure who lugged a heavy casserole that seemed too heavy for her frame. Concealed in the dark cloak, she toted the casserole to the corner, set it on the serving table, and stood back as Cole announced, "Madame DeVere, let me present my Marianne who prepares excellent repasts and launders my *vêtements*...a painter's smock." He swept off her cloak as if unveiling a sculpture.

"How do you do?" I said.

"Enchanté," said the woman whose skirt and shirt-waist loosely hung on thin shoulders and hips that could charitably be called fine-boned or slender. Large dark eyes so dominated her narrow face that I barely noticed other features except for her fingers, which were knuckled like a worker's hands.

Or like miners' hands in the West, I thought. Like my papa's hands. She saw me stare too long at her bare fingers and nails that were darkened from kitchen work. "At a coal stove," she said, "the cook wears no jewels...and let us to lunch. And we will speak English, yes?" Her voice sounded vaguely British.

Serving a slow-cooked French stew, a *daube*, Marianne said she grew up in the French-speaking Canada and learned English from an English teacher. She gave André a little smile when he said, *"Professeur d'Angleterre."* He uncorked red wine and poured three glasses.

We toasted my portrait. At its completion, Cole promised we would celebrate with champagne. My seat at the table put me in broadest light, but neither André nor Marianne offered to pull down a blind or close the tied-back curtain. André forked his *daube* while Marianne asked about my earrings.

"Amethyst," I said. Calista had chosen them, but I did not recall the details that Marianne sought as she leaned close to my right ear, then asked me to turn my head. "They match," I said. "Or they should."

"Oh, indeed," Marianne replied. "The stones so distinct, and your ears...nice."

The woman's enormous eyes seemed to drink in my face until I reached for my napkin and then for my wineglass to interrupt her gaze. Ideas about appropriate distances between people varied from one country to another, as I knew, but Marianne's interest in my ears and earrings brought her face awfully close to mine. Maybe a Canadian custom.

"A lovely lunch," I said to her, "but Mister Cole knows that I have another appointment, and so...."

"So, you will leave us so soon," Marianne said. "But André must know of your wishes for the background...your portrait background."

André looked up from his *daube* and grinned. "Ah, Marianne, *ma femme*."

The two peered at me until Marianne said, "I fear my dear André might make a regrettable mistake, Mrs. DeVere. Suppose he fancies you wearing a leopard skin stole? Or a Scottish tartan against the Highlands?"

"Scots? I don't think so."

"And then, your lifetime symbols?"

"What sort of symbols?" I asked.

"What you decide...for André Cole fills a cabinet with enticing symbols. He has a stuffed parrot. He has a head of John the Baptist."

"John the...." I shuddered.

"He has Japanese fans...and a scimitar too."

"Scimitar?" My mouth went dry.

"Or perhaps Mister DeVere would have a say...?"

I started for the door. "A say...yes, he will have a say. Indeed, he must."

Chapter Eleven

A FAST HOUR IN the carriage from Catherine Street to Seabright saw me seething over André Cole's scimitar. A sword, yes? Not a dagger but a sword. Did Marianne know the difference? Did any modern portrait feature a blade? Ladies cradled flowers. Gentlemen held walking sticks. Marianne's list, from a parrot to the severed head of John the Baptist, and then the scimitar...it felt deliberate.

What to make of it? Was that final exchange an intentional echo of Eccles's murder—and mockery of me? Or was I invited to share a secret between André and Marianne? And Asa Durling too? Or were these thoughts imagination's overflow? Did Asa Durling's vision of the culprit hanged, drawn, and quartered tantalize the artist and Marianne?

At Seabright, I would probably hear Cassie hold forth about a burst water pipe in the cottage leased by the oleomargarine couple. She would bemoan the ruined plaster...the *cartouche*. So trivial.

I would try to be supportive. My friend hated being a landlady, even for a season. She should have put Stone Point on the market, found a buyer unaware of its calamitous history. Or indifferent to it. Or happy to flaunt it. For now, Cassie's butler or housekeeper could find plumbers and plasterers. A gracious note to the Rickers would suffice. No need to pay a call.

To my surprise, Cassie's carriage with a pair of matched Grays stood at Seabright's entrance. Her coachman, O'Boyle, saluted Noland as Cassie's groom assisted me from my carriage into her brougham.

"A carriage relay?" I asked lightly. "The ladies are going for a drive?"

"Ma'am," replied O'Boyle, "Mrs. Forster requests your company for an afternoon call. She expects to drive you home...so, if you might dismiss Mr. Noland?"

I did, just as my friend burst from her front door to climb inside the carriage, sit across from me, smooth her rose silk afternoon dress, and breathlessly call out, "Stone Point, O'Boyle...quickly."

I said, "The water pipes, is that it?"

"Exactly my fear."

"Must we go ourselves? Not send a servant? Your Hayes is an excellent butler, Cassie. I'm sure he would...."

She waved me to silence. "Early this morning, a cry for help came to me from Geneva Ricker. She pleaded that I personally assist in a 'most serious matter.'"

"But she did not say what 'matter?'"

"No. Her footman waited while I wrote promising to see her as soon as possible today. Then I wrote to beg you to come with me. I only hope we are not too late."

Late for what? Roddy warned that water could dissolve a dwelling as completely as fire could reduce it to ashes, which we knew all too well. Was this carriage speeding us to a cottage hollowed by flood? Would we find the Rickers in the garden soaking wet?

The carriage passed Crossways, the white Colonial-style summer home of Stuyvesant and Mamie Fish. In a few days, Roddy and I would attend a party at Crossways and listen to Mamie's much-vaunted insults that were laughed off as wit, even by guests she skewered.

Cassie nervously peered from the carriage and murmured that a four-horse team would already have us at Stone Point. The cottage, I seemed to recall, had passed ownership from a seascape artist to a banker before its third owner disgraced himself and, by extension, the property. Last summer, Cassie heard a last will and testament read in the cottage and learned of the vast inheritance that complicated her life. I had once been to a luncheon at Stone Point, never to an evening event.

Soon enough, we entered elaborate ironwork gates and were assisted from the carriage by uniformed grooms. At the entrance, a butler informed us that Mr. and Mrs. Ricker would receive us in the Opal reception room. Nothing appeared out of the ordinary as he led the way, nothing damp or wet. Perhaps that was the problem, pipes jammed.

The rooms we passed in this moment might have been interiors along Ocean Drive or Bellevue Avenue with their golden wall panels, Louis furnishings, candelabra, porcelains, tapestries, and paintings in gilded frames.

Would a gilt frame ever again appear, to my eye, like a mounting for a picture? Was I fated to see murder in every such frame? Drumcliffe had its share, as did our New York chateau at 620 Fifth Avenue. I saw them on the way to the Opal room, where a middle-aged couple stood side by side amid sofas and chairs dripping with fringe no longer thought to be stylish.

"Mrs. Forster, so good of you to come," said Geneva Ricker, rubbing her hands together.

"Mr. and Mrs. Ricker," said Cassie, "I would like you to meet my friend, Mrs. Roderick DeVere. I hope we can be of help...."

"We know you will help us, don't we, Mr. Ricker?" said the full-figured woman draped in a hibiscus pink tea gown with a cannonade of buttons from neck to slippers. Her light brown eyes flickered under eyebrows seeming penciled into sharply-drawn arches. A short upper lip gave Geneva Ricker's face a sad expression, though her eyes were bright and her voice pleasantly eager. "Don't we, dear?" she prompted her husband.

Ezra Ricker seemed uncertain whether to bow or extend his hand, so he laced fingers across the broad expanse of his waistcoat and said, "Welcome, and thank you for taking the trouble." At about five feet tall, he reached his wife's chin but stood with feet planted wide apart as if ready to grapple with whatever confronted him. His pewter-gray eyes darted back and forth as if watching for trouble—or opportunity.

"Tea," Mrs. Ricker said as if she surprised herself. "We must have tea." A footman in the doorway sprang to attention. We had not yet been invited to sit down.

"Mrs. Ricker," said Cassie, "we would of course enjoy hospitality, but your concern about a 'serious matter' brings us here. If you would please help us understand the problem? Does it concern the plumbing?"

At this, Ezra Ricker snickered. "Nothing of the kind. Salt or fresh water...take your pick."

"Then, what...?" My friend's gentle but firm voice ceased.

Ezra Ricker continued, "Ladies, back in Little Rock, my wife would handle this thing without a second thought."

"I would," Geneva said. "It's about a picture...where to hang a picture we bought yesterday."

Her husband pointed to a space above a seating arrangement. "Up there," he said, "where we could look at it after supper. The footman will put it up, but suppose his hammer cracks that fancy plaster...?"

He raised a thick finger, and we all looked at the ceiling and molding. Stunned at the sight, I fell silent. As many times as I had seen elaborate plasterwork, nothing compared with this—a composition abounding in medallions, clusters of fruit, birds nesting and in flight, flowers in bud and bloom. Like fine sculpture, the shapes rewarded the eye at every point. This plasterwork garden soared to a plane that was masterfully artful, and I now understood Cassie's fetish about the *cartouche* and the young man who could achieve all this with putty knives.

"Incredible," I murmured. "Gorgeous..."

Cassie asked the Rickers about their new painting. Was it large? Heavy? I expected my friend to ask who might have sold a painting to the Rickers, but Geneva was happy to fill us in.

"About ten o'clock yesterday morning," she said, "a young Italian workman came to the front door with a painting to sell. He said he had found it and hoped that Mrs. Forster would buy it from him. He seemed to think that we are members of the Forster family, and he offered us the painting, which was already in a fancy frame. He had a mean look to him, like we better buy his picture if we know what's good for us. But we liked it. Mr. Ricker paid him...what was it, Ezra?"

"Ten dollars," Mr. Ricker said. "He wanted twenty, but I bargained him down because I liked the picture, and Geneva was partial to the frame."

"Could we see it?" I asked.

Mr. Ricker nodded, and Geneva said, "Ezra, let the footman bring it. Oh, footman...."

In moments, the painting in a gilded frame was brought into the Opal room and propped against a Louis table leg. The Rickers stood back and smiled at a picture now familiar to them, an artwork needing Cassie's permission to hang it on the wall.

Cassie and I stood speechless. My friend wet her lips and took a step forward, then back. My feet felt planted on the floor. On this hot July afternoon, I gazed at snow, at soldiers, at cannon...

"Detaille..." Cassie murmured. "Eduard Detaille."

"*Artillery...*" I said. *"French Artillery...."*

"...*in Snowy Winter,*" my friend mumbled. We said these words once again, back and forth.

The Rickers looked bemused and then alarmed. Cassie finally drew herself up and asked, "Mr. and Mrs. Ricker, do you recall the name of the young man who sold you the painting?"

"Italian name," Geneva said, pronouncing it Eye-talian. "What was it, Ezra?"

"Marco," her husband answered. "No last name. So, can you let us hang it up? Will you take the risk with the plaster?"

"The risk...." Cassie repeated. She faced the Rickers, cleared her throat, and stood up every inch of her five foot, two inches. "Mr. and Mrs. Ricker," she said, "we need to call the police. Call the police immediately."

Chapter Twelve

THE TWO OFFICERS HAD no idea why they were summoned until Cassie said the words, "Travers Block" and "Cuveen Gallery."

They snapped to attention, took notes, and asked the exact time of the Stone Point purchase of the painting. For a description of "Marco," the Rickers recalled a swarthy face and broken English, but Cassie had seen the plasterer when he created the *cartouche*, and she remembered a single eyebrow across his low forehead and a religious medal around his neck. The police asked whether "Marco" offered to sell additional pictures to the Rickers. He had not. And where did he claim to have found *French Artillery in Snowy Winter*? They did not know. They had not thought to ask him. He made them uneasy. They wanted him gone.

Cassie and I stood aside as the couple tried to answer each question, mortified to learn their new painting was stolen.

Geneva blamed herself for ignorance of art, Ezra for squandering ten dollars. They agreed to be available for further questioning in the days ahead. They also understood the police must confiscate the stolen painting. Cassie suggested a soft clean cloth, and my friend supervised the wrapping in a bedsheet. The police took down Cassie's name and mine, careful about the capital "V" in DeVere. We bid farewell to the Rickers and were quiet in Cassie's carriage. We had not stayed for tea.

On Sunday, Roddy's and my midday meal was oddly interrupted. No sooner had we sat down and lifted soup spoons than the butler appeared to say the Newport Chief of Police was at the door.

"Chief Cherry here?" Roddy said. "On Sunday afternoon?"

"With another officer, most keen to have a word," Sands said, displeasure in his knit brows and clipped voice. "Shall I suggest a delay, sir?"

Vichyssoise, a cold potato soup set before us would precede an eggy pie called quiche. Hungry, we both eyed the soup and warm rolls, but lunch would be stressful with the police hovering.

"Did the chief indicate the purpose of the call?" Roddy asked.

"He did not, sir."

We signaled each other with our eyes until my husband said, "Show the officers to the foyer. We will join them momentarily."

"Do you think Chief Cherry is here to question us again?" I asked.

"At Drumcliffe? Ridiculous, I won't stand for it."

"Suppose it's about *French Artillery*?"

"Nonsense."

Without another word, we joined the uniformed Chief of Police and the officer familiar to me from the Market Street headquarters. He had taken notes when I was questioned and now clutched a manila folder. Both men wore dress uniforms as if for church. Neither wore a side arm.

"My apologies for this unscheduled call," Chief Cherry said, introducing Officer Seavers. The chief's ruddy cheeks flushed a deeper red as he continued to apologize for inconvenience in service to his duties for Newport. Beside him, Officer Seavers stood at attention. "So that you understand," the chief said, "I know nothing about art and artists, but our investigation leads directly to paintings that disappeared from the Cuveen Gallery."

"Disappeared?" Roddy said, his voice curt. "You mean stolen, sir? You may know that Mrs. DeVere and I have met with Mr. Asa Durling about a new portrait this season. Mr. Durling told us artwork was stolen from the Travers Block gallery the morning Mr. Eccles was killed. Do we assume the homicide resulted from robbery?"

"That is our finding to date, Mr. DeVere."

"And the police have interviewed Mr. Durling in regard to his whereabouts on that day?"

The chief fingered his moustache. "Mr. DeVere," he said, "We have questioned Mr. Durling. On the morning of the...the break-in, he was on Thames Street on an errand. He has furnished a list of the paintings in the gallery before it was closed...the inventory. We know what is accounted for...and what is gone."

Chief Cherry nodded to Officer Seavers, who opened the folder.

"The total inventory need not concern you, sir...ma'am," the chief said. "The artists' names and the titles of the pictures are mainly in the French language. Most of the painting names were entered in ink...black ink." He swallowed. "Except for one in pencil at the bottom."

"And what would that be?" I asked. The chief looked as though he must swallow a dose of castor oil. "The entry goes, 'Rosa B-o-n-h-e-u-r, *The Highland Shepherd.*' And the name is 'DeVere.'"

Our stunned silence lasted an eternal minute until Roddy said, "Officers, if you will please follow me." He took my arm and led us briskly to the alabaster reception room, halting in front of the Scotsman in tartan plaid leading a herd of sheep that looked overdo for shearing.

"This is the painting in question," Roddy announced. "The late Warren Eccles saw this painting when he called here with a photographer to take pictures of Mrs. DeVere."

"The photographer," I said, "is employed by *The Newport Daily News.* His name is Hugh Bullard."

Seavers consulted his list, and the chief stepped close to see the artist's signature on the lower left corner of the canvas. He said, "So, this painting has been here for...?"

"Years," Roddy said. "It was purchased by my parents a number of years ago. The late Mr. Eccles took particular interest in it."

"And why would that be?"

"I have no idea. Perhaps he planned to offer to buy it...on Mister Joseph Cuveen's recommendation. He commented on its increased value."

The chief shifted from one foot to the other. "Mr. DeVere," he said, "Is it possible to show us a bill of sale? A record of the transaction?"

Roddy's law practice had proven the advantage of tight control over temper in the courtroom, but my husband's clenched jaw meant he struggled. Facing the officers, he said, "Any record of the transaction would be filed at our home in New York City. For the summer, my parents are in Maine, and I am most reluctant to disturb them on this matter of a penciled scribble."

"Note," said Officer Seavers. "A penciled note."

At this, Roddy took a deep breath and made a decision that would keep the policemen here for the next hour and postpone our meal indefinitely, though I was too flustered to be hungry. Taking my arm again, my husband marched the officers from room to room, pausing before each painting to ask Officer Seavers whether his inventory of the Cuveen gallery included the painting in question. Through drawing rooms, reception rooms, the music room, the library, the sitting rooms, guestrooms, and the hallways we went. The officers declined to visit Roddy's upstairs suite, and my boudoir was out of the question. Otherwise, we paused before landscapes, waterfalls, still life paintings of fruit or flowers or hutches of bunny rabbits—each one tested against Officer Seavers's list.

The exercise was punitive, but still my husband persisted until we finally entered the Lafayette Room with its mishmash of paintings. Agog, Chief Cherry and Officer Seavers stared at walls virtually plastered with art.

"I believe we have seen enough," the chief said. "Let us thank you, Mr. and Mrs. DeVere for your courtesy this afternoon."

The two officers began to retreat until Seavers said, "What is that?"

"What?" the chief asked.

"In that crate. Over there." He pointed.

"Oh," Roddy said, "the painting we brought from New York."

The officers stared at the crate, wood with steel bands.

Roddy said, "I can tell you about it."

"No need," Chief Cherry said, but he hesitated, exchanging a glance with Seavers. "But sir," he said to Roddy, "if you would not mind...?"

"I would 'mind,' Chief Cherry. The painting inside that crate is from the Netherlands from the time of Rembrandt. It might be a Rembrandt. In any case, I ask you to take my word for it. I give you my word."

Roddy's word carved itself in the air like a challenge, a dare, a border not to be crossed. In the weeks to come, I would fervently wish he had ordered the crate opened.

Chapter Thirteen

THE EVENING OF WEDNESDAY July 19 started with a quarrel over the cruise on Felix Vanderbilt's *Conquest*. Roddy suggested we send regrets.

"Absolutely not," I said.

Dismay was written in every line of my husband's face. "Val, I received a word of advice at the Reading Room from George Gould. Speaking gentleman-to-gentleman, he suggested we withdraw for the time being."

"Withdraw? Nuns 'withdraw' for spiritual lives in convents." I sucked in my breath. Angry tears welled up. "This is about showing spirit in Society. Hiding is out of the question. I will not be driven into social exile in Newport."

My husband straightened his shoulders and said, "I believe the request is intended for the protection of your feelings...and other ladies' feelings."

"Protection…oh, please! I will hold my own, and besides, those social queens are a tough bunch, Roddy, and you know it. At times, they remind me of the New York gangs, fighting over territory. If you are anxious about crossing George Gould, I will speak to him myself."

"Val, you are free to speak to whomever you like. But you might care to avoid a repetition of Alva Belmont's luncheon."

Roddy had a point, but I was too riled up to back off. "Speaking of slights," I said, "I listened in silence while you and Joseph Cuveen talked about the Lafayette table. You and I spent all afternoon looking at portraits in the Lafayette Room that first day in Newport, and you still have not shown me the inscribed antique table."

At this, my husband flushed, his eyes downcast.

Arms akimbo, I said, "Well…?"

"I could not show you the table, Val. It is no longer in the Lafayette Room."

"Where is it?"

The air grew very quiet. "Sold," my husband said softly. "My parents sold it."

"When?" Seeing Roddy's face in that moment, I could guess exactly when Rufus and Eleanor sold the valuable table. They sold it when their finances crashed. "Oh," I said, "That's why you didn't…."

My husband nodded. "It was a troublesome time, Val. My parents let some of the silver go. Mother's jewelry and furnishings too. And the 'antiques' in the Lafayette Room are not originals. Mother held fast to the paintings, and they would have gone next, except...."

"Except that the DeVeres journeyed westward, resulting in...in us."

"Us...." Roddy said it softly, took my hand, and met my gaze. "We are what matters."

"If only I had listened to you at the Cuveen gallery last Monday morning," I said, "none of this...."

My husband shushed me with a kiss. "No regrets. The police are searching all-out for the plasterer, and they will soon find him. For now, we go forward. I have mixed feelings, as you well know, but let us dress and be off to the Yacht Club station. When *Conquest* weighs anchor, we will be aboard."

Our carriage reached the waterfront with minutes to spare. The sleek Vanderbilt motor launch with **CONQUEST** on the rail head bobbed among the gigs and cutters, and a crewman assisted ladies and gentlemen aboard and sped us into the harbor to the moored yacht. We held onto our hats, assisted up the ladder and onto *Conquest*'s deck by crewmen in matching sailors' uniforms edged with the Vanderbilt signature dark red.

"Welcome aboard, Mr. and Mrs. DeVere...Roderick and Valentine."

"Mr. Vanderbilt...Felix."

I toggled between last and first names of a man I knew from dinners and one dance at Rosecliff, the cottage with a heart-shaped staircase. In his yachting cap, bow tie, and white shoes, the railroad director looked jaunty, and his former wide-wing moustache was trimmed to the lip line.

"Lulu is aboard and looks forward to seeing you both," he said, referring to Mrs. Vanderbilt, whom I recalled as a languid woman ideally suited to a chaise longue.

"I look forward to seeing the sails raised," I said.

"Sorry to disappoint you," Vanderbilt replied mildly, "but we won't be under sail this evening. *Conquest* is a screw steamer."

The term sounded risqué. I smiled.

Felix Vanderbilt waved Roddy and me toward burnished mahogany decks arrayed with groupings of deeply cushioned chairs of Genoa red velvet, sofas, Persian rugs, and rosewood tables. Guests stood chatting while soft melodies rippled from a baby grand piano played by a young man I recognized from a complicated country house visit just weeks ago. The musician, Jack Barrott, was said to earn his way as a useful guest, earning lengthy stints from wealthy benefactors. He smiled at me, took a lady's request, and smoothly shifted from "A Lemon in the garden of Love" to "Blue-Eyed Stranger."

Once underway, most of us would sit down. "Let's stand at the railing near the front," I said.

"The bow," said a voice at my shoulder.

"Theo...."

"Valentine and Roderick DeVere," said our friend with a little salute. "Do use precise nautical terms, especially since you, Valentine, plan to become a sailor this summer. Have you got yourself a boat?"

"Not quite yet," I said. "How goes life at the Bannister House?"

"Settled for the summer," Theo said. "A chimney sweep has swept both chimneys, and the hardware store has my order for extinguishers. The gardener is preparing the grounds for my picnic. Invitations will go out soon. How have you been?"

"Busy," I said, "as you might guess."

Our friend looked from Roddy to me. "So I understand."

"It seems all Newport 'understands,'" Roddy said, "no thanks to the lying reporters who write fiction instead of facts. At least the *News* now puts the murdering plasterer on Page One."

"Gliano," Theo said. "Marco Gliano. Everyone in Newport knows the name, and every servant swears to spot the eye-browed workman, reap the reward, and never again touch a mop or chamois cloth."

"Five hundred dollars from anonymous donors," I said. "He will soon be captured."

My husband looked past my shoulder. "Excuse me for a moment. George and Edith Gould have come aboard...just a quick word with them." Roddy hastened to the Goulds.

"Just so you know, Theo," I said, "George Gould urges us to hibernate this summer. It seems that this outlier from the West is out of season."

"You will weather this, Valentine, especially when the plasterer is behind bars. You and Roderick have the right idea. Go about and smile until your cheeks ache. And then smile some more. Now then, champagne?"

Servants in sailors' togs circulated with champagne and lobster tidbits that Cassie called *en croute*. We nibbled, touched glasses and sipped. "Theo," I said, "do you know that Boston was the late Warren Eccles's birthplace?"

"Quite disconcerting to see it in the *Daily News*, I must admit. But if you wish, I will ask my aunts and cousins."

"Please."

"No high hopes, Valentine. My relatives are Beacon Hill loyalists. They barely recognize the Back Bay, and all else is *Terra Incognita*." He sipped. "Unless Eccles attended art school...perhaps on a scholarship. I will inquire. Oh, we are underway."

Conquest had slipped its mooring so smoothly that no one's wine rippled. Guests barely noticed. "I see your hubby with the Goulds," Theo said, "so let us observe what other splendid vessels are lying at anchor as we glide by."

We faced the harbor as *Conquest* moved toward the open sea within this panorama of sailing craft. "There's Astor's *Nourmahal*," Theo said, pointing a finger. "And next up, J.P. Morgan's latest *Corsair*, so fast it is called a 'greyhound of the seas'...oh, and that's the *Gloriana*, only for racing, never for leisure cruising...."

Theo stepped forward to view the grandest ocean-going yachts as *Conquest* made its way amid countless vessels, some just right for a person taking sailing lessons. Imagining myself at the helm of the small boats, I did not notice the three gentlemen nearing the rail until I heard one of them say, "Let us ask her, let's do," and turned to see Felix Vanderbilt with two friends I vaguely recalled from past Newport summers.

"Mrs. DeVere...Valentine" he said, "I believe you remember Mr. Randolph Cowley and Mr. Willard Battersby... Randolph and Willard?"

Smiling, I strained to remember the bewhiskered Mr. Cowley and the goateed Willard Battersby. Had we been dinner partners? Danced at a ball? At The Breakers? Greystone? Should we use first names?

Still smiling, I said, "Lovely to be on *Conquest* this evening, gentlemen. I marvel at the captain who can weave us through this maze of anchored vessels."

"Felix's captain knows this harbor like the back of his hand," Mr. Cowley chortled. "And he masters the high seas in all weathers. Anything less, he would not be at a Vanderbilt helm."

We all agreed. "Salt water is the challenge on the coasts," said Willard Battersby, "whereas the western mountains pose their own particular tests of skill...do they not?"

The three men looked knowingly at me. All Society knew Roderick DeVere's wife came from the West, and I expected a reference to silver mining or prospecting. Instead, the goateed Willard Battersby remarked that years ago New York's Governor, Theodore Roosevelt, had gone west with a hunting knife made for him by Tiffany.

"I did not know that," I said.

"So much nowadays about the Governor's escapades in the war in Cuba, all that folderol about Rough Riders," said Randolph Cowley through his cloud of whiskers. "But Roosevelt took a hunting knife out west."

"Useful, no doubt," I said, declining a second lobster tidbit.

"A hunter's tool," remarked Felix Vanderbilt, "and a utensil at mealtime, I would think."

"Both," I said. The men looked expectant, as if I owed them more on the topic. "A Bowie knife," I said, "has many uses in the West."

"I'll wager it does out there," said Randolph Cowley, "and the watchword is 'Dead or Alive.'"

"Watchword?"

"Better 'Dead,' isn't it? The motto of the West?"

"No such thing," I said.

"At best a rifle," Willard Battersby continued, "but otherwise, is a jack knife just right?"

"I can say something about that," I replied, my cheeks feeling flushed. "A jack knife folds, but a Bowie knife has a fixed blade." Surely these men knew the difference. Was feigning ignorance an aid to polite conversation with ladies? The three looked eager. Should I tell them my papa's jack knife is now my letter opener? His Bowie knife a keepsake? No, I would not.

A servant wearing a sailor's middy blouse proffered champagne, and Willard Battersby took a fresh glass and held it toward me. "Valentine DeVere, a lady must have her best chilled bubbles." He signaled the servant to take away the glass in my hand.

I switched glasses for politeness and sipped when Willard toasted, "To the season" and sipped again when Randolph Cowley offered a second tribute to cruising on *Conquest.* My little joke about champagne and seasickness prompted the men to laugh too heartily and exchange glances.

"About Roosevelt's hunting knife," Randolph Cowley said, "he called it 'stout and sharp.' Did you know that the Governor cut up the animals he killed?"

"He dressed his game," I said. "It's called 'dressing.'"

"And Valentine," said Felix Vanderbilt, "would you tell us whether western women 'dress' game? Do they? Do they dress their game? Kill it and skin it and 'dress' it up?"

The question came at me like a punch at body and mind. I had overheard their words at the beginning—the "Let us ask her, let's do."

I swallowed the red rage now rising in my chest, a fury that took me over. These men wanted to know, *"Did you, Valentine Mackle DeVere, plunge your knife blade into animal flesh in the West? And where else did you plunge a blade?"* The yacht shuddered slightly as it entered the open sea, and wrath surged to my fingertips. In the next instant, the champagne glass smashed in my hand.

Chapter Fourteen

FOG BLANKETED THE DRUMCLIFFE loggia and erased the moon and stars, but I paced back and forth with the crashing waves. Holding up my bandaged hand, I marched from one end of the loggia to the other, heels snapping on the tiles.

"Val, must you?" My husband's voice neared exasperation. He stood beside a wicker chair, touching my elbow each time I pivoted. "How much longer?" he asked. "It feels past midnight out here."

"It feels like rage, Roddy." My back was turned to my husband, who asked me to repeat those words. "A fitting end to the evening cruise," I said, "working off rage."

Roddy heard, "Cage," which stopped me. "That's what I feel like, Roddy, a creature in a cage...on display in a zoological garden."

Taking my arm, my husband led me indoors without a word and marched us to a drawing room with tufted velvet furniture and a fireplace. I sat, crossed my arms and shivered in the fog-damp outfit from the yacht. This chilly July night called for a fire, and Roddy laid crushed paper, kindling wood, and birch logs.

In Nevada, the logs would be pine. Suppose Roddy had joined me in the West when we married?. Why was life in Nevada out of the question? Why did the wives and heirs of Silver Kings to bolt from the West? Theresa Fair was now Tessie Fair Oelrichs of Newport, the mistress of Rosecliff. Louise Mackay lived in Paris. Why not Virginia City?

The "why" of it was clear as a bronze bell. The onetime silver boomtown had gone bust. By the time Papa died, the mines were played out and very few tons of ore refined into silver bars. Virginia City threatened to become a ghost town like so many in the West. San Francisco and Denver were alive, of course, and Chicago rising high, but nothing compared to my husband's New York.

Or Newport.

A member of the Vanderbilt family clan had written, "No city on earth is as hostile toward outsiders as Newport." No truer words, but how many times must I be forced to learn them?

In moments, flames glowed and crackled. Roddy reached for a bottle and two small glasses in a cabinet, poured, and brought both drinks to the velvet sofa. "The fire and cherry brandy will warm us both," he said. "Tiny sips, please. It's strong."

My husband sat beside me on the sofa that faced the fire. "How does your hand feel?"

"Beyond scratched," I replied, "but no need for a doctor." Roddy's frown said otherwise. "We'll see tomorrow."

"Val, it is tomorrow."

"Then, daylight," I said.

The brandy streaked my throat. "One smashed crystal glass," I said, "and the deckhands sprang into action...first, tend to the passenger, then sweep up the glass."

"Val, if I had been at your side when it happened...."

I faced my husband to look into his eyes. "Roddy, believe me, if that glass had not smashed in my hand, one of three 'gentlemen' would be nursing a broken jaw."

I had not yet described the deck encounter to my husband, who was chatting with the Goulds when the crystal smashed. The three 'gentlemen' fled, and a deckhand picked shards from my hand and brought iodine and a bandage while his mate swept the deck. Felix Vanderbilt gallantly suggested we return to the harbor so that I might be taken to the Newport Hospital in a Vanderbilt coach.

I refused. "The sea is a pleasure," I said, "and *Conquest* rides the waves like a mustang in the West. So, let us enjoy the evening to the fullest."

Jack Barrott struck up a tune, and I turned to guests whose questions about my bandage enlivened their evening. Questions flew, and I bantered with offhand shrugs. "Not at all painful...good wine lost...amusement for the deckhands."

I had a word with Daisy Harriman, a friend who offered to take me sailing in her catboat. Weather permitting, we will go for a sail in the morning. I showed a pleasant face to one and all until we returned to Drumcliffe, where my perplexed husband followed me to the loggia to see me pace like a crazed sentry.

I now told Roddy about the 'gentlemen' who cornered me."

"Accused you, Val? They accused you?"

"They strongly hinted that I wielded the knife that killed Warren Eccles."

My husband's knuckles whitened on the liqueur glass. "Your hand is clenched, Roddy, as mine did. I was furious... am furious."

Roddy put his liqueur glass on a table, poked at the fire, and sat back down. "I am thinking," he said, "of their train of thought."

"You give them credit for thought? They leapt to conclusions from *The Newport Daily News* and Madeline Glendorick's dramatic charade. What else could it be?"

Roddy hesitated, then said, "Women with blades...."

"Blades? All of us use blades, almost every day...dinner knives, fish knives, fruit knives. Every lady learns her cutlery, as Cassie has patiently taught me."

"I am thinking beyond the dining table, Val. Remember last month on the steamboat...the Temperance woman who took a hatchet to the saloon's woodwork?"

I well remembered. Protesting against a brandy punch Roddy had devised for steamboat passengers on the Hudson

River, the woman attacked the woodwork with her hatchet. Roddy will represent the steamboat owners in court in the early autumn.

"The steamboat episode was not widely publicized," I said.

"But everyone knows about the hatchet brandished by Caroline Amelia Nation…Carrie Nation."

True, the dour Temperance crusader often appeared in the newspapers clutching her weapon to vanquish Demon Rum. Bartenders from Kansas to Texas feared she would burst through their swinging doors with her hatchet aimed at bottles and kegs. Her events were known as "hatchetations."

"Roddy, does Newport compare me to that woman?"

"Nothing of the kind, Val, but I am thinking in general of women and sharp blades…ever since Lizzie Borden."

"The axe murderer," I blurted, recalling Lizzie was acquitted of killing her father and stepmother in Massachusetts. Yet doubts persisted. Her name sent shivers up spines. "Roddy, what is your point?"

"Quite simply, capability…the havoc that women are capable of wreaking with blades."

"Then, you must include surgery."

My husband blinked.

"When my papa's appendix became inflamed," I said, "we went to Carson City, Nevada, and Doctor Eliza Cook operated on him. I saw the blade."

"Scalpel," Roddy said.

We glared, mismatched. The fire crackled, and live embers skittered on the hearth, inches from the wood floor.

Roddy had not put the screen over the open fire. He reached for the hearth broom.

I murmured, "Fire...and blood."

"What?"

"The Newport fires," I said, "and the woman found dead in the burned-out house on Gill Street. She gets no attention in the newspaper."

Roddy put the broom back.

"I assume her identity is not yet known. And when it is, how much notice will she get? A few lines on a back page. Meanwhile, the *News* gives whole columns to the Travers Block. It reruns Warren Eccles's stabbing and the search for Marco Gliano. It prints a childish drawing of a villain with a heavy eyebrow and reports that patrolmen are on guard at St. Mary's Catholic Church in case the killer shows up to confess or seek asylum.

I sipped my drink. "The fact is, Newport eats up the story of homicide in an art gallery on Bellevue Avenue, but cares nothing about a woman who died in a side street fire. If she turns out to be a cousin of the Astors," I continued, "she will be moved to the front page. Otherwise, it won't matter that she was overcome by smoke and died without her shoes." That detail lingered in mind, no shoes.

"Val," Roddy said softly, "do I detect in your words some sympathy that might be misplaced?"

"Absolutely not. Do not psychologize on me, Roddy," I said. "This is about the public and the press."

"Then may I have a word about the 'other' press?"

As if slapped, I croaked, "Not *Town Topics*...."

In a low voice, my husband repeated, "*Town Topics*."

"Oh, Roddy...not again this year." One year ago, the weekly scandal sheet that titillated Newport with outrageous rumors had published an exposé of me bathing in the nude at Bailey's Beach. In fact, a riptide threatened Cassie, an uncertain swimmer, and I shed the heavy wet wool bathing costume to swim to her aid. Saving her from drowning, I was touted as the "Mermaid" who gave beachgoers low-tide entertainment.

I seethed, but the publisher, a wily Civil War Colonel, kept *Town Topic*'s language within the law. His reporters ran down tips from paid informants and others seeking revenge. Colonel Mann had eyes and ears everywhere.

"Roddy, isn't it likely that one of Mann's toadies has heard Madeline Glendorick's story? Is he editing the paragraphs so we can't sue him?"

The logs needed stoking, but my husband slid the fire screen in place and sat back down. He put his hand gently on my shoulder and said, "Mann also works by other means, Val. He asks for investments in the book he plans to publish, then...."

"Extorts? Blackmails?"

Roddy hesitated. It was rumored that *Town Topic* stories were halted when hefty "investments" buried accounts of illicit affairs, gambling debts, jilted lovers, shoplifting heiresses, and whatever else soiled Society. In each case, a bank cheque or cash "investment" became a cleansing agent.

My husband's hand warmed my shoulder, his gaze soft and yet firm. "Roddy," I said, "tell me you didn't...?"

"I took care of the matter. *Town Topics* will not report what Mrs. Glendorick purports to have witnessed. We need not discuss the matter in detail."

My protest stopped with Roddy's stern gaze. "Be disappointed if you will, Val, but I acted for the sake of our privacy and protection. My conversation with the Goulds convinces me that I acted wisely."

"What do you mean?"

"Simply put, Edith Gould made the strongest case for both of us to circulate in Society. George repeated the points he made in the Reading Room about decorum. But Edith would not hear of it. She insists that we not deprive Society of our sparkling presence."

"She called us 'sparkling?'"

Roddy's cheeks slightly flushed. "Remember, Val, that Edith Gould was on the stage before she married George. She understands performance. She plans to make certain that our names are not struck from invitations and says we must appear front and center before the footlights and not go dark."

"Not go dark? What is 'dark?'" My bandaged hand began to pulse. Whatever "dark" meant in the Broadway theatre world, Edith Gould put Roddy and me on a stage where I was believed to be capable of knifing a man to death. In theatrical terms, Newport convinced itself the dagger belonged to me and I used it to murder Warren Eccles.

Chapter Fifteen

THE NEWPORT SKY WAS deep blue without clouds at 10:30 when I met Daisy Harriman at the docks where the small boats were cleated. The New York Yacht Club owned most of them for racing by members' children. A few were in private hands, such as Daisy's *Catnip*. Stepping quickly, I inhaled the briny scent, eager for my first lesson on the water.

"Good morning, Captain Daisy."

"A fine day for a sail, Valentine," replied the friend who had spent summers in Newport since girlhood, when she rode her pony when not otherwise on the water sailing *Catnip*. Daisy was now Mrs. J. Borden Harriman, married to a prominent banker she affectionately called Bordie. The two of us had met at a New York meeting of the Consumers League, an organization devoted to good wages and safe working conditions, especially for women. Daisy was a charter member of the League.

"Valentine, I see you took my advice about apparel."

I had chosen a dark culottes skirt and tailored white shirtwaist open at the neck. ("You will need a wide reach if we get a fresh breeze," Daisy had said last evening on *Conquest*. "And your sleeves must not become sails.") She had promised headgear and presented me with a navy-blue yacht cap with silk trim, identical to hers.

"Perfect fit," she said, adjusting the bill. "And how's the hand?"

"Good as new in a few days," I replied with a wave. A new, smaller bandage had been taped by Calista this morning.

"Ready to go aboard?"

"Aye, aye, Captain Daisy. One question, do you ever use your given name?"

"Florence? Never."

We laughed. By now, I knew Daisy Harriman well enough to appreciate the outlook of this lady with a narrow face, apple cheeks, a pointed chin, an hourglass figure, perfect posture, and up-to-date fashions. To all appearances, Daisy Harriman was every inch a lady. Her dove-gray eyes, however, saw the world beyond "fuss and feathers," her dismissive fillip about Society. Equally at ease in ballrooms or fox hunts, Daisy had surveyed the workaday world and declared she never heard of anyone making a living riding to hounds, jumping hurdles, or dancing quadrilles in ballrooms. She declared that she had moved from pinafores to politics and social fairness. Friends and family were both dismayed and bemused, for Daisy's lineage squared with Roddy's and Cassie's, all families with the highest regard for one another.

"Welcome aboard, Valentine. Take a seat on the starboard side, and let me acquaint you with *Catnip*, all sixteen feet from stem to stern." With manicured fingers, Daisy began the survey. "The wood shell is the hull, and that tall timber is the mast. The single sail is the mainsail, which you see furled over the boom. The sail will be raised by a line called the halyard and let out or trimmed by a line called a sheet. *Catnip* has a 'barn door' centerboard that will be shoved down for stability...like a keel. And this wood shaft is the tiller, which steers the boat. Catboats are stable but will never win prizes for speed." She winked at me. "Got it?"

"Trying."

"Trust me, you will learn fast. What's the slang for beginners in the West?"

"Greenhorns."

"On salt water, Valentine, they are landlubbers, but you will soon be an 'old salt.' Ready?"

"Ready."

Daisy deftly freed lines, and in moments we were underway in a light breeze. The hoisted sail filled out, and Daisy set our course toward the outer harbor. With a hand on the tiller, she kept her gaze on the water, on the sail, and on me.

"Valentine, a few words, please...."

"By all means." We neared open water.

"First of all, that photograph of you in the newspaper alongside the murdered man was an abomination. I wrote a letter to the editor. No, do not thank me.

"Daisy, I can explain. The situation—"

"—was an unfortunate circumstance. Say no more. The noisy gabble will quiet down as soon as the police catch the murdering thief. He cannot hide forever. He'll need water and food, and every servant in Newport, every store clerk and tradesman is alert for Marco-the-murdering-plasterer. Do we know who offered the reward?"

"Anonymous," I said, "but my guess is Joseph Cuveen. Two valuable paintings are still missing, and the reward is Cuveen's bid to get them back. He probably cabled his clerk in the Meunchinger Hotel to set the reward but keep the source hush-hush."

Daisy adjusted the sail. "Count on this, the killer will be caught and punished. And Madeline will eat her shameful words. In the meantime, you must keep busy. What is ahead for the summer beyond sailing and tennis?"

"I am planning a summer camp in the Hudson Valley for the children of the Lower East Side," I said. "So, a few hours' research on camps at the Redwood Library."

"Excellent. The Consumers League will applaud the children in fresh air and sunshine instead of factories. I hear you will sit for a portrait by that new man...Cole."

"I will."

"Remarkable skin tones on those portraits at the reception. I believe they were painted last winter in the city to show off his talent." Daisy cocked an eyebrow. "But mark my words, Valentine...do not look at your portrait until Cole pronounces it completely finished. Take one early peek, and he will banish you from his studio and destroy the canvas.

A cousin of Bordie learned the hard way. She broke his rule and watched him slash the canvas and stomp it underfoot. He frightened her. It was like a fairy tale where the maiden breaks a vow and is punished forever."

"Daisy, the portrait is for my husband. I can obey that rule. A few quiet hours in front of the easel might even be welcome."

She let out a line, and the sail seemed fuller. "But you and Roderick must also go about in society. Bordie and I agree the best strategy is visibility. You must be seen. We will make certain the DeVeres are not stricken from invitation lists."

Daisy frowned as the breeze shifted. "We will now go about, so duck your head, the boom will swing."

I ducked, the boom swung, the sail filled out, and we sailed in a new direction. Daisy said, "The point of sailing is, basically, to make the seas obey the canvas, wood, metal, and hemp rope lines." She invited me to take over the tiller and the sheet line that managed the sail. With Daisy's cues, I began to grasp the rudiments of sailing.

My friend had not finished her advice. "Another thing, Valentine...you ought to be seen shopping the Travers Block."

"Return to the scene of the crime?"

"Nonsense. Be above the fray. Pick up a bauble at Tiffany. Dip into Worth and see the new satin brocades with the latest motifs of tulips and birds. I had a chat with the Worth saleslady a day or two ago. It seems she was acquainted with the deceased manager."

"Eccles?"

"She met him in New York last winter when she clerked at one of the department stores where he leased space for an art gallery. He struck an arrangement with her."

"What arrangement?"

"To send customers his way."

"What's her name?"

Just then, the wind gusted, and Daisy called, "hard-a-lee, going about...."

The boom swung, and we veered in a new direction toward the shoreline. "We will begin to start back now, Valentine, but notice that the wind is against us. To reach the shore, we must tack, meaning we will sail in a zig-zag. We hope the tide is with us, but a strong tide can feel like a headwind while we go back-and-forth, tacking each time."

"Tacking, I said. "It sounds like a strategy for life."

Daisy was in no mood for philosophy. She offered the loan of *Catnip* until I found the right boat and suggested a premier marine designer. My mind, however, stayed on the term I remembered best from the morning. In the weeks ahead when headwinds surged with hurricane force, I would tack to save my life.

❧

Roddy and I kept close to Ocean Drive and Bellevue Avenue while the search for Marco Gliano continued. We notified Cassie of our plan and asked that she communicate with the Rickers and with anyone else who, to her knowledge, employed the plasterer earlier this spring.

He had not been caught by July 22nd when Roddy joined a foursome on the croquet lawn at the Casino and I took my first tennis lesson on the ladies' court, hoping to improve my backhand stroke. At Drumcliffe, Roddy signed papers for an orange grove in central Florida and told me he might need to take a flying trip to the city to consult about a cocktail for a hotel, though he declined to name it, keeping mum as always. The Redwood librarian wrote to say magazine articles on archery and woodcraft might help my planning for the children's summer camp. The articles were set aside for me.

A shipment of fire extinguishers finally reached Newport, and Cavell's delivery wagon brought three of the cumbersome units to our rear entrance, whereupon Sands and Mrs. thwaite debated placement and mounting. It was agreed the kitchen must have an extinguisher. Roddy and I were seldom drawn into domestic matters, but fire pre-vention was a worthy exception. I insisted an extinguisher be located in the servants' apartments, and Roddy ordered the third unit put in the butler's pantry.

Mrs. Thwaite took me aside to warn against a "new species" of maid-servants' uniforms of blue cloth with gilt buttons. "Whereas, ma'am, the black dresses with plain white aprons remain the most suitable...if you please." She added, "Mrs. DeVere kept the loggia closed off, ma'am... to prevent drafts." As always, her "Mrs. DeVere" meant Roddy's mother, who probably had been informed of my loggia infraction, thanks to a two-cent stamp to Bar Harbor, Maine. In her long gray dress with a keyring dangling from a black leather belt, the housekeeper could audition for a job as a prison matron or a spy. My recommendation to any new employer would be stellar.

The Newport Daily News reported the continuing search for the killer of Warren Eccles. The plasterer was said to be glimpsed rifling a harborside waste barrel for food scraps, but the police could find no sign of him. The reward was raised to $600 in gold.

We ordered Sands and Mrs. Thwaite to alert Calista and Roddy's valet immediately if *The Newport Daily News* reported the arrest of "Marco" or anyone thought to be involved in the Cuveen Gallery death. They were told to awaken us at the earliest when the morning newspaper reported a capture. The butler and housekeeper nodded solemnly as if neither had heard of the gruesome homicide which all Newport gossiped about from the oceanfront cottages to the humblest tumbledown shack.

After lunch on July 22, we went for a drive in the open-air Victoria with Roddy holding the reins of Apollo and Atlas. We had studiously avoided discussing the specifics of our Cuveen Gallery encounter. I was now able to fork the brightest red tomato slices without a qualm and enjoy raspberries with cream. Cassie called it on-the-mend recovery.

"I still cannot figure out why a plasterer would be any-where near the Travers Block," I said as our Victoria left Drumcliffe to enter Ocean Drive.

Roddy explained, "Crews of workers descend on Newport in earliest springtime for carpentry, tile work, plaster...for upkeep and repair of the cottages and businesses too. Marco and the others would have arrived weeks before the season began."

"Where do they stay? Surely not the Muenchinger Hotel."

Roddy laughed. "Gus and Amanda Muenchinger would sooner fold their tent, so to speak. No, those workers stay on scows in the harbor. The Travers family earns a pretty penny from summer leases, so the plasterer would be busy on the Block when the shops and gallery needed interior work."

"And Marco could have seen the paintings delivered," I said, "but Cassie told me how strictly he focused on his work. He told Cassie he fashioned grape clusters with leaves and vines with different putty knives for delicate shapes."

"What did you say Ricker paid him, Val? Ten dollars? A skilled plasterer should have earned enough to pay his own way home without thievery."

Roddy reined in the horses to keep them at a walk. "But why did he not depart when the work crews returned to the city. The calendar works like a curfew. He should have been gone before the cottagers began to arrive. It makes no sense that Marco Gliano would loiter in Newport to steal paintings."

"Or peddle them at cottage doors," I said. "Maybe he got stranded when the scows left without him...so the gallery heist promised cash for a ticket out."

Roddy and I spoke mainly of robbery, avoiding the deathly scenario when Marco confronted Eccles.

When the plasterer became a murderer.

⁊⁊⁊

The news broke on Monday, July 24 when Roddy burst into my bedchamber at dawn tugging the newspaper and pointing to a headline:

Cliff Walk Claims Killer!

I sat up and reached for the paper, but Roddy gripped it tight. "'Body found on rocks below Ochre Court,'" he read, "'...worker sought in murder of Travers Block gallery manager Warren Eccles...art thief and killer identified by plaster tools in pockets and name, Marco Gliano, on jacket flap...body discovered at dawn on rocks below Cliff Walk in front of Ochre Court. Police called when servant sounded alarm....'"

Roddy perched at the foot of my bed. "It goes on, Val...'Cuveen Gallery assailant met death after nightfall, Police say. They ask, was footing lost in darkness or was plunge inspired by guilt? 'We may never know the answer,' says Police Chief Ronald Cherry, 'but justice is served...peace restored to Newport.' The search for stolen art continues."

The report went on to say a Goelet servant had discovered the body at dawn, and the newspaper was filled with disparaging remarks about "foreigners," adding the Irish to

Italians and calling for American young men to take up the trades so the country's borders can be closed at long last.

"Peace restored and case closed," Roddy said. "And clear sailing for you."

"Clear sailing! Clear sailing!" I said it twice to put conviction behind words that somehow fell far short of jubilation.

Chapter Sixteen

WITHIN A DAY, THE Cliff Walk attracted out-of-towners who halted in front of Ochre Point to stare at the rocks below and take photographs with Kodak box cameras. Ordinarily, these same tourists would have craned necks toward the mansions silhouetted across the emerald lawns of the Vanderbilts or the Goelets. Instead, they stood at the edge of Cliff Walk, risking life and limb to see the spot where the corpse of a murderer had lain on the rocks or rolled in the swelling waves. A few laid bouquets along the Walk. Others scattered flowers toward the water in some sort of tribute. To be sure, the body of Marco Gliano had been removed, but the Newport police stationed an officer at the Cliff Walk site in case an overeager tourist took a tumble. *The Newport Daily News* reported ferries at capacity and the police safeguarding visitors on Cliff Walk.

"Can't the Walk be closed for a few weeks until the story fades?" I asked at breakfast on our loggia on a misty Wednesday morning, July 26. The dog lounged at our feet. "Can't it be closed, Roddy?"

"Only briefly in front of Ochre Point while the police investigate."

"Why not close the whole Walk for a few weeks?" My husband shook his head. "Why not?" I reached for a blueberry muffin.

Roddy's crooked little smile was familiar from moments when knotty laws were to be explained. He put his teacup down. "The Cliff Walk goes back to a colonial charter from the King of England and to Rhode Island's founding documents that guarantee rights to the shoreline. The first principle was fishing rights."

"Centuries ago, but the law still holds?"

Roddy nodded.

"Then...the Ochre Point property has never extended to the waterline?"

"No."

"Nor the Breakers? Nor Marble House...nor the others?" I had imagined that public spirit moved the cottagers to keep Cliff Walk open for townspeople to stroll in the fresh sea air.

"Val, every legal effort has been exerted to privatize Cliff Walk. When the courts provided no relief, the cottagers cleverly lowered the Walk."

"To limit prying eyes?" Roddy nodded. I bit the muffin. So much for public spirit.

Roddy saw my disappointment. "Be realistic, Val. For years, the tourists trespassed onto lawns and demanded refreshments at the cottage doors. My parents recalled such stories, and today's *Daily News* reports visitors off the ferries literally beating the bushes. Shrubbery is trampled and fences smashed in the search for the two stolen paintings that are still missing. It's a treasure hunt. The tourists have become a public nuisance."

My husband was not the first to condemn Newport's day-trippers. Our servants were given last evening off to attend the wedding of a footman and a parlor maid employed at the Villa Rosa estate. The nuptials took place in the Chapel of Hope and were followed by celebratory cake and punch in town. Chalmers and Bronson asked to attend, and I suggested that Calista and Roddy's valet Norbert might also appreciate the extra night off for the wedding celebration. This morning, they all had curt words about the visitors who noisily waited for the last ferry of the night. "The likes of them nearly drowned out the wedding toasts," Chalmers murmured when Roddy inquired. Calista told me the wedding ceremony was beautiful, but the cake and punch might have been better served in the quiet churchyard.

The dog stirred, went to her water bowl for a drink, and looked at each of us in hopes of another biscuit. "Never enough," Roddy said.

I shifted on the chair cushion. "Enough..." I echoed. "Enough of the rumors and innuendos about us...about me."

Roddy reached for my hand across the wicker chairs. "These difficult days are behind us," he said softly.

"Awful," I said. "The death grip on the picture frame... Eccles's cream-colored suit...the blood. Then Madeline Glendorick...and Alva's luncheon. And those men on *Conquest*." I almost added Marianne's ghoulish symbols for my portrait.

Roddy lightly held my hand. "The bandage is off. Your hand has healed."

"And my reputation likewise 'healed,'" I said. "Hideous that the plasterer committed murder...hideous that he fell to his death. But the newspaper has been filled with the account, and the police have closed the case. Everyone knows who killed Warren Eccles. No more snide comments about Valentine Mackle DeVere. No more sidelong glances. I am vindicated, exonerated...free."

And ready for the party at Crossways tonight," Roddy said.

"Ready for Mamie Fish and all of Newport," I said. "Meanwhile," my first sitting for André Cole early this afternoon."

"So, here's to your portrait, Val DeVere. I hereby propose a late morning cocktail to celebrate your portrait and the summer season we can finally enjoy."

"The season we deserve."

Roddy had his bar cart wheeled to the loggia. The dog's interest matched mine as Roddy reached for ice tongs and began a cocktail I recorded in my journal.

The Anticipation

Ingredients:

- ½ ounce sherry wine
- ½ ounce Italian vermouth
- 1 dash absinthe
- 2 dashes gum syrup

Directions:

1. Fill mixing glass with chipped ice.
2. Add gum syrup.
3. Add sherry and vermouth.
4. Add absinthe.
5. Stir until mixture is its coldest.
6. Strain and serve.

"Salud, Val. What do you think?"

"I like the ice and especially the name, 'Anticipation.' It suits the summer that is about to begin...for us."

"For us!" Roddy leaned for a long, sweet kiss. We put our drinks down, held hands, went upstairs to Roddy's suite, and enjoyed the next hour in lush privacy, riding free on a feather bed, time suspended as we discovered one another again...and again.

Our jubilation was not dampened by the telephone call from police headquarters inviting us—Mr. and Mrs. Roderick DeVere—to call at our "convenience." We dressed in linen streetwear for the visit to the Market Square station this midday, July 26, sixteen days from the Travers

Block horror and our interrogation. The afternoon promised sunshine and rain showers, according to our footmen's favorite almanac. An umbrella was tucked between us on the dogcart.

Past the Jamestown Ferry office and Albro's Fish market, Roddy tied up at a lamp post, and a belltower struck 12:30 when we entered the station house and were promptly ushered into Chief Cherry's office.

"Mrs. DeVere, Mr. DeVere, thank you for helping Newport in this time of such...difficulty," The chief sounded apologetic. "I mean to thank you in person. Won't you please be seated?"

Officer Seavers stood by, but Chief Cherry held my chair and joined Roddy and me at a small round table, bypassing his massive oak desk with a flag stand and papers anchored by a brick.

"Please understand this headquarters is the pride of Newport," the chief began, "and the center of law enforcement and keeping of the peace." He smoothed his thick white moustache and glanced from Roddy to me. "Perhaps you have heard it said that crime cannot pay in Newport because we are an island? Thieves cannot escape? Murder is out of the question?" He looked intently at Roddy with bloodshot eyes.

My husband nodded and said, "It is common knowledge, Chief Cherry, that criminals will be stopped at the ferry."

"A disservice to us, Mr. DeVere, a failure to take the Newport Police work into account. Or to credit our service."

The chief wiped his eyes with a handkerchief. Was this outpouring self-pity or righteous indignation? Or both?

Officer Seavers swatted at a fly that landed on the oak desk. I cast sidelong glances to see whether *French Artillery in Snowy Winter* was here in the chief's office. Neither the bedsheet bundle nor the painting was in view. An illustrated wall calendar for a carriage works marked off the days of the month.

"Mrs. DeVere," the chief said, "we appreciate how helpful you and Mrs. Forster were to our officers. Your identification of the stolen painting broke a murder case wide open."

"I am pleased that we could help," I said.

"Furthermore, we have talked further with the murdered man's assistant, Mr. Asa Durling. He verifies the picture of the soldiers in the snow was in the Cuveen Gallery collection. It is the biggest of the pictures that we know to be missing... stolen. Two others are smaller. They are...Seavers, you took down the names."

He turned to Officer Seavers, who missed the fly again but opened a notebook and read aloud, "It's *Cows Crossing a Ford* and *Potato Planters*. The painters are M-i-l-l-e-t and D-u-p-r-e with an accent mark over the 'e.' We do not know the exact inches, sir, but we were told...about like so." Seavers spread his hands up and down. I guessed no more than a foot in width or length, paintings easily hidden or carried under an arm.

Roddy said, "Chief Cherry, we assume your men are searching for the paintings?"

"As best we can, Mr. DeVere."

Roddy and I exchanged a glance. Were we summoned here for the Chief of Police to tell us of the search? To ask our help? Could we leave now?

Chief Cherry leaned closer to us. "I want to tell you face-to-face, Mr. and Mrs. DeVere, that I hope we have no misunderstanding. So, Officer Seavers, if you will return Mrs. DeVere's property."

The young policeman clicked his heels together, slipped into another room, and returned with my stiff blood-stained gloves tweezered between his thumb and forefinger. I had no choice but to take them in my gloved fingers with a "thank-you."

"So, you both are free of any connection to this terrible crime," Chief Cherry said. "Your citizenship is beyond reproach. No one can think otherwise."

"Thank you," Roddy said.

"Much appreciated," I added, beginning to rise.

The chief had not finished.

"And Mr. Durling confirms he made your acquaintance,"

"He did." I said no more. Despite the chief's cordiality, this was no social call. My stiffened gloves would go into the nearest rubbish barrel.

"We inquired whether Mr. Durling might know about the painting in your cottage," Chief Cherry continued.

"Oh?" Roddy said.

"The one in the crate."

My husband's jaw tightened.

"Mr. Durling says he knows nothing about a crate," the chief said.

"And need not," my husband replied.

I gazed at the chief and at Seavers who stood at attention. We were supposedly model citizens, invited here for an apology. But these men were obsessed by the crate. They thought us somehow connected to the Cuveen Gallery theft.

To Marco's death too?

The apology was a mere pretext.

We could settle this easily. We could describe *The Counting House*. We could invite Chief Cherry and Seavers to the Lafayette Room to open the crate. The embarrassment would be theirs, their apologies redoubled and sincere.

The angle of Roddy's jawline, however, told me he would not begin to consider such a thing. His narrowed eyes told me of anger under greatest restraint. He would not give Chief Ronald Cherry the satisfaction, for Roderick Windham DeVere was a gentleman and a man of his word.

My husband, in short, would not allow the chief to peer inside the steel-banded wooden crate to see the mud-brown, lackluster picture I wished we had never brought to Newport. Roddy's headstrong pride put us under suspicion that was soon to make us one more story in a book to be titled *Tragic Mansions of Newport.*

Chapter Seventeen

I DROVE A PONY cart to the Catherine Street studio and found a granite hitching post to tie up Shamrock, our shaggy Connemara pony. Roddy so often took the reins that I needed practice driving and insisted on going myself. The Market Square mix-up over the crated painting was sure to ricochet one way or another. *The Counting House* might be a Rembrandt or worthless, but it could be a boomerang. My husband's gentlemanly faith in Knickerbocker ancestry as social armor struck me as naïve. For now, the pony cart and artist's studio were a welcome distraction.

Calista suggested I wear a silk bodice that could be lowered off the shoulders if desired. Any such lowering, I told her, would be negotiated between the artist and myself.

André Cole opened the studio door at 2:00 p.m. and ushered me inside with a deep bow and sweep of his black suede beret. The curtains were drawn, and the parlor-studio was rose-scented.

"Madame DeVere, it is my pleasure to welcome you for our first *rendez-vous*."

"*Rendez-vous?*"

"'Appointment,' if you like. The language of France suffers when it must cross the waters to English, does it not?"

I wished Cassie were here to translate. Cole put the beret back on, angled carefully across his forehead. His artist's smock was a box-pleated garment that freed his hands but resembled a waistcoat, apparently sewed and laundered by Marianne. It fit flawlessly.

"May I escort you to your seat of honor?"

Cole offered his arm to lead me past as the sizeable blank canvas resting on his easel and a crock sprouting brushes on the side table. Marianne was not here, and the table in the corner was set for two.

A vase of freshly cut red roses stood on the table beside the upholstered chair. "Madame DeVere," Cole said, "in the States, the rose blooms on the *fête de Saint Valentin*...as you say, Valentine's Day. To honor you with a touch of chivalry, André Cole takes the *liberté* with your name to present *un bouquet...les roses for* your pleasure. You are pleased?"

"Very thoughtful."

Smiling, he helped me onto the chair, then stepped close and murmured, "You are prepared, Madame?" Circling the chair, he bent to one knee, gazed upward, and said, "For your portrait, we are *ensemble*...together as one. The portrait lives when the artist sees the truth of all that is possible."

He reached toward my upswept hair, released a pin, and loosened a lock with the skill of a hairdresser or lady's maid. "*Les tresses*, Madame," he said, "...and for the shoulders, if you please...." He touched the bodice, and I suddenly posed for the off-the-shoulder portrait.

"There now...Madame is comfortable as in the Tuileries Garden. For you, it is the leisure, but for André Cole, the *challenge se montrer à la hauteur*...to meet the test and rise highest."

Tempted to remind him that he had demanded—and received—photographs of my face, I held back. This was for Roddy. I had promised my husband the gift of my portrait. I would cope with André Cole.

"My one commandment, Madame...." He stationed himself behind the easel. "That you see your portrait only when complete, *fini*. Do we agree?"

I agreed.

"Because this is supremely important."

"I promise not to look until your work is finished."

He cringed at the word "work," said something in French about art, and took up his palette and a brush.

I sat for the next two hours commanding every muscle to stay still. My ornery mind took me west to the mining camps with recollections of rocks to climb and cold rushing streams to cross. Then random thoughts brought me here to the Narragansett Bay, where I passed the next hour sailing Daisy Harriman's catboat. The tiller and the sail obeyed every order, and I ducked the boom when I came about. My afternoon on the water was interrupted by one fifteen-minute interlude when André Cole insisted I rise and turn my head so my face could regain its coloring. I would later recall that his fingernails were perfectly clean this afternoon, that no trace of paint was visible at the cuticle.

Roddy was waiting for me later that afternoon when I handed Shamrock to a groom. "Welcome home, my dear. How was it?"

"Nothing unusual to report, Roddy. I posed in a chair for two hours, and André Cole was quite the *artiste* in a suede beret and a smock custom fitted for him. Sorry to say, I have nothing to report about the painting. He covered it up before releasing me from the chair, and I took an oath not to peek before he finishes."

"An oath?"

"So to speak."

"Did he say how many hours? Or sittings? Asa Durling was vague when I spoke with him."

So, Roddy had gone to the Muenchinger Hotel suite to bargain about a price for the portrait. My next sitting would be arranged by Mr. Durling.

"But your portrait is underway," Roddy said pleasantly.

"Launched on canvas, yes."

"Are you hungry, Val? You must be hungry."

"Famished."

"Let's have something. You'll want time to dress for Crossways."

Indeed, I would. Our clocks struck 5:00 p.m. when Roddy and I sat in the inglenook over melted cheese on toast with crisp bacon strips. My husband sipped a mug of ale but for me, mineral water. A late night hosted by Mamie Fish required sobriety. "Time to get ready," I said. "Fashion awaits."

Calista drew me a warm bath scented with verbena and laid out two possible evening ensembles. I said yes to the satin gown with a sleeveless bodice and smooth skirt in golden yellow tones.

In my dressing room after the bath, Calista fastened me into a "ventilated" corset of whalebone and cotton with silk trimming.

"This is new, ma'am, for summer air to circulate."

"All for it," I said. My maid looked so trim in her uniform. "Were you corseted on the coastal steamers, Calista?"

"Managed to avoid them, ma'am. Now if you please, hosiery...then your hair." My maid held out a robe-like wrapper and seated me before the mirror at the dressing table. For the second time today, I sat for someone who would be paid to do my "portrait," the one on canvas, the other fashioning me into a living mannequin.

The fact was, I could not dress for the evening without assistance. Nor could any lady do so. The hooks and snaps from the base of the spine to the neck, the undergarments and accessories all required a second set of hands—deft hands and agile fingers. Ladies' maids had been dismissed for being "all thumbs."

"Your hair this evening, ma'am…I suggest the combs with diamonds and seed pearls. The gold, of course."

"Of course."

Calista opened a locked jewelry safe while I asked myself when gold and diamonds had become routine. Not in Virginia City, the improbable Nevada boomtown that had its share of riches in the glory years. Champagne and lobsters by the carload came on the V&T Railroad, which also brought Papa's formal suits and my special dresses from San Francisco. For my sixteenth birthday, Papa gave me a gold locket, but I never craved jewelry that must be kept under lock and key nor gowns from a Parisian couturier.

"Ma'am…? Your hair, ma'am…are you pleased?"

"Sorry, Calista, my mind wandered." Reaching for the hand mirror, I admired my maid's skill from every angle and murmured, "Lovely…perfect," then asked, "Have you decided on your autumn trip to Athens?"

"I think October, ma'am. My nieces and nephews are so pleased. It's been years…and travel so dear."

She meant expensive. I insisted that Calista Adrianakis travel cabin class to be freshest for her visit. Our servants had paid vacations and extra funds for travel. The least I could do. "Now, for the gown?"

"A tiny minute, ma'am…if you will?"

Hearing her tone, I turned on the stool. "Of course."

"You know, ma'am, I am not one to tell tales."

"I know that, Calista. Is something wrong at Drumcliffe?"

"Oh, no. not Drumcliffe. It's the wedding last night... the cake and punch afterwards. Servants from the cottages, everybody gabbed."

"I would hope so."

"...about Ochre Court...."

How could it be otherwise, the talk of all Newport, upstairs and down?

"A footman at Ochre Court called the police at dawn, ma'am. He told us he saw someone down on the rocks...and he went inside the cottage and used the pull for the police."

All the Bellevue Avenue cottages had silent bell pulls for direct contact with the police department. "So I understand," I said. "The newspaper has reported it."

"But another footman saw something else, ma'am. I know you and Mr. DeVere take an interest in things."

"What 'things,' Calista?"

"What the other footman saw...from the Ochre Court lawn. He told how he walks the lawn every night to pick up any rubbish thrown up from the Cliff Walk or blown by the wind."

"Housekeeping," I said, eyeing the gown lying across my bed, knowing Roddy was downstairs waiting to go. My maid, however, gazed with a quiet intensity. "So," I said, "the other footman made his rounds."

"It's what he saw looking over the edge of the lawn, ma'am.... He says he heard voices and saw two people on the Cliff Walk."

"And then?"

"And then, one of the two disappeared...disappeared from his sight. All of a sudden, one of the two was gone."

Chapter Eighteen

MINIATURE LANTERNS GUIDED GUESTS along the serpentine pathway to the entrance of Crossways, the plantation-style house Mamie Fish declared to be *all American*. On the path, Ladies' voices chirped in anticipation, and men answered briefly in low tones as our lineup of gowns and swallowtail coats processed smartly ahead. A high-pitched voice nearby asked whether a fortune teller would enliven the party tonight, or perhaps a celebrity, since Mamie Fish invited stage performers and athletes. Last year, the champion Prizefighter John L. Sullivan had been a guest and demonstrated how he earned his nickname, "The Boston Strong Boy."

Just ahead of Roddy and me, a couple stepped inside to hear our hostess's unrivaled greeting, "Howdy-do, howdy-do." Mamie Fish famously refused to memorize guests' names, so we all were "lambs" or "pets." Somehow, this grand dame of Society got away with grating insults that passed as humor.

With a "Howdy-do," she ordered us to the dining room. Her white-on-white dress shimmered with a diamond fringe across the bosom, and a tiara sparkled in jet-black hair. "Step lively, pets," she said, shooing us to make way for the next guests in numbers exceeding one hundred for dinner and games.

Roddy murmured, "Remember the dinner pace, Val, soup to nuts...."

"I remember," I murmured. "Cassie also warned me."

Anyone expecting a leisurely dinner at Crossways would be astonished by Mamie Fish's momentum. Footmen snatched away plates before knives could slice a chop or a tiny fork pierce an oyster. Marian Anthon Fish had not been raised in a military family, but her guests learned to "chow down" for the sake of speed, lest a slow dinner become a sedative.

On a foyer table, each gentleman now sought his name on a small envelope containing the name of the lady he would escort to the dining room. I eyed Teddy Wharton and wondered who would be his wife Edith's dinner partner. It would not be Edwin Glendorick who took Grace Vanderbilt's arm nor Henry Chanler who escorted Elizabeth Lehr. Roddy gave me a little wave as he opened his envelope and promptly took the arm of the amiable Anita Holbrooke.

Then I heard, "Mrs. DeVere, we dine once again."

Annoyance rose at the sight of the man I must allow to hold my chair and sit beside me. "Mr. Bourne," I said. "Mr. Chadwick Bourne...not since last winter in the city."

"Where we smoked after-dinner cigarettes rolled in banknotes, if you recall...?" He chuckled, amused at a recollection I had found appalling, watching hundred-dollar bills go up in smoke as a party favor.

I took his arm but turned my head to avoid his Patchouli scent and stay clear of his puffy side whiskers. Bound to dine at Chadwick Bourne's side, I suspected our hostess played a trick on me. Stuffing my name into his dinner envelope, Mamie partnered me with the spouse of the woman who taunted me at Alva's luncheon earlier this month. Mamie's bloodstone jewelry was its own barb, while Paulina Bourne had led off with a reference to the Travers Block, ready to target me in the presence of two guests until Cassie defused the moment.

Tonight, Chadwick Bourne could have been cued by his wife to pick at me. Lifting my glass for a sip of water was the reminder that my hand had healed. No crystal would shatter at this place setting.

"I take it Stuyvesant is not with us tonight," Chadwick Bourne said. "He was not with Mamie to greet us."

Chadwick meant our host, Stuyvesant Fish, who was often in Illinois tending to his railroad while Mamie entertained. It was said that Mr. Fish preferred the Illinois Central to the ballrooms where his wife held court.

"I'm afraid he will miss tonight's festivities," I said. "We will miss him."

"And he will miss these *canapés de crevettes*,"

"Shrimp toasts," I snapped, dreading a replay of last winter's dinner when Chadwick Bourne translated every dish for the bumpkin from the West. I had replied in crudest English, my fish eggs to his *caviar* and so on, tit for tat and tedious.

"Do you know, Mrs. DeVere, that we are honored with British royalty this evening?"

"Ah," I replied, "the Glendoricks' daughter must be here, the Countess of Cleave."

"To be sure," Bourne replied, "the Countess is here for a family visit, but I meant the reigning sovereign of the London stage who is seated by our hostess—Miss Ellen Terry."

"Oh, very nice."

"No actress more celebrated than Ellen Terry in Shakespearean roles."

I recognized her name but braced for Chadwick Bourne's quotation from the Bard. He would challenge me to identify the play, the act, the scene. My recollections of *Romeo and Juliet* and *Hamlet* were few, and the history plays yet to be confronted. My western upbringing loomed like a scourge.

Instead, we fell silent as footmen snatched away the shrimp toast and brought plates featuring tiny roasted birds enshrined in greenery.

"Quail," said Bourne uncertainly. "No, my mistake. We have woodcock."

"Woodcock," I repeated, surveying my silver. So, the small knife with the odd curve must be a game knife.

Up and down the dining tables, every guest took up this knife and a miniscule fork to begin to carve. I might offer a quip about speed, but Chadwick Bourne leaned closer and said, "Mr. Belmont's valet would make short work of this dish, would he not?"

"His valet?"

"His man, Azar, the Egyptian."

"I would not know."

"You are not aware that Azar sleeps at the threshold of Mr. Belmont's suite?"

"Why would I know such a thing, Mr. Bourne?"

"You among others would know, Mrs. DeVere...." He leered at me. "...that Azar would protect Oliver Belmont at the risk of his own life...and so, he sleeps with a dagger between his teeth."

I murmured "dagger" as his leer continued. He scanned my face as if the two of us shared a secret. I was to remember this moment. Looking back, it seemed a prelude to what followed—and was planned.

Distracted by the fevered pace of the food, I pushed Azar's dagger from my mind and downed an extra glass of champagne, sipping easily since Mamie served it freely, convinced that wine made guests sleepy and apt to overstay. Soon enough, the footmen served us Bavarian cream with fruits (*"Bavarois aux fruits,"* according to Chadwick), then a spot of coffee, and we listened to the husky, blonde Harry

Lehr crack jokes with Mamie, her brash gaiety matching his exaggerated falsetto. The two had become chums, Newport's court jester and the Crossways comedienne.

Ellen Terry, the famous actress in a burgundy velvet gown with a single strand of pearls, appeared amused by the repartee. Sitting beside her, Madeline Glendorick held the hand of a lissome young woman I recognized as the Glendoricks' daughter Emily, now the Countess of Cleave. She laughed lightly, as did her mother who rose to catch my eye and beckon me to an empty chair, as if the chair were reserved just for me.

"If you'll excuse me," I said to Chadwick Bourne, who dispatched me directly to the designated chair.

A curtsy always felt like a square dance move, but I curtsied before Emily and said, "Countess, so good to see you in Newport."

"With my dear parents at Owls Roost," she replied with a slight lisp, "and with our house guest, Miss Terry."

At which I was introduced to the actress by Madeline, who gushed that Owls Roost was glorified by Ellen Terry's presence.

With expressive eyes and lips appearing ready for tragedy or comedy, the actress replied in a clipped British voice that she found Newport to be "exclusively, absolutely American." She added, "Neither Tenby nor Brighton resembles it the least bit."

"So," I said, "Newport offers contrasts along with...."

"With portrait art," the countess said in an assertive voice, as if she might fade by keeping silent. "I have told

Miss Terry that my portrait is being painted this summer by Antonio Boldini. I have begun to sit for him."

"And I have informed the countess," said Ellen Terry, "that my portrait was done without a single sedentary hour. A decade ago, John Singer Sargent painted me in the role of Lady Macbeth." She smiled ruefully. "In the portrait, I am crowning myself, though no such moment occurs in Shakespeare's play. You might amuse yourself when next in London, Mrs. DeVere, for Sargent's portrait hangs in the National Gallery."

"Your most famous role, Miss Terry, is it not?" a male voice cut in. I turned to see Felix Vanderbilt and one of the two men from the *Conqueror* episode, the goateed one, Battersby...Willard Battersby.

"You play the monster that goads her husband to commit bloody murder, and the audience eats it up," Battersby went on. Slightly stumbling around some chairs, he sidled up to Ellen Terry, straightened his shoulders, closed his eyes and addressed the ballroom in a thunderous voice. "'Is this a dagger which I see before me, the handle toward my hand? Come, let me clutch thee.'"

A smattering of applause, and the ballroom grew quiet. Ellen Terry looked forbearing and murmured, "Act two, scene one."

"Always thought Lady Macbeth should have that speech," Battersby continued. "Always thought Shakespeare wasted it on the husband."

Felix Vanderbilt softly said, "Willard, please...."

Battersby did not budge, and Ellen Terry apparently felt called to respond. In arch tones that carried across the ballroom, she stood and said, "Let us remember that Lady Macbeth prepares the daggers for her husband, bloodies her hands, and is overcome at last with the scope of the deed she has put into motion."

At that moment, the actress faced the ballroom and moved her hands and fingers in gestures that focused every eye. "'Out, damned spot! Out, I say.... Here's the smell of the blood still. All the perfumes of Arabia will not sweeten this little hand. Oh, oh, oh!'"

For a full moment, the Crossways ballroom was silent as a tomb, then exploded in applause. Ellen Terry waved the room to silence, faced Willard Battersby, and said clearly for all to hear, "Do recall, sir, that Lady Macbeth at last goes mad and commits suicide."

Battersby nodded, slightly swayed, and pointed to me. "Newport got its dagger scene," he bawled out. "Lady Mac... Mackle. Got the scene right here."

He pushed forward and stood over me. "Lady with a dagger...newspapers all about it. American Lady Mac...."

He stopped when Felix Vanderbilt clamped a hand on his shoulder. The tableau at that instant might have lasted seconds or minutes. Halfway rising from my chair, I looked back to see the faces familiar from three years in Newport, the same faces I saw in New York. The gowns, the jewels, the men in white-tie formals. There were Alva and Oliver Belmont and near them, the Goulds, George and Edith. And the Lehrs, Elizabeth and Harry whose laughter had died. And Grace Wilson, now Vanderbilt. And the Whartons, the Dovedales, the Goelets, and the others in the far back. No one made a sound. Mamie Fish's tiara was tilted, and I could not see Roddy in the crowd. No one came to help. No one said a word.

Chapter Nineteen

CARRIAGE HEADLAMPS CAST AN ochre light into the darkness, each hoofbeat a dreary drumbeat. Roddy and I sat silent. I had refused my husband's help when Mamie's grooms assisted me into the carriage and coachman Noland mounted the box and flicked the reins.

Where was Roddy when I looked over the Crossways throng? Where was he when the drunken Willard Battersby pointed his stubby finger and called me "Lady Mac?"

I wanted to scream when Felix Vanderbilt excused his friend's "incident," but my voice would entertain the ballroom for another agonizing hour before I could bid farewell to Mamie Fish.

Where was Roddy at that critical moment?

Nowhere.

I avoided his glance in the carriage. The ride was short, just over a mile to Drumcliffe. All too soon as we entered our crushed shell drive and came to a stop at the entrance, where Chalmers opened the door and bowed. On orders, the household turned in by midnight except for one footman who took his turn at the door and offered whatever services we wished, such as opening or closing windows.

In the lamplight, Chalmers maintained the placid front required for his job. Roddy asked whether all was well at Drumcliffe this evening.

"Yes, sir...ma'am. All's well. And would you wish something from the kitchen?"

Knowing where we had dined, the footman expected to provide a hearty snack. The pace of Mamie's dinners doubtless made its way into cottage-to-cottage gossip, a news wire all its own.

"Perhaps a snack?" Chalmers repeated.

I said, "Thank you, Chalmers, but we will say good night."

Roddy added his "good night," and the next minute found us awkwardly in the foyer. If our dog were not in her crate, Velvet might well wriggle and jump to get us going, but no such luck.

Roddy said, "Shall we wake the dog?"

Two minds in parallel, but I did not relent. A deep-throated clock struck 1:00 a.m.

Roddy said, "Let us not retire without coming to terms."

"Terms? How lawyer-ish."

"My dear, we must not take to our beds in bitterness. At the very least, allow me to unfasten your gown."

I let my husband unhook the gown from the neck down, deft and practical, nothing like a night of love.

"There now...drape the cloak over your shoulders and let us sit down."

Roddy led us to the inglenook where he lighted a wall sconce candle and sat opposite me at the small table. With tie loose and collar opened, he leaned forward on his elbows. "Val, what happened tonight? From the garden, I heard the guests applaud, and then—"

"—the garden? So, you were in the garden? Why?"

"To assist my dinner partner, Anita Holbrooke. She felt unwell and asked me to step outside for a few minutes for fresh air. I think we missed half the courses before we returned to the table. Then I saw Felix Vanderbilt lead his friend away from Ellen Terry and you. The man looked unsteady on his feet, tipsy."

"Drunk, Roddy. The man was drunk, and he insulted me. Put another way, he felt free to insult me precisely because he was drunk among friends. Mamie's champagne came at a cost tonight. What's that phrase, *in vino...*?"

"*Veritas*...in wine, truth."

"The truth, Roddy, is that Mamie targeted me, and so did Willard Battersby. The truth is, I have become this season's joke...Newport's plaything."

My husband's eyes squeezed shut. "Let us not jump to such a conclusion."

"Us? It's me they ridicule." I drew my cloak tighter. "Roddy, tell me what you know about Oliver Belmont's valet."

"The Egyptian? They say he is phobic about dogs...calls them vermin. Why?"

"I'll tell you why. He sleeps at Oliver Belmont's threshold with a dagger in his teeth, which I learned from my dinner partner Chadwick Bourne who made a great point of it. Or were you and Anita already outside when we carved roasted birds?"

"No, we coped with the game birds."

"And with game knives, Roddy. Blades."

My husband sat back and rubbed his cheek. "You think Mr. Bourne deliberately mentioned the valet's dagger?"

"Not merely mentioned, Roddy. He beamed. He scored. And then my maiden name gave Battersby the license to call me Lady Macbeth."

My husband had a "surely not" expression on his face, his eyes crinkling and lips taut.

"Listen to me, Roddy." I cleared my throat and worked to keep my voice low and steady. "First, Battersby bellowed a few lines from Shakespeare about a dagger, and then Ellen Terry recited as if performing for an audience in a theatre. She was brilliant. The ballroom burst into applause, which you heard in the garden. That should have been the end of it, but Battersby held the floor. He took 'Mac' from 'Mackle' and called me Newport's dagger lady. Nobody said a word. Nobody did a thing to help."

Roddy's eyes widened, then narrowed.

At that moment, I wanted to say something about my papa's good name twisted for Newport's amusement.

Instead, I heard my voice rising as I jabbered, "The tale of me holding the bloody dagger lives on, Roddy, and I have become a character in a cartoon. A man was murdered, and the police have closed the case, but...but there is reason to think the killer is out there...loose."

I panted, breathless, and the stillness at that moment continued after the clock struck 2:00 a.m. on this fourth Wednesday of the month. It continued as Roddy's cufflink rasped across the table and my cloak slipped from my shoulders.

My husband rubbed his eyes. "Are you sleepy, Val?"

"Hardly."

"Then wait here. Give me a minute."

Shedding his coat, Roddy reached for the candle and disappeared into the darkness, returning with two glasses, a bottle, a corkscrew, and a tin box under his arm while also managing the candle. "Shortbread cookies," he said, "and *vin santo* from Santorini...a dessert wine."

"Italy?"

"Island in Greece," he replied, replacing the candle and uncorking the bottle. He poured two glasses, moved one toward me, and opened the cookie tin. "Shortbread snack," he said. "No point waking anyone for kitchen duty."

"No."

"So, cookies. Aren't you hungry?"

"To be frank, I cannot tell hunger from anger."

Roddy took two shortbreads, ate them, and nodded with the gravity familiar from critical junctures in our life together. "Val, you have made a sweeping charge...in anger? Or do you have reasons?"

I sipped the sweet wine. "If you are asking for evidence, Roddy, I have none. If you want to know who really killed Warren Eccles, I have no idea."

I pulled the cloak over my shoulders. "The murder has its own logic. The art gallery manager came upon a thieving workman named Marco, tried to stop him, and paid with his life. The thief-turned-murderer, a skilled plasterer, sold one of three stolen paintings at a cottage door and was immediately revealed as the killer...and you know the rest."

Reaching for his wine, Roddy nodded. "His body was found on the rocks in front of Ochre Court...at dawn." With his glass held for a pensive moment, my husband continued, "and his guilt was confirmed by the tradesman's knives found in his pockets."

"And his identity verified by a clothing tag...Marco Gliano. And the remaining question is how to account for his fall from the Cliff Walk. He either slipped from the path, or...."

"Or jumped when guilt overcame him." Roddy sipped. "The police are satisfied, and the murder case is closed. The search for two stolen paintings continues." My husband shrugged. "What else, Val?"

I started to reply, but Roddy held up his palm. "You are asking, why was the man on Cliff Walk, especially at night? No one frequents Cliff Walk after dark because the path is not lighted. Isn't that it?" My husband's tone seemed dismissive. "

"Don't make light of this, Roddy, not after Crossways."

"I do not...would not. I have mulled over that very question with no answer."

"Roddy," I said, "there is something else. Calista heard an Ochre Point servant talking at the wedding reception last Friday night...not the servant who discovered the body, but a footman who made the rounds of the property the previous night. He claims he saw two figures on Cliff Walk, then only one."

"Did the footman hear voices?"

"I don't think so. Calista heard the footman say he observed two figures below Ochre Court on Cliff Walk, and then just one left standing. My maid is no gossip, Roddy, but the murder has been on everyone's mind. The plasterer worked at cottages, and he might have made acquaintance with household servants."

"In other words, Newport's servants might suspect the plasterer was not Eccles's killer." Roddy paused, and I nodded. "But Val, why would our maid trouble you with such hearsay?"

In the silence that followed, the candle flame cast faint shadows across the tabletop. Our thoughts might have converged, or perhaps intersected. "Roddy," I said, "a year has passed since we first exposed a murderer here in Newport. And then the others...Central Park, the opera...Chicago. And last month in the Hudson Valley...so awful." I shivered despite my cloak. "Word has got around about us."

"So it seems."

I gripped my husband's hand. "Now, yet again…? You know the police will not be interested."

Roddy smiled ruefully. "I'm afraid my pride makes me *persona non grata* at Market Square."

"I'm afraid you are correct, Roderick DeVere." At this moment, I wanted to ask, was *The Counting House* worth it? Is your Knickerbocker gentlemanly pride more important than helping the police help you? Roddy seemed downright nonchalant.

My stake in the Travers Block murder, on the other hand, was palpable. I was driven to heal a social wound that would otherwise fester all summerlong and follow me to the city in the fall. If Marco's innocence could be proven and Eccles's killer exposed, Newport would be forced to eat its words. Its dish would be humble pie. My flashing eyes would be the daggers.

The clock struck 3:00 a.m. on this July 26, my head beginning to ache in these wee hours that lent themselves to flights of fancy. I would realize in the light of day that Newport would not so readily reconcile with me.

Chapter Twenty

AT MY REQUEST, CASSIE invited me for an afternoon drive with a stop for lemonade at the Casino. My morning was spent at the Redwood Library immersed in articles on "Open Air Pursuits," "Campfires," and "Woodcraft," all with advice for the children's camp that I was eager to set in motion.

The Forster Victoria arrived on the hour at 2:00 p.m. "Good afternoon, Mrs. Forster."

"Good afternoon to you, Mrs. DeVere."

"And your children are...?"

"At Bailey's Beach with nanny Cara." Cassie leaned toward her coachman and said, "To the Casino, O'Boyle."

Cassie and I had not seen one another since the afternoon at Stone Point with the Rickers, the police, and *French Artillery in Snowy Winter*. This afternoon we would catch up and deliberately eavesdrop at the Casino's Horseshoe

Piazza. Overheard gossip might be leads that I could pursue on my own, and my friend would join me in listening to the ladies' conversation at surrounding tables. The piazza air would surely hum with chatter about Marco Gliano's fall from Cliff Walk, and perhaps May Goelet would stop by with friends. As mistress of Ochre Court, she possibly had heard her footman speak of the figures he saw on Cliff Walk in the darkness, the two persons who somehow reduced to just the one.

"How are you feeling, Val?"

"Hopeful about a summer camp for needy children," I said, knowing my friend was asking a different question. "And I hope your effort with the birds might fit with my camp. Also, if you care to know my feelings about *The Newport Daily News*, I can shed light on the subject."

Cassie made a face. "I am so sorry...."

"And if you wish to know my views on Madeline Glendorick...or Paulina Bourne at Alva's luncheon?"

Cassie's cringed her ladylike cringe.

I said, "Cassie, you appeared just when Paulina was moving in for the kill."

"Trying to save the moment with distraction," my friend replied, "because Paulina Bourne put you in a terrible position...forced to defend yourself against you-know-what."

"Against murder, Cassie. Go ahead, say it. And I wish you had been at Crossways the night before last. You missed quite a spectacle. I was ridiculed as a semi-comic murderess. Have you ever seen a performance of *Macbeth*?"

"Shakespeare's *Macbeth*?" My friend suddenly tensed in the green faille afternoon dress. "Mother forced me to see it twice, Val. She decided ghosts onstage at the theatre would cure my visions. *Macbeth* was terrifying...there's a murdered man's ghost, Banquo's ghost. And in *Hamlet*, a ghost of a murdered father. Mother looked up more such plays, but my father called a halt to Shakespeare except for *A Midsummer Night's Dream*. Even so, I cringed at 'damned spirits' and dragons in the clouds. I think Shakespeare knew about the 'unseen' world. I told my parents he would understand me, which was a mistake. I was sent to my bedroom for a week."

Cassie smoothed her gloves and touched my arm. "Forgive this outburst, Val. *Macbeth* has another meaning for you, doesn't it? All that stabbing...."

From the frown on Cassie Forster's delicate face, I guessed she might have heard something about the *Macbeth* debacle at Crossways. She would tell me if I asked, but my thoughts circled back to the Cuveen Gallery reception when I learned my friend arrived early and had left within minutes.

"Cassie, you know that I am sitting for a portrait by André Cole?"

"I do know. I mentioned it in my letter to Dudley...to Fiji." She now looked straight ahead.

"Cole's portraits were on view at the Cuveen reception," I said. "You saw them?"

Cassie nodded with her face turned aside.

"Glowing skin tones on all three portraits," I said, "so it seemed like a good idea for Cole to have the DeVere commission. My portrait is for Roddy, for his study in the city."

My friend looked toward the sea. I was not sure she heard me, so I raised my voice. "I'm afraid you and I have been out of touch," I said, "except for that upsetting afternoon at Stone Point. You did promise to attend the reception. I looked for you. I heard you left shortly after the opening."

The Forsters' Grays moved smartly under O'Boyle's whip. Minutes passed with the sea on one side of us and dappled sunlight through the trees on the other. At last, Cassie turned toward me. "I did promise, Val, and I went into the gallery but felt...woozy." She touched the throat of her dress. "Something about that gallery," she said. "Or someone's fragrance." She smoothed her gloves.

It was not like Cassie Forster to be evasive. Tactful yes, but not to dodge an issue. Was she touching lightly on the matter that inflamed her life? Shying away from saying her Sixth Sense took hold at the Cuveen Gallery?

These days, Cassie tried her best to tamp down episodes that struck without warning. She had promised her husband to ward them off for the sake of their family. If necessary, she agreed to go to Switzerland for a treatment involving ice and electricity. I decided Cassie said "woozy" and "fragrance" rather than admit the Cuveen Gallery sent her into the otherworldly realm. Whatever caused her "spell" that evening on the Travers Block, I needed to find out.

My friend responded generously this afternoon because the Cliff Walk was no favorite of hers, especially the section in front of Ochre Court. Cassie remarked without explanation that her children were forbidden to walk there. Their nanny had strict instructions. I did not ask why but gazed at the sea and watched the surf roll and crash against the rocks. We smiled and waved at a crisscrossing carriage. If we passed a second time, we would smile but not wave. The third time, we would ignore one another as etiquette decreed.

Cassie said, "Val, I'm happy to have lemonade on the piazza and listen to chit-chat at the other tables, but you seem not quite yourself this afternoon. Neither of us cares to pry, but would you like to tell me something...?"

"Cassie," I said, "at this very hour Roddy is at the Reading Room listening to conversations prompted by whiskey. He will listen for hearsay about the Cliff Walk death of your plasterer."

"Marco..." she murmured, "the artist of *cartouche*...the late artist."

I would remember her phrasing, for Cassie did not say "killer." O'Boyle reined us to a stop in front of the Casino and assisted us from the carriage. I said, "Let us take our turn on the piazza. We will order lemonade and overhear every word around us."

At my request, the Casino butler, Mr. Ives, directed a waiter to seat Cassie and me at a piazza table surrounded by ladies wearing broad-brimmed, feathered hats. Several acknowledged us with twisted little smiles that meant word was around about me and the knife. Quite possibly *Macbeth* as well. Norma Doolittle's lips puckered, and Charlotte Drayton raised an eyebrow. Mrs. Astor's divorcée daughter Charlotte presided at a table of five. Everyone sipped tea or cool soft drinks and chatted within earshot.

"Cassie," I said as we sat down, "the ostrich plumes around us could inspire your bird protection idea."

"Not only ostriches, Val. I see flamingo feathers…and herons too. I tried to bring up the feathers at Alva's luncheon, but no one was interested. I'm thinking of a luncheon to honor a guest from London. The Royal Society for the Protection of Birds puts the English far ahead of us in bird protection. And Americans follow England like goslings paddling after Mother Goose."

We laughed lightly. "Or suppose," I said, "that we decided on fewer hats? Suppose we could take our cue from Mr. Ives's hair?" The Casino butler sported a glistening tower of salt-and-pepper waves that rose from his forehead to give him four inches of additional height. Neither rain nor wind budged the man's hair. Nicknamed Sir Pompadour, Mr. Ives had proven himself indispensable on numerous occasions, whether supplying pocket money or helping inebriated members. It was considered a stroke of genius that the Casino founder, the newspaper heir James Gordon Bennett, Jr. found Mr. Ives and installed him as butler.

Our lemonades arrived, and we tilted our heads to hear phrases from other tables. I heard couturier gowns debated between the House of Worth and Redfern, tulle versus satin, and whether a gown could be worn a second time or must be discarded.

Cassie murmured that jewelry was the topic uppermost at Charlotte Drayton's table, whether bracelets by Boucheron or Marcus set off diamonds to best advantage. Then Cassie held up a finger to signal quiet, leaned forward, and whispered, "Fire extinguishers."

"What about them?"

She sat back again, then leaned. "A fire at *Beaulieu*...extinguished."

"Not *Beaulieu*...on Bellevue."

"Shhh, Val...not so loud." Another back and forth, and Cassie said, "Small fire on first floor, footman used extinguisher. Minor damage."

"Still...." We sipped, and I thought of the body found in the fire-ravaged ruins of the house on Gill Street. Before I could add a word about fire equipment, Cassie shushed me with a raised finger, then murmured, "Barbizon School, Val."

"What school?"

"Art," she said softly. "Wherever the killer hid the two missing French paintings...the Millet and Dupré." Cassie leaned closer and said, "Charlotte imagines them thrown into the sea."

"By Marco?"

She nodded. "...because he felt guilty. She thinks fishermen will find them and claim the reward." Cassie paused, listening. "Charlotte thinks the reward will be denied... water damage."

We sipped our lemonade. A smooth voice at a table behind me said, "Murderous riff-raff...Italian temper...hot head with knives...our hallway replastered immediately. Ill at the very sight...."

Cassie said, "That's Norma Doolittle. I recall Marco worked for her."

The phrases floated as the afternoon lengthened, wisps of theories about Marco Gliano and the Eccles murder. One exchange caught my attention, the way Marco Gliano landed when he plunged from Cliff Walk. Somehow, a trapeze acrobat came into the conversation, a man who had fallen from the aerial bar a few years ago when the circus came to Newport. Did he land on his back or flat on his face? The voices debated the question. The deceased Marco and the trapeze fatality became a heads-or-tails argument without solution.

On the sidewalk minutes later in front of the Casino, my friend took deep breaths to steady herself. While we waited for her carriage, Cassie leaned close and took my arm for support. "You know that Cliff Walk is odious to me, Val. It was always so. Saffira warned me of trouble in that place."

"Cassie, you needn't explain about Saffira." She meant the nursemaid who opened the gates of unseen worlds to little Cassandra, all before her mother fired the nurse and sent her back to the Islands. "You needn't explain, Cassie."

"But I must. My early memory...Saffira would not speak the word, 'Newport.' She would say 'Aquidneck Island of Peace.' She spoke of tribes long ago...then of troubles that would have no end in that place. My mother forced Saffira to take me to Cliff Walk, Val. It was terrible. No wonder Mr. Goelet fell ill and died. No wonder Marco Gliani met his end at Cliff Walk. There will be others. Believe me, there will be others."

Chapter Twenty-One

THE DRUMCLIFFE GARDENS GLOWED in the early evening sunlight, especially the royal blue-violet hydrangeas, a seasonal display everywhere in Newport in the month of July. Roddy was outside walking our dog, said the footman who assisted me from Cassie's carriage. From the Casino to Drumcliffe, my friend's gloom became mine, and the lush hydrangeas were a tonic, every bloom visually delicious.

Winding along the crushed shell path, I heard Roddy's sharp, "No, Velvet...no," then caught sight of my husband and the dog in a tug-of-war over a feathery object set tight in Velvet's jaws.

"No, Velvet...give it up...no."

Our French bulldog neither growled nor obeyed. Roddy muttered "damnable dog," then yanked the object loose and hurled it skyward. Velvet strained at her leash, and

I blurted, "Velvet, you killed a bird! Roddy, did she kill that bird?"

"She did not." My husband dug into a jacket pocket. "Here, girl...a biscuit just for you." Roddy pointed to a second floor window. "The bird flew headfirst at the window and fell into the garden. And that was that."

"Poor bird." I glanced up at the polished windowpane. "Suppose Mrs. Thwaite allowed dust to gather on a few windows...and salt brine too?" It seemed farfetched, but I would speak to the housekeeper.

My mood had darkened. "Shall we stroll, Roddy? I'll tell you about the Casino, and you report on the Reading Room. I'll go first because there is very little to report. Every lady presumes Marco Gliano is the murderer. It was suggested he threw the two missing paintings into the sea, to be recovered in fishermen's nets. The only disagreement concerns Marco's plummet from the Cliff Walk, whether he landed on his back or his face."

"That's all?"

"The gist of it." I withheld Cassie's forebodings. "Your turn," I said. "What did you hear?"

We paused beside a rose bush with few buds and no flowers. "It took a while, Val. Two whiskeys with soda for this reluctant member."

I knew how reluctant. Roddy seldom took advantage of his membership in the Reading Room, that most exclusive gentlemen's club in Newport. My husband objected to its stodginess, though I sensed something to do with cocktails and perhaps with his father, who adored the Reading Room. Rufus DeVere's greatest regret was leaving it when he and Eleanor decamped for summers in Bar Harbor, Maine. I suspected the members balked at Roddy's special cocktails, holding fast to soda and ice as the sole additions to their whiskey or gin. I guessed my husband felt rebuffed and took it personally.

"It took a while for conversation to turn to the murder," Roddy said. "The members first talked about property... vacant lots recently cleared for builders. Which lots do you imagine they meant?"

I shrugged. "No idea."

"It's the property now vacant because of the fires. Three houses gone, and purchase of the lots and a few tumbledown houses create an opportunity. Would I care to invest?"

"You're joking?"

"I wish I were. The Reading Room conversation was deliberately roundabout. But the Gill Street fires present commercial possibilities...a new Travers Block by a major architect."

"But no mention of the woman who died?"

"Not in my hearing. I know how you feel, Val. Let us hope she is identified. Let us hope the fires are found to be accidental. The members did bring up extinguishers, how every house ought to have at least one. In fact, Randolph Cowley regretted none of the three houses had an extinguisher. He's a major stockholder in the Pyrene Company."

"Cowley...he was on *Conquest*. He is one of my tormentors. Who else was in the chummy circle this afternoon?"

Roddy tugged Velvet's leash. "Val, we have enough on our minds right now. I went to the Reading Room for the same reason you and Cassandra went to the Casino. Perhaps I should have waited to bring up the vacant lots and fires. Perhaps I spoke out of turn just now, but our afternoon plan was to seek specific information."

My husband's cool gaze said he would offer the Reading Room names only if pressed. I finally said, "Roddy, tell me what you heard over your second whiskey and soda."

"I heard the strong suspicion that Eccles's assistant killed his employer."

"Not Marco?"

"The Plasterer was involved, but the prime candidate at the Reading Room is Asa Durling."

That possibility had lingered in the back of our minds, but we relied on the police confirming Durling's alibi. I asked, "Because Eccles was a ruthless boss?"

"Start with Durling's appearance. An albino in Newport is something of a white whale. The members are convinced that Durling killed his employer in a foiled robbery. One gentleman's sister decided to have André Cole paint her and he went to make arrangements at the hotel suite. He was struck by Durling's kerfuffle over insurance claims."

"Which we remember," I said.

"The man thinks it was a ruse, Val. He thinks Durling tangles with the insurance company to avoid detection. Or because he feels guilty. It's something to consider, but the

Reading Room debate mainly centered on whether Durling was in league with the plasterer."

"Conspiring...."

"But not on equal terms. They think Durling made Marco his foil, set him up to be targeted as the thief and killer."

I waved away a bee. "And do they think Asa Durling sent Marco to the Stone Point cottage door with stolen art?"

Roddy swatted at the same bee. "They think any cottage on Bellevue or Ocean Drive would suit Durling's plan. The Reading Room seems to think the *French Artillery* painting was expendable, far less valuable than the pictures of peasants planting potatoes or cattle crossing a ford. Don't ask me why. Maybe Napoleon's defeat and exile devalue the artillery men in the snow. Maybe the snow is not appealing in July."

"Or the soldiers' corpses?"

"Or the fallen, yes."

We turned back and retraced our steps, pausing to let Velvet sniff and paw at a boxwood. "Roddy," I said, "isn't it plausible that Reading Room members are correct, that Eccles came to the gallery at dawn and found Durling pulling paintings from the walls? Maybe Durling had a handcart. Maybe he panicked when Eccles appeared and questioned him. The dagger was nearby, a decorative piece. And then... the rest." Eyes shut, I took a deep breath, dreading memory's reprise of that morning.

"If it happened in that order," Roddy said, "the paintings would have been hidden according to Durling's initial plan, which was theft. And if the plasterer was an accomplice, he stowed the paintings in the hiding place."

"For retrieval at a later date," I said. "So, if Marco was in league with Asa Durling, is it possible that he was offered *French Artillery* as his share of the robbery?"

"Quite possible," Roddy said. "Let's say Durling gave Marco the painting as payment and suggested he sell it for cash. He knew the naïve plasterer would be caught and arrested for Eccles's murder, especially since the man struck everyone as brutish."

"Or maybe Marco snatched it from the hiding place when Durling failed to pay him," I said. "It's the largest painting of the three, and Marco might have mistaken size for worth."

"Either way, Val, the Reading Room believes Durling is the mastermind, the murderer and thief. And he will try to recover the two paintings before day-tourists find them and reap the reward. At that crucial moment, he might expose himself as the killer. Discovery of the paintings might be the lever to reopen the murder case. That, in sum, is the Reading Room theory."

"And the members will go to the police with these ideas?"

"Certainly not." My husband stiffened. "Out of the question."

"Oh...because gentlemen do not lower themselves. Is that it?"

Roddy did not answer, and I did not to pursue this point, especially after that standoff over *The Counting House*. My husband's disdain for the Reading Room had not moved him to resign his membership. It seems meddling in Police work was not for Knickerbocker gentlemen for whom lineage and propriety mattered so greatly.

My next question should have been answered before I asked. "What about the portraits being arranged at the Meunchinger suite? What about André Cole? Who sits for his portraits? Surely not the Reading Room gentleman's sister."

My husband gave me a fish-eyed glance. "She has cancelled."

"So," I said, "crass rich people will sit, but not the crème de la crème of Society?" I might have asked where Valentine Mackle DeVere fits in the grand scheme of things but instead asked about my next scheduled sitting on Catherine Street.

"Actually, Val, you are due tomorrow morning at 10 a.m." Roddy cleared his throat. "I called on the suite this morning to authorize a bank draft...before the Reading Room visit." He tugged Velvet's leash. "Val, if you care to cancel the portrait, say the word."

I was sorely tempted, but the gift to my husband was already underway. We would need to find another artist, probably drag the business into the autumn.

"And Val," Roddy said, "if you cancel, you will close an avenue of possible information...whatever Cole knows about Eccles. And Durling too."

My husband was right. Cole might let go a useful snippet in the studio while fawning over Madame DeVere. I would try to keep him talking while he wielded his brushes and dispensed flattery.

For now, Marco Gliano was officially Eccles's sole killer, and he was dead. Still, the debate at the Casino stayed in mind, the question of how the plasterer landed on the rocks below Cliff Walk...below Ochre Court. Was he found face down, or on his back? The difference could split the case open like a thunderclap on a sunny morning.

Chapter Twenty-two

I TIED SHAMROCK AT the granite post on this overcast Newport morning and straightened the tan kersey jacket that would not attract attention later today in downtown Newport. First, however, two hours of posing at the Catherine Street studio. A light tap on the door, and in seconds the suede beret swept low as André Cole crooned, *"Bonjour,* Madame DeVere."

"Good morning, Mr. Cole."

Once again, the artist in his box-pleated smock took me to my chair. Odors of wine topped the scents of roses and turpentine, and the table by the window held one glass and an emptied bottle.

"You are in the chair *confortable,* Madame?"

"Comfortable, yes, Mr. Cole." The glass and bottle were unnerving. If he drank, his mistakes would mean more sittings to repair errors. I could be bound to this chair for the better part of the summer.

"Madame is *inquiet*? How you say...fretting?"

"Fretful? No, I'm fine...fine." I smiled, reminding myself this portrait was for Roddy. What's more, the lady in the chair must be disarming to learn about recent portrait cancellations. She must be tranquil to somehow introduce the names Eccles and Durling in the studio. Maybe the wine would loosen Cole's tongue, though his words would be French.

"Madame's *veste*?" He made unbuttoning motions, and I released the horn buttons to let the soft cloth slip to the collar bone.

Cole swooped the drapery from his easel in a motion I had seen in magazine pictures of matadors in bullrings. "Ah, Madame," he said, "the morning is *encore* for us. We begin again."

"We do," I said pleasantly.

"And again, *la loi*...the first law of this studio?"

"Never to look at my portrait until you say it is complete."

"*Oui! Mais oui!*"

The sounds of liquids mixed with grit filled the next minutes, then a brush scuffing against canvas. "These lovely summer days pass ever so quickly," I said. "I do so hope that you take the time to go about Newport. I feel sure that Marianne would enjoy sight-seeing."

"Ah, *ma Marianne*," he said, "*si seulemont*...if only. Marianne is in romance with the kitchen. For me, I am *mettre en prison*...the prisoner of my art. The work summons me, Madame DeVere, and I must obey."

He asked for silence for a *"très délicate"* maneuver which gave me time to plan my approach. It would not do to mention Eccles or Durling just yet.

"Monsieur Cole," I said as he stepped back to regard his work. "On the topic of art," I said, "do you know of the paintings that are now missing...stolen from the gallery here in Newport? Two important paintings are gone."

He waved his brush in the air and spat at the tarpaulin on the floor. *"De l'école Barbizon*? Jean-François Millet? Jules Dupré? What is their art, madame? *Les images des vaches...* cows. And *paysans* that labor in the dirt."

So much for the slantwise push. To André Cole, those artists' names were curses. The Barbizon painters' success insulting. He stepped toward me, his eyes hot. "Madame DeVere, be not deceived. The soul of a man or a woman speaks in the face and form. The artist must worship, ever *modeste...*humble before the face and form."

I dared not bring up *French Artillery* and risk another fit of temper and my portrait as well.

Perhaps the man was jealous. Not one of his sample portraits had been stolen. The emptied wine bottle could be solace for cancelled portraits. Cole's income was possibly at risk, and the rent for the Catherine and Cottage Street cottages would come due, assuming the leases were not pre-paid by Joseph Cuveen. Or did Eccles have oversight of the rentals? And now Durling?

His brush scratched at the canvas, and I tried mentally to sail Daisy Harriman's *Catnip*, just as Cole abruptly brought up the West, asking if I was related to "Boofallow Bill?"

"His name is William Cody," I said, "and I am not a relative."

"But the West of America, so vaste."

"Yes, vast."

"*Les montagnes*."

"Mountains, yes...mountains." His brush scratched, and I lapsed into memories of the Rocky Mountain waterfalls in summer, the sunny slopes, the towering rock and diamond-bright rivers. "Mr. Cole," I asked, "could the background of my portrait be...mountains?"

"*Les montagnes*, Madame? *Pour la distance....? Certainement.*"

"My "Merci" rounded out this sitting. The portrait could have something for me, something from my past before this season of social stain and mockery, before whispered suspicion at every turn. Before murder.

I found myself time-traveling to Pikes Peak in the Sawatch Range of the Rockies. Later, I would ask Cassie to write down the French phrases and bring them here next time. They must be America's Rockies, not the Alps. I would make sure of it. At last released from the chair in a near giddy instant, I bid "Adieu" to André Cole and skipped to the pony cart. My plan had started in reverie, a daydream, though by afternoon I would be grounded in the hard fact of this craggy shoreline. I had briefly sipped memory's wine, but cold sobriety waited just ahead.

A delivery boy took a shiny coin to look after my pony at the Catherine Street hitching post with the promise of another coin on my return later this afternoon. I then waited for an electric trolley to head downtown. Newport's trolleys chauffeured servants into town or to Easton's Beach on their days off.

The trolley with number **20** blazoned in gilt across the front stopped for four of us, a young couple and a woman whose resemblance to our housekeeper was so uncanny that I nearly cried out, Mrs. Thwaite. The woman smiled with such warmth at the motorman that the resemblance vanished when we paid our nickels and settled on the bench seats for a swift downhill ride.

My destination was the Holly Tree Coffee House at the corner of Thames Street and Commercial Wharf. My invited guest would probably prefer a barroom, for it was common knowledge that newspapermen frequented taverns. However, a cup of coffee and the promise of profitable work in his spare time might lure *The Newport Daily News* photographer Hugh Bullard to my table. Early this morning I had sent him a note saying I would be at the Holly Tree from 2:00 to 4:00 p.m. and hoped he would have time to join me to discuss photographs that I would like to have taken as a surprise gift for my husband.

The ride was breezy, and the Holly Tree Coffee House a short walk from my stop. The modest clapboard building with large front windows felt more like a depot where patrons hastily drank coffee at a dozen pine tables with ladderback chairs and woven rush seats. Women in long skirts, long-sleeved jackets and feathered straw hats chatted at the tables, while men in corduroys and celluloid collars folded and unfolded trolley schedules. No one seemed relaxed. The waitresses scurried breathlessly with cups and little plates. People paid upon being served.

"Black coffee and a corn muffin, please," I said. My table faced the door. If Hugh Bullard came in, I would see him at once. A wall clock read 1:46 p.m. Would he recognize me? Would I know the man in the derby hat who operated his camera with a black cloth tenting his body? Looking up as a derby was doffed at the door, I pulled my smile and averted my gaze. The man was not the photographer.

The waitress brought the first of several cups and was paid promptly from the coin purse tucked in my skirt pocket. The coffee was weak, the muffin delicious. Roddy told me that coffee in France or Italy was a slow-motion experience, that Americans bolted the brew on the fly. Maybe we Americans lost out when life demanded bustle and speed without cease.

Imagine the surprise when the Holly Tree customers suddenly surged to the door like a tide rushing out. The waitress said an outdoor bell announced a trolley's arrival at the stop alongside the coffee house. "Don't you worry, ma'am," she said. "Other folks will come in sooner than we can grind the beans and brew the next pot. You take all the time you can spare."

True, harried men and women soon filled the room. Women sat heavily, thankful to get off their feet. A man loosened his tie and slipped off his arm garters. The clock said 2:43 as I nibbled and sipped. Two derby hats, but no Hugh Bullard. My note of invitation was delivered by a footman early this morning when the photographer was said to be "out early on assignment." I knew nothing about a newspaper photographer's hours.

By 3:35, the Holly Tree Coffee House had emptied out and filled up twice again. In less than half an hour, I would board a trolley and return to my patient Shamrock and return to Drumcliffe.

At my fourth coffee and second muffin, however, the door was opened by a thickset man in a gray worsted suit and derby hat. The clock said 3:52. With hat off, he looked about, and I waved, forgetting etiquette. He started toward me, paused to wipe his face with a handkerchief, then took the chair across from me. Hugh Bullard scanned my face as if focusing the camera for a photograph. He ordered coffee with cream. His eyes never left my face.

"Mr. Bullard," I said, "thank you for finding time to join me this afternoon. I trust you recall taking pictures of me earlier this month at my...." I hesitated to say cottage, false humility for a mansion. I also omitted Eccles's name. "I am Mrs. DeVere, and we met when you took my photograph at the request of the artist, Mr. André Cole. I assume that Mr. Cole is pleased?"

"Said he was." The coffee arrived, and Ballard's coin beat mine to the waitress.

"I recall," I said, "that you told my husband and me to look for your photograph of a burning house to appear in the *News* the next day. Which it did, a vivid picture."

"Such is the job, One day a parade, the next a fire. I never know." He sipped.

I fought temptation to ask about the woman who fell victim to that very fire. Perhaps the newsroom had ideas about her, but Hugh Bullard would be unlikely to tell me. Also, I had my plan and my questions. He would not sit here for a second cup.

"Mr. Ballard, I am hoping to persuade you to return to our property to take photographs of the beautiful hydrangea blooms in our garden. Of course, for full compensation in your free time."

The hazel eyes squinted. "Flowers?"

"The garden hydrangeas," I said. "A surprise for my husband's birthday."

He sat back, sipped his coffee and said, "Lady, you will want color. One of these days, a camera and darkroom might do the trick, but not now. Photographs are black, white, and gray. Sorry to disappoint you, but let's not waste your money or my time."

I hoped my laugh sounded silvery. "Oh, Mr. Bullard, to be clear, I plan to have the photographs tinted...tinted by hand. We Ladies do enjoy our activities." I gave him a soulful glance. "Trifling activities...so unlike your profession." I touched my throat. "Your presence in demand at scenes of devastation."

I slowly shook my head. He briefly closed his eyes.

"At tragedies," I said. "Fires, accidents...those who have breathed their last."

He tugged at his collar. "Tough work at times."

"I cannot begin to imagine," I said. "Of course, the *Daily News* did report my husband and I had the misfortune to be at the Travers Block on that terrible day earlier this month." I spoke in lowest tones. "Terrible...."

"You might say."

I sipped my coffee. He sipped his. I must not hasten. "A day when you, Mr. Bullard, were called upon to verify that most unspeakable event. Disastrous."

He nodded slightly.

"Your photographs never to be seen by the public," I said, as if musing in the moment. "Never in the newspaper, but in your experience...deep in memory."

"Camera work for the chief," he mumbled. "Police files."

"Good works," I said. "A service to all." I lifted my cup. "And then, so soon called to Cliff Walk." I glanced upward as if to the sky. "Just at dawn, we understood from the *Daily News* reports. Your photographs of the rocks...only of the rocks. You pointed your camera down from the Walk?"

"Cursed birds," he said.

"Birds?"

"Gulls in the way, in the air, on the rocks, on the... on him."

On the body. On Marco Gliano's body. I sipped my coffee. "The News gave us your photographs of craggy rocks in front of Ochre Court," I said, "but we were spared the sight...the sight of what you saw."

Bullard did not respond.

I leaned closer to him. "That young killer did plastering work," I said, "for people who said he had a young face...like an angry boy...a very angry face."

He finished his coffee and fixed me with those hazel eyes. "Let them, Mrs. DeVere. Let them." He turned the cup over. "The face on those rocks had a broken nose and busted jaw, like he went bare fist for a round and got the worst of it. For sure, Mrs. DeVere, what I saw was no boy's face."

Chapter Twenty-three

PAST THE MASSIVE BLACK stone fireplace and dark leatherbound books, I found Roddy holding a mixing glass in front of a window, swirling the contents and peering like a chemist. Already dressed for dinner, he was probably working on a cocktail for someone in New York. Or a business. His tuxedoed back was turned, and he did not hear me come in.

Not to startle him, I spoke softly. "Roddy...Roddy...."

He turned, annoyance and relief gathering in his narrowed eyes. "Val, where have you been? I sent Bronson to Catherine Street to inquire. He saw your pony and cart. André Cole said you left his studio by noon and knew nothing of your whereabouts. I had Sands telephone Seabright in case you were visiting Cassandra, then had him telephone the Casino to page Ives. The Redwood librarian had not seen you. Where did you go? Where have you been?"

"At the Holly Tree Coffee House," I said.

Expecting my husband's "Why on earth?" I was not prepared for Roddy's accusation. "It was about Votes for Women, wasn't it, Val? Let me guess. You found out the coffee house was started by the abolitionist lady...Sophia what's-her-name...Sophia Little. She led the Abolitionists, and now the Civil War is history, and the next push is Votes for Women. Answer me this—is the Holly Tree Coffee House your new summer headquarters?

"Roddy, of course not.... Let us sit down," I said, looking for a bright spot in this gloomy library and finally pointing to the Empire sofa against a mud-brown wall supposedly painted in rich mahogany tones.

We sat. "First of all," I said, "the coffee house history was unknown to me, and Votes-for-Women was furthest from my mind this afternoon. Let us not renew that debate... not now."

My husband nodded grudgingly. Our longstanding disagreement about women and the ballot pitted Roddy's "eventually" against my "right now." We had agreed to disagree, though the issue bubbled at the worst times.

"Someday I want to hear about the beginnings of the Holly Tree," I said, "but today's visit really began when Cassie and I went to the Casino yesterday."

I now made the mistake of telling about Cassie's childhood nursemaid from The Islands who forecast death near Cliff Walk where Ogden Goelet bought property for his Ochre Court cottage.

Roddy jiggled the mixing glass. "My dear Valentine," he said, "do recall that Ogden Goelet passed away two years ago at Cowes, the Isle of Wight. He died aboard his yacht in Britain, two thousand miles from Newport."

I could remind my husband that Cassie's otherworldly visions crossed space and time. But the point would set us wrangling. I simply reminded Roddy that ladies at the Casino disagreed over whether the murderous Marco had landed on his back or his front when he plunged from Cliff Walk.

"They remembered the circus when a trapeze performer missed the bar and fell," I said, "and their question stayed with me."

My husband put the mixing glass on a table, his gaze no longer quite so dismissive.

"Marco's body was found at dawn," I said. "And the police came immediately, as we know. The reporters and the photographer also came right away, but the *Daily News* published pictures only of the rocks."

"Of course," Roddy said. "Fully understandable."

"But the photographer saw the body, Roddy. Standing on Cliff Walk with his camera, he looked down and saw Marco Gliano on the rocks...his body either face down... or face up." I swallowed. "Roddy, if Marco fell, he would probably have landed on his face."

"Probably."

"And if he jumped, overcome with guilt...same thing."

"Probably so."

"But if he was pushed...?"

"Val, please, no guessing games."

"Probabilities, Roddy. I am saying that If Marco was pushed, he would land on his back, face up. Especially if he struggled against an opponent who shoved him off the Walk."

My husband waited with the practiced patience of an attorney who would take his turn to argue.

"In sum," I said, "the photographer saw the body on the rocks, and I talked to him at the Holly Tree Coffee House this afternoon...by invitation."

"You invited Hugh Bullard?" Those blue eyes widened.

"Hugh Bullard," I said firmly. "He will come to Drumcliffe to photograph our hydrangeas for the promised sum of fifty dollars. So, Roddy, for fifty dollars I learned that Marco Gliano was found face-up on the rocks...face-up with a broken nose and jaw."

Roddy sucked his cheek, always a sign of serious interest. I should have allowed these things to steep. Instead, I pushed on. "So, let us factor in Calista's rumor that a servant saw two figures on the Walk, then only one...it means that Marco was pushed off the Walk. He was murdered."

Roddy raised his palm for a *stop*. My slide into certainty tripped me up so often. My husband's handsome brow furrowed. "Val, let us take our time about this. Probability is not proof."

"Suppose it was Durling," I said. "Your Reading Room friends convicted Asa Durling."

I lip-read Roddy's objection to "friends" as I dug myself deeper with this accusation. "Durling," I said, "would have doubts about Marco because the plasterer might confess if the police caught him. Suppose his broken English was not broken enough, which Durling would have known. So, the co-conspirator must be eliminated, meaning Durling had a motive." My voice grew shrill. A few minutes ago, I was steady, Roddy upset. Now we reversed.

Roddy took my hand. "My dear, I would have enjoyed watching your clever maneuver in the coffee house but let us please take a step back." He eyed the mixing glass as if its contents might expire.

"Roddy, if you would rather finish what you were doing? Talk about all this later?"

"No, it's a pent-up topic, and we should deal with it before dinner...clear the air as much as we can."

This strenuous day ought to wind down with a pleasant drink, but a cocktail would feel trivial, and the bottles on the library table looked more like a laboratory than a cocktail bar.

"So, Val..." Roddy said, "let me propose an alternate theory of how Marco Gliano died and was discovered lying on his back...and face up."

Warily, I nodded.

"Let us suppose that he either fell or else jumped from Cliff Walk to take his own life. In his forward plunge, he broke his nose and jaw upon impact."

"But in that case, he would lie face down," I said, my impatience mounting.

"Only if he died instantly," Roddy said slowly. "But if gravely injured, he perhaps managed to turn himself over and cried out in pain or tried to call for help before he perished."

I shuddered. "In the nighttime, Roddy...dying at night on the rocks. Hugh Bullard complained about seagulls. Think of seagulls flying over Marco's body...the birds on his body as he lay dying...." I choked.

"Another possibility, Val, and very grim."

"Which is...?"

"That the body was dumped onto the rocks."

"Already dead," I murmured. The kersey cloth felt clammy.

"And without an autopsy," Roddy continued, "we lack the physical facts to help settle any of these possibilities, including your Marco Gliano fighting off an attacker who pushed him to his death."

"*My* Marco? *Mine*?"

"Your theory." Roddy held my hand firmly.

"The police closed the case so fast," I said. "An open-and-shut case, isn't that what it is called? And Newport likes it that way?"

"Val, the police acted on reasonable evidence. Circumstantial, but persuasive." My husband's lawyerly voice held steady and firm. "Asa Durling's alibi held up, and Marco Gliano appeared with a painting stolen from the gallery on the morning Eccles was killed. The plasterer had worked on the Travers Block this spring, and he was found on the rocks with tools of his trade, steel putty knives sharp enough to kill."

Roddy gripped my fingers. "The police saw those connections. An autopsy at public expense might seem reasonable to you and me, but not to year-round residents. And not to certain cottagers we could name."

I could name Mamie Fish and Tessie Oelrichs, two very rich penny pinchers of Crossways and Rosecliff.

"I don't suppose the police could be persuaded to reopen the case," I said, stopping myself from bringing up a sore point. The cottagers often worked with police when issues concerned them both, such as prowlers or thieves. Last summer at The Elms, our host Edward Berwind told us a raid on his wine cellar was foiled when he partnered with Chief Cherry. Mr. Berwind quipped that the "case" saved The Elms cases of rare vintages and cooperation was the keynote. This summer, however, *The Counting House* affair ruled out any such alliance with Roddy.

My husband's eyes had softened with concern. "Val," he said, "we might be shouldering an impossible task. To root out gossip and innuendo, we are working against slimmest odds. A betting parlor would find us laughable...two credulous amateurs. And what have our efforts got us? Rumors at the Reading Room and a coffee house gambit with a *Daily News* photographer."

Roddy laced his hands together and sat back. "I have been thinking that we need not stay in Newport in the summer."

"What do you mean?"

His tenor voice grew throaty. "I mean my dear wife is bearing up bravely against Newport at its nastiest. Those ladies at lunch, then *Conquest* and the *Macbeth* episode at Crossways.... It's poisonous for you, Val, and each time you were all by yourself. I worry about you being targeted when I happened to be in a garden helping a lady get her fresh air. It's your fresh air I worry about, Val. It's you."

Roddy gestured at the bottles of liquors and flavorings he called his Libation Foundation. "I can set up my workstation elsewhere...such as Southampton."

"Long Island?"

"We could sell Drumcliffe and find a house to rent or buy in Southampton. Society is known to be more accepting. We would make new friends."

Did I hear a plaintive tone beneath these bold words? I reached for my husband's hand, but his fingers had locked together. "Roddy," I said, "I won't hear of it. I look forward to horseback riding and sailing, and I will take Daisy Harriman's advice to shop and be seen on the Travers Block. I meant to go before this...before the police closed the Eccles case. Now I will go upstairs and dress for dinner. I trust the Drumcliffe air is clear enough, but to remind you, my dear, I was not raised to cut and run."

Chapter Twenty-four

NOLAND DROVE ME TO the Travers Block in our seldom-used brougham with the flamboyant DeVere crest on the door. He would wait curbside during my morning of conspicuous shopping. As Daisy Harriman urged, I had come to the Travers Block to brazen my way without regard for Society. Wearing a double-breasted twill reefer suit and a narrow brim hat, I would invite onlookers to stare. I would flaunt in full.

In plain sight, unknown to Daisy or Newport at large, I would also carry out a secret plan.

A bicycle horn announced Gertrude Vanderbilt Whitney wheeling up, and we both said, "Good morning to you...fine day," at which she parked her bike and entered Black, Starr & Frost, jewelers. Perhaps Gertrude would tell Newport that Valentine DeVere was shopping near the scene of the heinous crime. The elegant sign—*J.*

Cuveen Fine Arts—had been stripped and the windows draped in black.

Gertrude did not glance at the crooked "Closed for the Season" sign, and I hastened past, strolling very slowly from one purveyor of luxury goods to the next. The gems and leather goods beckoned behind polished plate glass, and I gazed at each carriage that passed along Bellevue Avenue and noted the faces gawking from carriage windows.

I would thank Daisy Harriman for her good advice to be seen on Travers Block. She would not learn, however, of the plan she unwittingly set in motion. While sailing, Daisy mentioned the saleswoman at the House of Worth salon as someone who knew Warren Eccles in New York when he leased art gallery space inside a department store last winter. The woman sent customers to his gallery, according to Daisy. Yet the gallery failed, which Roddy and I learned when Theo warned us to stay clear of the Cuveen manager.

On *Catnip*, the saleswoman's name went unspoken when Daisy suddenly called, "going about." Still, the woman's recent talk about Eccles seemed promising for my purposes. His violent death apparently jogged her memory and prompted words of commiseration, especially since Daisy was sympathetic, as I planned to be. Even if the saleswoman and Eccles parted company on frosty terms, she might reminisce willingly.

I planned to find out who settled scores with Warren Eccles. Who committed premeditated murder? Or killed him in sudden rage? Roddy and I agreed that his death possibly had its origin in Italy but was hastened in New York. His forgery could have caught up with him, as it did in the loss of his villa and payoffs. Talking it over, Roddy and I agreed a reasonable start would be inquiring about the saleswoman's New York days with Eccles. Did she sense discord between the curator and his overworked assistant? If so, did Asa Durling boil with murderous rage here in Newport? And if Marco Gliano's death was murder, was it committed as a cover-up? Or did someone involved with greyhound dogs grow so bitter and angry in New York that he came to Newport to wreak vengeance? Did anyone else come to mind? Transportation between the city and Newport was well established with frequent rail and ferry service. A killer could easily come—and slip away. Who could it have been?

With a smile and a wave to a couple in a four-wheeled trap, I struck a pose at the Tiffany entrance, then opened the door and prepared to seek "baubles" on the Travers Block.

Shopping was not a favorite pastime, though gift selection could be pleasant. I quickly chose a gold tie clasp for Roddy and a bonbonniere for Cassie, for whom a jeweled mint dispenser was preferable to a sapphire-studded cigarette case. My friend was trying to stop smoking cigarettes, so far with mixed success. For me, the treat at Tiffany was the artistry of giftwrapping, from the soft hush of tissue papers to the heavy luxe wrapping, the silk ribbons and satin bows.

The speed of my selections, however, took the store clerks aback and amiss. My purchases would be delivered to Drumcliffe, but I had skipped the careful musing on goods presented on little velvet pillows while the salesclerks consulted and paid compliments. Leisure set the pace, but I broke an unwritten rule. Furthermore, the clerks' whispered words to one another meant they recognized this customer as the lady on the sidewalk with a gentleman when police swarmed the Cuveen Gallery—the very same lady pictured in *The Newport Daily News*. My signature set off more whispers. Nonetheless, I must be patient and above-it-all at the Worth salon this late morning, the 29th day of July.

The door with *House of Worth* in gold leaf on the glass opened easily. Early for my appointment, I caught my breath because the air hung heavy with perfume. A woman in dark silk voile with an atomizer misted the air as she greeted me. "Welcome to the House of Worth…today's fragrance is *Violette de Parme* with notes of Frankincense and amber… exclusive to Worth."

I stifled a sneeze in this thickly carpeted space with upholstered chairs and an oak table cleared to display the latest fabrics from Europe's looms.

She set the atomizer down. "I am Miss Sabine Haines at your service. And I have the honor of assisting Mrs… DeVere?"

"Early for my appointment," I said, "but yes, I am Mrs. Roderick DeVere."

Unlike the Tiffany clerks, she did not wince or curl a lip at my name. I fought a sneeze, and my eyes watered.

"Won't you please be seated, Mrs. DeVere?"

On the wall across the table, niches and cabinets burst with fabrics. Ladies would make selections, but fittings would take place in Paris according to measurements on file, though ladies would preferably appear in person at the Worth atelier when traveling abroad.

I patted my eyes with a handkerchief and sat down.

"Perhaps madame would like to see our latest fabrics from Paris…? It would be my pleasure, Mrs. DeVere."

I said, "Yes, please" and blinked my watery eyes as she reached into the niches. Miss Haines was in Newport, she explained, as a representative of the couturier and would serve ladies for the summer season, having come from a New York department store with plans to return to the city at the conclusion of the summer. I guessed her age to be late twenties.

She spoke in murmurs, almost purring. Miss Haines did not, however, name the department store that sold the Worth fabric and leased gallery space to Eccles. For the sake of timing, I must not ask yet.

"If you are ready, Mrs. DeVere, I will introduce our Jacquared-woven silk."

"Ready."

Miss Haines pirouetted to the niche wall, though her upper body seemed better suited to a gymnasium. The flattering lines of lightweight silk voile could not conceal brawny contours. Her fingers fluttered like birds' wings, but the fabric rolls in outstretched arms suggested a hunter with captured game.

The perfume had settled, and I tucked the handkerchief in my skirt pocket as she announced, "Madame, for your pleasure...the Jacquard elegance and detail." Miss Haines unrolled the fabric and spoke as though she memorized her words. "...so lifelike one can almost touch, taste, and breathe the aromatic orange in the weave."

"Heavenly," I said. Truly, the fabric came alive with clusters of oranges and green leaves that disappeared into the midnight black background of heavy silk.

"Or this one?" With a flick of the wrist, she unfurled another roll "For a dinner gown, Madame, midnight blue velvet highlighted with embroidered birds and moths in flight."

"Moths? Really, moths?" Did she hear my alarm at a pest that devoured wool? Moths ate into our blankets in the Colorado mining camps and chewed holes in Papa's best suit in Virginia City, the one he planned to wear at dinner with President Grant. Moths were the insects that Cassie's little Charlie collected in a jar, insects that his scientific explorer father—Cassie's husband Dudley—called by Latin names.

The saleswoman held her upright posture, but her purring grew strained when she said, "This is a motif, Mrs. DeVere...you understand, a motif from colored thread...hand sewing...needles...embroidery."

"Many possibilities," I said.

"The again, perhaps taffeta...?" The purring returned. "Or your satins?"

My satins would wait. I wished Cassie were here to help with this woman. My friend often went with me to a dressmaker to offer advice on fashion, fabric, and flattering colors. Today's solo outing needed a wedge into my topic, my goal.

Which turned out to be the perfume. While I paused between the two fabric samples, Miss Haines reached for the atomizer, squeezed the rubber bulb, and sent me into a fit of sneezing.

"No, not again...." She dropped the atomizer and clenched her hands as if to crush the vapors. "Second time today," she muttered, then slumped on a stool across the table.

It took a moment until I could say, "No more perfume. Please, no more."

"You and my last customer. It drove the lady out, but I have my orders, Mrs. DeVere. The *Violette de Parme* is for sale."

"Here? Really?"

"Fabrics and fragrance. It's not my idea, but Worth and the department store...they lined up."

I shook my head to express sympathy. Her purr became a protest with anger at the edge.

"Didn't I memorize the Jacquard, Mrs. DeVere? Didn't you hear me say 'the aromatic orange in the weave.'"

"I did."

"And for the Dutch tulip pattern, I am supposed to say, 'the alchemy of success.'"

"And now perfume," I said.

"Perfume, Mrs. DeVere, that nobody wanted in the first place. All summer I am to say 'notes' of this and 'wisps' of that. They got it cheap."

Her protest sounded logical, but did Sabine Haines feel hired on the cheap? Did her Newport earnings depend on perfume sales?"

"Miss Haines," I said, "won't you come sit over here?" I patted a nearby chair cushion. "That stool cannot be comfortable."

Her eyes darted toward the door. "There's a rule about that."

I patted the chair again.

With a moment's hesitation, she went to the door, turned the bolt, and pulled down a blind. "For just a few minutes," she said.

"Now, then..." I said, "a little time to ease up, especially with long hours ahead."

She perched uneasily on the chair. "Longer than you ladies know, Mrs. DeVere. The other stores at Travers Block have two or three behind the counters, but it's just me here. I get in early and stay late. There's tidying up, and then deliveries ...excelsior flies out of the crates."

"Packing material," I said, "such a nuisance."

"Pain in the...yes, nuisance. The stock boys dealt with it at the Arnold Constable store."

"Ah," I said, "Among department stores, the renowned Palace of Trade."

I mentally mapped the Ladies Mile shopping district with the Arnold Constable store at Nineteenth Street and Fifth Avenue.

"They started me upstairs in yard goods," she said, "chintz and cottons, but my goal was the first floor. So, gloves."

"And did customers soon find you at the glove counter?"

"I knew my ladies," she said. "Long gloves to the elbow, opera, church...lace, kidskin, silk. I knew who ordered by the dozens, by the season.... They came to me, asked for me."

"But Miss Haines," I said with a soft smile, "you speak as though your service is in the past."

"I would be Assistant Buyer in the Glove Department, except I helped somebody, and it cost me."

"Perhaps your good intentions were misunderstood?"

"Made me welcome as ground glass in coffee...with the managers, anyway."

"Store managers?"

"They gave away space that belonged to gloves, gave it to an art gallery. But I did not complain. I helped. If Missus So-and-So ordered two dozen kidskin to the elbow, I steered her to the art. I would get a bonus if my ladies purchased his paintings. So did girls in hosiery and stationary. Our wages could double if ladies bought his paintings, but nobody did."

"Miss Haines," I said, "I fear you are losing me. Whose paintings do you mean?"

She rolled her shoulders, and her voice dropped to a whisper. "Mr. Eccles...the man that got me this job and died here. He ran the gallery that's closed. It was terrible. Didn't you hear? The assistant with the ghost-white skin and hair handles whatever is left. We don't speak. He is too foreign."

I turned sideways and folded my hands. Was it possible she knew nothing of the lady seated in this chair? My name escaped her notice? Sabine Haines in a cloistered existence in Newport? Could it be?

I said, "Sudden death is indeed a terrible thing, Miss Haines, especially the death of a friend."

"I wouldn't say 'friend.' Mr. Eccles thanked me for a big favor."

"Here in Newport?"

"No, at Arnold Constable's. I stopped a man who tried to steal a painting."

"My goodness...." I batted my eyes.

"A big picture of skinny gray dogs. A man came in and went right to that picture of dogs and grabbed it when Mr. Eccles stepped away for a few minutes. I said, 'Sir, you must not touch the painting,' but he tried to steal it and got very angry. I held it tight and hung on. The frame broke. He ran off."

"Mercy...how upsetting." I touched my throat. "And then...?"

"A customer fainted, and I was 'dismissed'... fired. But Mr. Eccles stood up for me. He's the reason I'm here. It gets lonesome all by myself. Mr. Eccles said I would make new friends, but not so far, and he is gone forever. I say life is cheap in Newport."

She stood as if to collect herself. "So, Mrs. DeVere, I have taken up your morning, and another lady is almost due. So, thank you for your visit and remember that *Violette de Parme* comes in classic Lalique crystal and makes a very nice gift for many occasions."

Chapter Twenty-five

BACK FROM THE TRAVERS Block, I found Roddy at a desk near a window with legal papers and an inkstand. Right now, the lawyer outweighed the cocktail maestro.

Roddy sneezed and wrinkled his nose as I bent for a kiss. Velvet sped to a far corner.

"Val, what is that odor?"

"Scent," I said. "A French perfume in my clothing. I call it the price of information. And Roddy, I do have new information. I'll be right back."

The library windows were wide open when I returned wearing a skirt and shirtwaist. On the desk, Roddy's papers were held down with a stone gargoyle paperweight. Velvet let me pet her head.

"All morning on an upcoming court case?" I asked.

"The *Mary Powell* steamboat attack by the Temperance women," he said, "a property crime and thereby assault." He capped his inkwell. "And solicitation ought to be charged because the two women who destroyed mirrors and light fixtures were encouraged by the principal to commit criminal acts."

The word "principal" always reminded me of school. "It sounds like a straightforward case," I said.

Roddy's smile confirmed my naiveté. "The three are church ladies, Val, and their minister will testify to their sterling character. The jury will hear the steamboat owners denounced as greedy promoters of Demon Rum."

The catchphrase rankled because Roddy carefully crafted his rum cocktails. "In any case," he continued, "I must take a flying trip to the city. A signature cocktail for a large organization is in question, and I have been asked to intervene 'at my convenience' in the beastly hot city."

"So many requests 'at convenience,'" I said. "But Roddy, I will go too. I must nose around the ground floor of the Arnold Constable department store. This Travers Block morning has opened a big lead in the Eccles murder.... Tell me, do you recall seeing a painting of greyhound dogs in the Cuveen Gallery the night of the reception?"

"Not unless the painting was out of our sight. Why?"

"Because a man stormed into the Arnold Constable store and tried to steal one of Eccles's gallery paintings...of 'skinny gray dogs.'"

Roddy raised an eyebrow. "Greyhounds."

"I feel sure of it. The saleswoman, Miss Sabine Haines, fought off the thief. She wrested the painting from him, and he fled. The disturbance got her fired, but Eccles was appreciative and helped her get the job in Newport. So, I am going to the beastly hot city with you. How about tomorrow?"

Roddy began to scratch Velvet's back, which often meant he needed a minute to think. "Did Miss...Aines is it?"

"Haines."

"Did she describe the man who grabbed the painting?"

"I did not ask her, Roddy. The moment was not favorable. Do you mean his physique? Was he large?"

"Or was he armed? Were the police called?"

Annoyed, I beckoned Velvet to my side, but the dog refused to budge. "Roddy," I said, "to remind you, I was not at Worth to interrogate Sabine Haines. I went to find out about her acquaintance with Eccles and whatever she might say about his assistant. Which is simply that she and Asa Durling do not speak. She is repelled by his skin and hair. Also, she apparently knows nothing whatsoever about my presence at the Cuveen Gallery on the tenth day of July. Unlike the snide clerks at Tiffany, I might add."

Roddy scratched Velvel's belly, and the dog lay in canine nirvana.

"Something is on your mind," I said. "When Velvet gets a full massage, you are meditating. So, if you please...?"

"I please to see you avoid danger. The department store district is for ladies only, isn't it?"

"The Ladies Mile," I said, "is the only part of New York City where a lady can go by herself without an escort or a woman companion."

"So," Roddy said, "the thief violated the ladies-only code and then physically grappled with the saleswoman. He knew exactly what he wanted and where to find it. He was bold...and determined. And violent. The saleswoman could have been harmed."

"Miss Haines is a sturdy woman, Roddy. I'd say robust." My husband's gaze turned vigilant, his blue eyes grim. "But it's really about me, isn't it? You picture me with the art thief, fighting him off...alone and injured."

A clock chimed, and the moment turned poignant. My husband's forehead furrowed with worry, and I recalled a photograph of boyhood Roddy with toy knights in armor. His chivalry now cast me as a damsel, the self I deplored but found touching in this moment.

"Roddy, dear," I said softly, "I only plan to stroll the ground floor of the Arnold Constable department store. I will shop for...hair ribbons, perhaps gloves, such as the long gloves you like to tug loose on certain nights. I will order a dozen."

"Dozens," my husband replied in a sultry voice. "Dozens for the future...our future." His eyes had moistened. "Val, I will admit the flying trip concerned me, and no gentleman or lady descends on the city in the depths of the summer. But we might make a day or two a treat for us."

"For us," I echoed.

A final rub on our Frenchie's chest, and my husband gave me a deep, lingering kiss. "I will suggest a certain hotel over lunch," he said, "and I propose that we toast our flying trip with the very lightest of cocktails?"

My qualms about a midday drink turned into interest in a new device Roddy set on the library table when he opened and ice bucket and dropped chunks into a contraption with a crank. "Grinds ice at the turn of a handle," he said. "Close your ears and prepare for a Soda Cocktail."

The grinding sent Velvet to the corner while I watched my husband turn the crank, then reach for glasses, a lemon and small bottle. He promised this would surely be the mildest cocktail ever served.

Soda Cocktail

Ingredients:

- Teaspoon refined sugar
- Lemon
- Ice, finely chopped or crushed
- Orange bitters
- Soda water

Directions:

1. Add ice to mixing glass.
2. Add sugar to mixing glass.
3. Squeeze peel of lemon into mixing glass (to release citrus oil)
4. Add two dashes bitters.
5. Slowly fill mixing glass with soda water with left hand while gently stirring mixture with right hand.
6. Pour cocktail into Collins glass (strain if desired).

Roddy's kiss came first, then the refreshing drink. "Salud, Val. Here's to our 'flying trip' to the city...as early as tomorrow on the Fall River Line." He kissed me once again. "And here's to us."

We registered at the Waldorf-Astoria on Sunday at 5:15 p.m. as the sun mercifully began its descent from a day that baked the city and left our clothing limp. Roddy whispered that "limp" was not in his personal lexicon and would prove it. I whispered back as the elevator took us to our sixteenth-floor suite with Arabian and Renaissance hangings that set off the woodwork and French furniture. We had traveled without Roddy's valet or my maid. Calista quickly packed a small trunk for me, and Roddy's Norbert did the same for him, though the 90-degree heat would cancel fashion, no matter what we chose to wear.

"Forget the frills and furbelows," Roddy said when the bellman had closed the door, leaving us alone. "My idea... follow me."

He led us to the bath with its gleaming porcelain tiles of an up-to-date shower. Roddy said, "Our spa, my dearest Val, and we will bathe...as one. Are you ready?"

I murmured, "Yes," and he whispered that we would bathe *au natural* with our own waterfall, then reached to send sprays of water rushing just beyond us.

Soon to envelope us.

Roddy's fingers played slowly at my lips and throat, then worked the buttons and hooks of my traveling costume until it dropped to the floor. Petticoats off, my hosiery rolled down in his hands until I knelt before him to untie his shoes and then slowly pull off his stockings. My fingers reached for his shirt studs. "Clothing that defies...and entices too," I murmured, my fingers trembling as I felt at the buttons of his trousers.

"And promises..." he answered in a husky voice.

All clothing on the floor beside us, Roddy lifted me to him, lifted with muscles sleek with the sweat I knew from our first time together, the scent I breathed and tasted with my face against his chest as he took me in his arms.

"Shall we dance, my Val? Dance into our own rain shower?" His hands cradled my throat, my breasts, and we danced in rhythm into the cool water. The rivulets played, and his touch had never been tenderer as his tongue plunged deep with a searching caress. We both played at bathing until desire took us to the undertow of currents we would ride together, unbound and unbounded in a flashing flood of desire that thundered and consumed us in time out of time.

Afterward, the spraying cool water left us laughing and then toweling one another, too relaxed to recite reasons for our presence in a New York hotel suite in the depths of the summer. "We could order drinks and dinner in our suite," I said. Until now, we had avoided the new feature of hotel room service which meant dining close to a bed chamber. "How about it, Roddy? Dinner here on the sixteenth floor?"

I had no idea why this suggestion tugged us into the present, restarting a clock and calendar that love-making had blessedly paused. When my husband replied firmly that we must dine here at the Waldorf-Astoria main dining room, I nodded without objection, more concerned with drying my hair and finding a dinner dress in the trunk. We rummaged for Roddy's dinner suit and my lilac silk dress with embroidered fleur-de-lis at the neckline and a short train. With a kiss to my neck, Roddy fastened my dress and the amethyst necklace that matched the drop earrings. Calista packed a fan with advice to use it in the sweltering city.

"Shall we?"

"We shall."

The main dining room featured columns of "midnight sun" marble imported from Russia and rose silk draperies that set off a painting of a country scene. The Italian Renaissance room was also identified with a maître d'hotel who had not been here a year ago when Roddy and I dined at the Waldorf Palm Court. The renowned Oscar Tschirsky—Oscar of the Waldorf—presided over the hotel's banquets, balls, and private dinners for royalty. In season, the main dining room was in high demand, and Oscar had devised a rope covered with red velvet to keep crowds in check.

The dining room had no need of a velvet rope tonight. Just two tables were occupied when Oscar greeted us with a crisp, "Madame and Monsieur DeVere, if you please..."and led us to our table as though we were honored guests. A small orchestra played tunes that seemed to wander but filled space that otherwise would feel cavernous.

"Roddy," I said, "I prefer everything cold...salads, fish, water and wine too." Our waiter seemed relieved to hear Monsieur DeVere speak English, though the menu was in French, as I recalled from previous dinners in this hotel. Roddy said all the Waldorf-Astoria waiters were required to speak French and be clean-shaven. "Oscar's orders," he said.

Opening my fan, I felt like a time traveler invented by Jules Verne to spin like a top from place to place. We had rushed this plan, sent regrets for missing a ball at Rosecliff and my special apology to Cassie for absence from her luncheon honoring the Britisher who would appeal for the protection of birds. I sent her flowers with regrets. My scheduled sitting with André Cole was posponed but the artist could continue my portrait with the three photographs in his possession. We would reschedule upon return to Newport.

Roddy surveyed the room as if sensing a lawsuit in the making. Or was the cocktail mixologist troubled by the drinks being served at a nearby table? My lover was another person now, preoccupied with private plans. He had insisted we stay at the Waldorf-Astoria and did not explain when I pleaded for the Plaza, which was just a few blocks from our house.

"So," Roddy said as we sat over chilled champagne, "we will go separate ways tomorrow. I will visit the Hudson River steamship company office, and you will go to the department store."

"And I am tempted, Roddy, to visit our house."

"But it's closed for the season."

"It is tended by five servants," I replied, not naming each of the Irish young women whose jobs in our household gave them a foothold in America. I had slipped each of them an extra sum for ice cream in Central Park and amusements at Coney Island. They must not be "closed for the summer."

The waiter was at my elbow with shrimp on a bed of ice and a dozen blue point oysters for Roddy. He poured a dry white wine and disappeared. The orchestra drifted into another tune.

"Val...your hand is cold." Roddy had taken the fan from my fingers and held my hand. "You seemed so far away just now. Where were you?"

What could I say? Blocks away from this hotel, a saleswoman had grappled with a thief who tried to steal a painting from a man who was knifed to death. I was here to find out what happened. I was here out of season, as always. Shamed and shunned, I was here on my own rescue mission.

Chapter Twenty-six

THE TEMPERATURE SHOT INTO the high eighties under a sullen sun at 10:00 a.m. when we stepped outside into air thickened with a city mix of horses, asphalt, and tar. Roddy's seersucker suit and Ecuador straw hat would be tested, as would my ivory linen jacket and skirt plus a tiny straw hat and kidskin short gloves. The doorman summoned a hansom cab with orders to drive me to the Ladies Mile. Roddy would go to the steamship office in a second cab and meet me back here in late afternoon, if not earlier. He also said a mysterious word about his cocktail consultation, but I knew not to press for details. The day would offer no relief from the heat under a leaden sky that denied the city a cleansing rain.

The Arnold Constable "Palace of Trade" stood at Fifth Avenue and 19th Street, but the hansom had gone only two blocks when I tapped my parasol handle against the door, as I had seen Roddy do with his walking stick.

The driver knew to stop. "A change of direction," I said. "Please take me to Fourth Avenue and 22nd Street." He hesitated, doubtless suspecting I was cheating on the man who had just paid him. In fact, I did not tell Roddy of my plan to visit a certain office before going to the Ladies Mile. He would object, and it was too hot to argue. "The building at 22nd Street," I called to the driver, "is rather a church."

In a manner of speaking, the United Charities Building was a godly structure because it housed the offices of several charities on four floors. A philanthropist had purchased the old stone church, had it refurbished, and invited the charitable organizations to consolidate under one roof to curtail expenses. Each one now paid a modest rent but kept its mission separate from the others.

Just after 11:15 a.m., with the hansom waiting in the shade of a nearby pin oak tree, I walked down the United Charities hallway past the New York City Mission and Tract Society and glimpsed the door of the Association for Improving the Condition of the Poor. A stairway took me to the second floor's Children's Aid Society and the Charity Organization Society until I reached the doorframe of my destination, The National Consumers League.

A typewriter clacked furiously inside, followed by a ripping sound and a short sigh. I knocked on the doorframe. "Miss Flowers? It's Mrs. DeVere.... Miss Flowers?"

A firm alto voice said, "I shall be with you presently, Mrs. DeVere." A slim figure in a high-necked shirtwaist craned her neck from behind a partition, pushed back her office chair, eyed my wrinkled linen and said, "I did not see your name on this month's appointment calendar, Mrs. DeVere. If you are here to see Mrs. Kelley, she is not here. As Executive Secretary of the League, she is in demand upstate at Chautauqua. She is speaking on 'Workers Rights and Wrongs.' We do not expect her back until next month."

"Actually, Miss Flowers, I am here to see you. May I have a few minutes?"

"Just a few. You may have a seat."

Familiar with this closet-sized office, I sat on the same hardwood visitor's chair familiar from past visits, most recently last month. That interview did not go well.

Annie Flowers smoothed her serviceable cotton skirt and turned her dark eyes on me with a pert gaze bordering on contempt.

Or was it pity?

We had met last summer in her Lower East Side flat when I helped Cassie seek information about a fatally ill cousin. Over the next months, Annie Flowers and I connected over Central Park's dark history and our mutual support for women's suffrage, though we differed radically on tactics. Her noisy performance with a hurdy-gurdy and ***Votes for Women*** sign landed her in jail as a public nuisance. Since then, she earned a certificate in clerical skills and was now employed by the National Consumers League, which is committed to the reform of treacherous workplaces. I have watched Annie flowers take minutes at meetings that I attend as a League member.

"I can give you fifteen minutes, Mrs. DeVere, because I have a good deal of typewriting to do, and this July heat is a handicap."

"I am sure, Miss Flowers, that you are up to speed."

"Sixty words per minute before this terrible heat," she said, "but only fifty-five this week. The Fowler Secretarial College suggests we talcum our fingers, but a handkerchief does it for me." She turned the face of her watch toward me. "Now then, how might I assist you?"

I pointed to the file cabinet behind her typing table. "As you might recall, Miss Flowers, I served on a committee chaired by Daisy...by Mrs. Borden Harriman. I agreed to see about the saleswomen at Macy's Department Store, where I learned the saleswomen are required to stand for long hours on hard floors for wages that barely keep a roof over their heads...and to dress fashionably in the store's clothing." I pointed again at the file cabinet. "My report is on file, I believe."

"Typed by me and filed under 'Conditions of Work, Female: Retail.'"

"Along with other department store reports...Lord & Taylor? And what about Arnold Constable? Has a League member reported on the Arnold Constable store?"

"Why do you ask, Mrs. DeVere?"

"Because I might shop at Arnold Constable and wish to familiarize myself with the situation behind the counters."

She straightened her shoulders. "Is this why you came here this morning, Mrs. DeVere, to read someone else's report without her permission?"

Somehow, this woman always bristled with tests of ethics. "Miss Flowers, this is a matter of importance."

"It was 'importance' that brought you here last month, Ms. DeVere, to ask that I spy on a secretary at another business firm."

Once again, I was in arears but did not remind Annie Flowers that she was sprung from jail when Roddy and I paid her fine. "I regret the incident last month," I said, "but my time is short, and perhaps you could lend a hand?"

"My hands are pledged to the Underwood typewriting machine, Mrs. DeVere." She reached for her watch.

"Never mind, Miss Flowers. I see fifteen minutes is up. I will be going." I gathered the limp linen folds of my skirt very slowly and deliberately to give her time for second thoughts. Annie Flowers and I would never be friendly, but could we trade on shared interests? She took dictation and typed for a cause that I supported, and we would see one another at League meetings resuming in September. Each time she looked up from her pad and pencil, I would be in sight. The National Consumers League linked us whether we liked it or not.

I was at the doorframe when she called me back. "Perhaps a few minutes, Mrs. DeVere. I propose a compromise."

Seated once again, I agreed to ask about the Arnold Constable report while Miss Flowers held the typewritten pages in her hands. She would judge which of my questions could be suitably answered. Opening the filing cabinet, she plucked out the report. "Please begin, Mrs. DeVere. What do you wish to know?"

Generalities seemed best to start. "I assume the League's 'shopper' surveyed several floors?" She nodded. Some of us did shop during inspections when we posed as customers." I had a closetful of Macy's ready-to-wear. "On several floors?"

"Yes."

"Including conditions on the ground floor?"

"Ground floor? Yes, I see it here."

"Hosiery, I would think," I said. "Perhaps neckwear and hair ribbons? Does the report happen to mention the Glove Department?

"I would not say 'happen,' Mrs. DeVere."

"Quite right," I said, "but gloves, a busy department...at least two saleswomen, I would think. My report on Macy's includes saleswomen's names, so when I shop for gloves at Arnold Constable, it would help to know...."

She cut me off. "Do not ask for any names, Mrs. DeVere."

Annie Flowers glanced at her watch, a reminder of budgeted minutes. "Very well," I said. "One further question, Miss Flowers. Does the report describe an art gallery on the ground floor?"

She ran a finger down the page. "Adjacent to the Glove Department."

"And favorably located for the saleswomen? Helpful to their situation? What is the date on the report, Miss Flowers?"

She turned a page, read and reread before looking directly at me. "The report is from last winter. It says one saleswoman in gloves appeared to be most upset."

"That's all?"

"That's enough. Whatever you are looking for, Mrs. DeVere, I hope you find it at the Arnold Constable store. It must be important to bring you into this ninety-degree city heat. I understand you spend summers with Mr. DeVere and your fancy little dog at the seaside. I wish you good day. I will see you in the autumn."

I reached Arnold Constable shortly after church bells rang the noon hour. The hansom driver perked up at the silver dollar from my reticule handbag, but his face glistened with sweat, and his horse looked desperate for the water trough and a stall. The streets looked nearly deserted, the Ladies Mile minus the ladies.

A doorman uniformed in wool opened the heavy doors and ushered me into a cooler scene of glass showcases and saleswomen busy behind numerous counters. Months ago, I learned from Macy's that each employee must be constantly occupied whether she helped a customer or not. She arranged and rearranged her merchandise and ever-so-subtly dusted her wares while keeping a small smile on her lips.

So it was in the Glove Department at Arnold Constable.

"Good morning...pardon me, I mean good afternoon." The young woman at the glove counter blushed at her mistake, which gave me added authority as I forgave her error.

"Morning or afternoon," I said with a smile, "one hardly knows in these terribly warm days."

Across the counter, the slender saleswoman with a moon-shaped face and cautious dark eyes looked relieved to have a customer, especially one who seemed pleasant from the start.

I put my reticule on the counter and peeled off my gloves to signal intention to shop at length. "I am Mrs. DeVere," I said. "You must be Miss Sabine Haines?"

"I am Miss Cardwell." A second blush bloomed. "Miss Haines no longer works...is not employed here. I would not know where she is, but if you will allow me to help you, Mrs. De...De...."

"DeVere." I gave a benevolent smile. "You see, Miss Cardwell, I have been abroad for several months...overseas, and greatly in need of gloves. A friend advised me to see Miss Haines. I assume she was your co-worker here in gloves?"

Her lips tightened. "She was, Mrs. DeVere, but I will do my best. Would you be needing short gloves? Kidskin or silk?"

"Both," I said. "And for this coming Fall season...?"

"Mrs. DeVere, we have just received suede fawn-colored gauntlets to the elbow. If I may show you...?"

"Yes, please do...." These pointless ladies' gloves must be worn in all weathers, including this record-breaking heat in New York City. At this moment, I remembered the sheepskin gloves and mittens from girlhood in the Rockies, bulky but toasty in winter. In warm weather, fingers flexed free.

My fingertips now touched the fawn suede from France. As at Macy's, I was cultivating acquaintance with the sales-clerk's wares, her job, and her. By the time I had ordered two dozen pairs of gloves and gauntlets, I knew Alice Cardwell had grown up in a large family in New Jersey and started at Arnold Constable in hair combs, then happily came to gloves.

"More suitable for me, Mrs. DeVere, because gloves need frequent replacement, and so this counter is busier. I admit time stands still in the summer when ladies are at the mountains or the seashore. I tell myself, be thankful for days when nothing much happens. Last winter was so hectic."

"Hectic? A strong word," I said, looking to the left and to the right, as if guarding the space from the stationary counter and the display of hair pins and combs. "How can the Glove Department possibly be hectic?" I asked in a low voice.

She hesitated, so I added another dozen pairs to my lambskin glove order and waited while she tallied the sale. Miss Cardwell then looked up as if deciding what to say. "Mrs. DeVere, can you imagine this glove counter squeezed to half this size?"

"Why would I imagine such a thing?"

"If you came in last winter, you would see our Glove Department shrunk to half.... Next to gloves, you would find an art gallery."

"A what?

"Pictures for sale...an experiment, we were told. The store rented space to a man who brought old pictures for sale. They said he brought them from Italy."

"My goodness."

"Not goodness, Mrs. DeVere, not by any means. Our customers did not know what to think, and our sales drooped, just like we thought they would. The art gallery was gone by the spring, but I believe it caused Miss Haines to lose her position."

I nearly whispered, "How could that be?"

"For a start, Mrs. DeVere, the ground floor salesclerks are all women for good reason. Here came this man last winter, dressed like a gentleman, shoes polished and suit creased and smooth talking to sell the pictures. When no lady customers were around, he showed them to Miss Haines. Her station was at the end of the counter."

"Close to the art?"

"No more than a foot away. I told her, keep your distance, Sabine. We are here to sell gloves. I said the word 'we' not to boss her, but no use."

I shook my head.

"He teased her, hot and cold. I saw it happen, right before my eyes. She got into a fog."

"You all work so hard in sales," I said. "It sounds like Miss Haines was daydreaming?"

"Worse than that, Mrs. DeVere. To this day, I believe she took a desperate measure, all over him."

I gave an inquisitive frown.

"That man took lunch each day, you see, and asked us to keep watch on his pictures, which our floor supervisor permitted us so do. Last February a man came in the front door and straight to the picture gallery. He grabbed at a painting, like to steal it."

"Mercy...."

"Scared us, all masked with mufflers and a cap pulled down, just one tuft of hair showing, white like snow. He grabbed the picture by the frame, and Miss Haines grabbed it too. They scuffled back and forth, and he ran out of the store. She held it up high like a trophy."

"It sounds like she prevented a theft."

"Some thought so, but our supervisor said Miss Haines was 'grandiose' and dismissed her."

"But you think she might have arranged the attempted theft?"

"I would say that Miss Haines was half crazed. The art gallery man was too much, and she lost her reason. Her feelings ran hot. Miss Haines is a larger person, Mrs. DeVere. Not that she used paints and powders but reminded me of one of my brothers in the arms and shoulders."

Miss Cardwell stood back and lifted a new pair of gloves. "Forgive my talking so much, Mrs. DeVere. This summer heat...they say it breaks a record. Now then, Arnold Constable will deliver your purchases, but you surely wish to wear a new pair from the store. If you'll please hold out your hands and let me help you...."

Chapter Twenty-seven

"RODDY, THERE IS A good chance Sabine Haines murdered Warren Eccles."

My husband squinted at me across the tea table. "Did you hear me, Roddy? I said...."

"I heard you, Val. Let's keep our voices down."

We were seated in the Waldorf-Astoria's Palm Garden that required a gentleman be accompanied by a lady or ladies. Roddy had waited in the lobby to waylay me for tea. He took my arm and marched me to the Palm Garden. His seersucker sagged, and my linen had collapsed, but he would not allow us time to change.

"The teatime hour is nearly up, Val, and this is important. You'll guess why in a few minutes."

Exasperated, I kept quiet, then repeated, "It's murder, Roddy. Did you listen?"

Was the man hard of hearing this afternoon? My new cream-colored gloves had wrinkled and darkened from perspiration, and the hansom from Arnold Constable to the hotel felt like an oven. The stone and brick walls of the Waldorf-Astoria barely cooled the enormous room, and the potted palms drooped.

Ready to screech *bloody murder*, I was trapped in a tearoom with out-of-towners seated close together to promote a sociable feeling. Near us, ladies in garden party hats laughed and fanned themselves, while a table with three generations of women murmured ear to ear. Fewer than half of the three hundred guests who would fill the Palm Garden in season occupied these tables.

"We could talk in our suite," I said tartly. "We could order tea from room service. I have to tell you, Roddy...I have to...."

My husband, however, grasped my hand but peered steadily at a waiter who circulated with a tea wagon. "Val, give me an hour. When the waiter comes, I will say that you wish an orange blossom."

"Orange? Orange Pekoe tea?"

"Blossom. Ordered in a teacup. And you will hear me request a Dewey, but no remarks, please."

Fuming, I wanted to slap a lady's fan against my palm the way high school teachers slapped rulers during our tests. Cassie told me fans can send secret messages, and she showed me a few moves. Right now, my fan would signal **A Murderer on My Mind**, but the tea wagon was at our table, the waiter ready to hear Roddy say, "...for the lady in a teacup, if you please, and for me...."

The waiter nimbly handled the cup, but also bottles like those Roddy stocked on our wheeled tea wagons at home. In moments, a china cup was before me and a drink in cut glass in front of Roddy. "Your tea, Madame, and the Dewey, sir..."

Roddy's hard gaze never left the waiter or his supplies. He took a sip from my cup, then from his Dewey cocktail, murmuring, "I thought so...Boldt will hear about this."

The tearoom crockery hid my cocktail, but Roddy's mention of the legendary hotel manager's name told me that his secret cocktail consultation involved the Trolley Bar of the Waldorf-Astoria Palm Garden. Roddy insisted "gin" demanded discrimination. I did not ask what he meant. I did not care.

In the suite sitting room, I shed my hat and jacket, and Roddy flung his seersucker coat onto a chair. The shades were drawn, the windows opened no more than one inch. The suite smelled like mildewed roses.

I told my husband our dinner must come from room service. "I cannot play the part of a gracious lady in the main dining room, Roddy. I have murder on my mind, and we need to talk."

The evening nonetheless stuttered until the lights were finally switched off. The space devoted to love-making just a day ago became a warren of doubts, confusion, and fumbling attempts to listen and be heard. Roddy ordered a room service dinner, and a platoon of white jacketed waiters lifted silver domes at eight o'clock to present a meal featuring the new "iceberg" lettuce. Meanwhile, Roddy described his upcoming steamboat case and said he would slip from the suite this evening for a scheduled word with George Boldt in the hotel manager's office, which he did while maid service turned down the beds. I took advantage of these moments to send a message to our "skeleton" household on Fifth Avenue, issuing orders to them, one and all, and signing my name.

My big mistake this evening was admitting I visited Annie Flowers at the Consumers League. Roddy was convinced the League was a front for socialists who would wreck the economy if they got the chance. What's more, Annie Flowers's noisy suffrage demonstration at the Coaching Club parade in Central Park infuriated my husband who swore never to hear Annie Flowers's name again.

I thought his grudge would be set aside at news of the report filed on the Arnold Constable art gallery and the "upset" saleswoman in gloves.

Maybe the heat scrambled my brains. "Roddy," I said, "the 'upset' woman was—and is—Sabine Haines. The saleswoman at the glove counter described her as hefty, which was also my impression. She was attracted to Eccles at his gallery, which was situated quite close to ladies' gloves. The point is this…Sabine Haines became highly emotional over Warren Eccles. He teased and flirted with her off and on."

"But appearances do not constitute evidence, Val."

"Then, try this…. According to the saleswoman I spoke with today, Sabine Haines and an accomplice staged a phony robbery at the gallery last February. She 'triumphed' by wresting the painting from the so-called thief, who disappeared. She lost her job for undue flamboyance, but Eccles was thankful and got her hired by the House of Worth for the summer in Newport. Miss Haines told me exactly that when I visited Travers Block."

"The woman expressed gratitude for employment, and she is thereby a killer?"

"Let me add something else, Roddy. The saleswoman remembers the robber's hair. He was bundled up, except for a lock of snow-white hair. She said white as snow."

"Any man of a certain age, Val."

"But he could be Asa Durling, Roddy. Suppose it was a scheme between Eccles and his assistant, and Sabine Haines as well? You will ask why, for what purpose, and I answer in two words, 'newspaper' and 'publicity.'"

Roddy tilted his head and looked sideways.

I raised my voice. "If the gallery was failing, a foiled robbery could pique interest in the art gallery and bring more customers to Arnold Constable. All New York would learn details in the *World*, the *Journal*, the *Herald*...the *Tribune*.... For Eccles, it would be a desperate measure."

"Val," Roddy said wearily, "we read all those papers. Do you recall any such news last winter?"

"I might have missed it."

Roddy sucked his cheek. "Would you wish to review last February's editions in the newspapers' morgues?"

The word for press storage rooms always jolted.

"We could stay in the city for another day or two and visit Newspaper Row, Val. The morgues are usually in base-ments, which might be cooler. Would you wish to extend our stay?"

We fell into sullen silence. The suite's upholstery felt like hot fur, and the ice was long gone from the water carafe. Patting his forehead with a handkerchief, Roddy said, "I concede it is possible that Eccles devised such a scheme, and that the Haines saleswoman could have fatally stabbed him."

"A crime of passion," I said. "Impulsive...deadly...."

"Perhaps, but the art robbery cannot be discounted... robbery by Asa Durling or someone else, quite possibly involving the plasterer. And two missing paintings that might lead police to the killer and solve the case."

"If day-tourists don't find them first and claim the reward." I ran a sleeve across my moist face. Neither of us spoke for long minutes. "I am ready to return to Newport," I said.

"We'll go first thing tomorrow. Do you know the city broke a record today? Ninety-seven degrees, Fahrenheit."

At that moment, I could have told my husband that my message to our entire Fifth Avenue household "skeleton" staff had issued this direct order: they were all to spend their days at Rockaway Beach until the heat broke. I would tell Roddy when heads were cooler.

The Drumcliffe staff welcomed us the next evening, and we approached one another carefully over a light supper in the inglenook. Our mood felt like a truce when a fight comes to a standstill. Saying Sabine Haines's name provoked my husband's lawyerly hedging and set me ranting on her murderous crime of passion. We went round and round.

At Drumcliffe, we opened our mail and sat over a cold cucumber soup, "Hot weather, hot tempers," I said, trying for a light tone.

"City like a furnace," my husband replied. "Now cool Newport..."

Under the table, our dog kept her distance, eyeing Roddy and me as though we were close relatives of Mrs. Thwaite.

"She's annoyed that we disappeared for two days," I said. "And she senses chilly air between us."

Roddy did not take my hint to warm up. He rolled his shoulders and salted his soup. "Summer resumes," he said. "So, croquet at the Casino, and a tennis lesson for you? And sailing?"

"Sailing," I repeated.

The soup took us through chitchat on Daisy Harriman's charming offer to crew for me, on Theo's picnic invitation, and on saddling Comet and Justice for horseback riding in the early morning hours. "Also," I said, "I'll want to find out about Cassie's luncheon for bird protection."

Roddy put his spoon down and hesitated. My chatter held back Sabine Haines who pulsed in my thoughts. The footman brought our next course, sliced capon that I mistook for chicken.

"I am ready for Catherine Street," I said.

"Good, Val. And I suppose you will revisit Travers Block to talk with that saleswoman."

"Sabine Haines, Roddy. Yes, I will learn whatever I can."

"And Val, just so you know, a letter was delivered this afternoon...to me."

"While we were on the ferry?"

"From Chief Cherry. He asks me to do him a favor."

"Not *The Counting House*, not again...."

"Something else. I don't know...."

"We don't know." Cold asparagus was served and was removed untouched, and then the footman presented melon with the inevitable fruit knives. Drumcliffe had two sets, one entirely of mother-of-pearl with nicely rounded blades. I reached for the mother-of-pearl handle, only to see the knife from the other set. The footman stood at attention as I gripped the handle, but his eyes followed me as I sliced into the fruit with a steel blade shaped exactly like a dagger.

Chapter Twenty-eight

I WOULD CONFRONT SABINE HAINES at the House of Worth salon after my third portrait sitting. I planned to ask carefully shaped questions, the sort of subtle questions that Cassie might ask.

Questions that I would coordinate with Cassie in advance of the appointment.

To pass a few days, Roddy and I rode horseback from Newport to Middletown, an excursion far from prying eyes. A sailing date was cancelled by hard rain showers, but Roddy and I wandered along Easton's Beach, the so-called common beach shunned by Society but enjoyed by the citizenry of Newport. Located exactly at the start of Cliff Walk, the beach reminded us of Marco Gliano and prompted a taut exchange about his death before we calmed ourselves gathering pebbles smoothed by sand and sea.

Roddy was in no rush to meet with Police Chief Cherry at Market Square or host him at Drumcliffe, so the two talked on the seat of a patrol wagon pulled up to the Drumcliffe gate. Ready to go for a tennis lesson at the Casino, I waited until the chief drove away and Roddy joined me in the foyer to say the "favor" for the Chief of Police was the surveillance of Newport's gentlemen.

"The chief got a blistering cable from Joseph Cuveen," Roddy explained. "Cuveen is furious about the paintings missing from his Newport gallery. He wants to send private detectives from New York to help recover his 'most valuable' works of art. The chief thinks the Newport force would suffer a terrible blow to morale."

"Especially if Cuveen's sleuths find the paintings," I said. "But why bring you into it, especially after *The Counting House* clash?"

"The chief thinks I might find out who has them. He seems to think a cottager might have bought them on the sly."

"At a back door?"

"Back or front. Ever since *French Artillery* showed up at Stone Point, the police suspect the plasterer might have sold off the other two paintings before his accident."

"Or his murder."

Outside, the pony cart waited for me, Shamrock's bridle held by a groom. "So, what are you supposed to do, Roddy? Ask the guests at Theo's picnic who bought *Cows Crossing a Ford*? Who has *Potato Planters*?"

"The chief asks me to keep my ears open at the Reading Room."

"Ah, yes...the Reading Room."

Actually, it made sense. Roddy had learned about the fires and the investment scheme while sipping a drink in the Reading Room. A few members probably did read books and newspapers, but conversation and gossip seemed more the rule.

I gripped my racquet. "But why choose you, Roderick DeVere? Wait, let me guess...it's because you marched Chief Cherry and the other officer on an inspection tour of Drumcliffe's art. That's it, isn't it? He doubts the missing paintings are in this cottage. He exempts you."

"Presumed innocent," Roddy said in sarcasm. "But Chief Cherry sounded nearly desperate."

"He should be desperate to find out who murdered Warren Eccles...and Marco Gliano. It sounds like he's afraid that Joseph Cuveen will embarrass him, but not afraid of a killer going free and clear. Maybe he'll arrest me on suspicion when I tell him about Sabine Haines."

"Ridiculous."

"Is it? Newport would like nothing better. Madeline Glendorick would gloat, and the vilest jokes spurt from Mamie Fish...like Old Faithful Geyser. Our social calendar is...is...."

"Plentiful," Roddy said.

"A juggernaut," I answered. A quick peck on the cheek, and I trooped out. The summer calendar would give us until the third week of August to prove that Sabine Haines murdered Warren Eccles and whether Asa Durling conspired with her and involved Marco. Or acted alone. Or whether the assistant who fancied the art thief hanged, drawn, and quartered was innocent, merely voicing murderous fantasies.

My tennis lesson went badly. The instructor declared my timing "off" and said I must "loosen" my shoulders. We would try again next week on the Casino's ladies' court. A visit to the Redwood Library found me presented with a camping manual on cooking over an outdoor fire while keeping young minds *pure, happy,* and *healthy.* "For both girls and boys," the watchful librarian said, having bookmarked a passage specially for me: *"Keep your thoughts clear as a crystal stream. Thinking evil thoughts blackens the soul."*

My dark thoughts? Did the Redwood librarian knife me with her whetted passage? Roddy said *paranoia* was an ancient Greek word and I must ignore the librarian as I overlooked the footman's glance when cutting the melon with a steel blade. It was little comfort when Cassie invited us to join her and her children the next afternoon at a site unknown to me: Hazard's Point.

"Off Hazard Avenue in Narragansett," Roddy said, "crashing surf and granite rocks."

"Nothing hazardous?"

"We'll avoid the slick black moss."

Cassie and the children arrived first at the rock-bound shore. Her groom and two footmen set up chairs and a table, then opened a net. The breaking waves thundered and foamed in the glaring sunlight, and I tied my chinstrap as little Bea and Charlie ran to greet us, disappointed that Velvet was not here. "Uncle" Roderick promised that Velvet would visit soon. "Auntie" Val doubly promised.

Cassie took our hands in hers and thanked us for joining this impromptu outing. Her gloves and sun hat veil would protect her alabaster complexion, but Cassie's smile glowed brightly behind the veil that slightly blurred her face.

The purpose of this afternoon was announced by Charlie. "We are having a crab roast! We will eat crabs cooked on the fire"

His sister proclaimed, "And I can help light the matches."

"I get to bait the net," Charlie boasted.

"Greasy bacon." Beatrice made a face. "Your fingers will smell bad."

The children joined the footman who spread the net while we were seated in canvas folding chairs by the second footman who opened a wicker hamper, and we three soon sipped chilled white wine and snacked on deviled eggs. I asked Cassie about her bird-protection luncheon and saw her lovely eyebrows knit in a frown.

"Everyone was polite," she said, "but every mind was made up before the carriages arrived. You should have seen ladies fingering their plumage as if terrified every feather would be snatched away."

"I am sorry," I said.

"Americans dislike restrictions," Roddy remarked. The groom lifted firewood sticks from Cassie's carriage, then began to lay a fire on the rocks several feet downwind from our chairs.

"To roast the crabs?" I asked.

"Cross your fingers that crabs are hungry for bacon chunks and will go into the net," Cassie said. "I have heard nothing but 'crab roast' since yesterday."

A footman unfolded a burlap sack, and Roddy said, "This brings back memories. If you ladies will please excuse me, I will join the crab catchers and relive boyhood good times."

Roddy stepped away, and Cassie peered at the sea. "Dudley will appreciate hearing that we have spent the afternoon on granite rock that dates from the Ice Age.

"He's in Fiji?" I asked.

"Fiji," she said softly, gazing at the sea as if his ship might magically appear. Even behind the veil, I had seen that same look on her face at this time last year. The moment grew quiet except for the surf.

"Cassie," I said, "may I impose upon you with questions... questions about questions?"

"I am all ears."

"Suppose you suspected someone of wrongdoing...let's say, you needed to know for certain that a member of your household transgressed."

"Transgressed?"

"Broke a rule...in violation. Something serious."

"Like our footman dismissed for 'visiting' the wine cellar? The butler dealt with him, Val."

"Something more consequential...grave."

My friend lifted her veil, looked at my face, and sipped her wine. "Is this truly a household matter, Val? How to question a maid? A cook?" She sipped and adjusted her veil. "Or is this something else?"

"Else..." I said at last. My word lisped, and the surf crashed. "Remember Alva's luncheon, Cassie, when you appeared so suddenly? I was about to explain what happened at the Cuveen Gallery when you interrupted."

"For your own good, Val."

"Suppose my 'own good' depends on questions that are fine-tuned, very subtle but sharp as...as...."

"Sharp as a knife? Sharp as a dagger?"

I caught my breath, speechless. Cassie lifted her veil and looked at me with eyes as frank as they were clouded. Her fingers clutched the wine glass, and she gazed at the rocks where a net was being pulled from the sea. The children squealed. The fire crackled.

"Roderick believes that I am superstitious," Cassie said, "and Dudley fears that I am ill. But you, Val, try to suspend your judgment. You try, and I appreciate that. I love you for it."

I nodded, silent in the moment.

"I try to shield those who need not know of my visions. I keep them to myself. But this summer they intrude in ways I cannot understand. Try as I might, the message fails me."

"What message, Cassie?"

A blush rose in her cheeks. "A dagger and Catholic saints...and a queen. And you. I cannot fathom any meaning.

I hardly know what to say, except it will be best when this summer is over and done with, when we get through it unharmed."

Chapter Twenty-nine

TEN MINUTES EARLY FOR my sitting, I tied Shamrock at the hitching post and paced the sidewalk while rehearsing questions I would put to Sabine Haines after posing for Cole this morning. At yesterday's crab roast, Cassie crafted a few phrases I memorized like a multiplication table. On this cool misty morning, I drew my cloak around the light blue silk day dress that Calista advised. A milk wagon clattered down the street, a dog barked behind a picket fence, and geraniums bloomed in window boxes. Except for my pacing, these cottages faced the world in homely harmony.

Inside the studio, one glance at the familiar scene showed a champagne bottle in an ice bucket with three glasses arranged on the corner table. My heart skipped a beat. Cole promised to celebrate the portrait's completion. Had he finished after two sittings, aided by the photographs?

Had he secretly invited Roddy for the unveiling? Champagne for the artist and the DeVeres?

"An early celebration? My portrait is *completer*?" At my fractured French, this excitable man shook his head and wagged a paint-stained finger.

"*Non, non*, Madame, but a little surprise today. You will see my Marianne."

"Oh...Marianne instead."

"And then a guest of your *connaissance*...your acquaintance."

He did not say who was coming, but it was not my husband. I burst my own balloon. And why would Marianne intrude while André did his job? Escorted past the draped easel, I felt Cole's heavily starched smock rub against my arm. The last time here, I worried about mistakes from his drinking too much wine. Could today's brushwork be foiled by a sleeve as stiff as a gentleman's "boiled" shirtfront? Could his arm reach the Rocky Mountains for the distance?

"Mister Cole," I said, "I hope you remember the background of my portrait, the mountains?"

"*Mais oui*, Madame. *Les* Rockies."

"Good."

Dreading the man's touch, I opened the top three buttons of my dress, and Cole immediately set to work. His right hand held a palette daubed with different paints, and he changed brushes frequently with his left hand. No need to charm the lady in the chair.

Not this time.

I guessed an hour passed when the door knocker signaled a change of mood, a lighter atmosphere. Cole quickly put down the palette and brush to greet Marianne with kisses on both cheeks. "And here is Madame DeVere, *ma Cherie.*"

"Lovely to see you," she said with a little wave. Her tan muslin dress looked sizes too large for her slender frame. Was she thinner from battling a balky coal stove for André? She had arrived with a covered tray she set on the table beside the champagne and said to me, "You must stay for our party."

Party? I wanted no festivity here, not until my portrait was finished. How many hours so far in this hothouse? Six? Eight? My appointment with Sabine Haines was next, and every minute in this chair brought me closer to the Travers Block. I would spend this time rehearsing my questions.

Marianne's enormous eyes lingered on me as she joined Cole behind the easel. They murmured together, gazing from me to the painting. Marianne suggested that my lips could be a bit fuller on the canvas.

"Dearest André," she said, "the pastry stone board is my easel, but you kindly make room for my fancies."

"An artist must value the eyesight of his love," Cole replied.

"Madame DeVere," Marianne said, "may I please approach to satisfy myself that full justice is being done to your fine features." She looked at Cole anxiously. "And André, you will not object?"

"*Ma Cherie*, I give you *carte blanche*." The two sounded stilted, maybe from scrambling two languages, especially if André Cole was not really French.

I wet my lips for Marianne's inspection, which extended to my cheekbones and chin. Her precise culinary work lent itself to this clinical gaze.

Behind the easel again, she advised a touch-up, and Cole reached for his palette and brush—but took them up in opposite hands. The brush and the palette were switched from right to left hands. I was sure of it. Or was I? I had not noticed previously. Some people were two-handed. Was Cole? Did it matter?

I shifted in my chair. "Might I have a look," I asked. "A quick peek?"

A horrified Cole let loose a stream of *non, non, non,* and Marianne squeezed her eyes shut.

"Never mind," I said. "I will obey Monsieur Cole's rule... not until my portrait is completely finished...*fini.*"

They resumed their cozy parley behind the easel. Cole dabbed at his palette and seemed to jab the brush at the canvas until a clock tower struck eleven o'clock.

"*Onze heures,*" Cole decreed. "The hour of our guest...."

Marianne jumped aside, taking André's brush and palette while he draped the easel. His matador's swirl with the cloth was familiar, but Marianne's ease with the brush and palette was novel, even fascinating . Perhaps she assisted Cole's work from time to time. A pastry brush and paint brush could be similar, a palette not unlike a baking sheet.

I was not invited to step from the chair but waited for their signal, only to be sitting in place when the door knocker rapped. Who should be invited inside but a hefty woman in dark voile silk carrying a basket with protruding rolls of fabric.

Cole said, "*Bienvenue*, Mademoiselle Haines!"

I clamped my jaw shut at the sight of this woman receiving André Cole's bow and a kiss on her hand. Aghast, I saw him lift the canoe-shaped basket from her arm while introducing Marianne, who had the decency to remember that Mrs. DeVere was in the room. "Do join us," she said to me.

"By all means please do, Mrs. DeVere," said Sabine.

Feeling half naked, I buttoned up my dress under her watchful eye, then was drawn in range of the bitter *Violette de Parme*.

"A delightful coincidence to see you here this morning, Mrs. DeVere. And of course, our appointment."

"Indeed," I said.

"But first, a look at Worth fabrics in the studio of a glorious artist."

"I am not sure I understand."

"For the backgrounds," Marianne broke in, coming closer to me. "You recall, Mrs. DeVere, that we spoke of the portrait backgrounds, the personal objects of great meaning...such as the parrot, the head of John the Baptist, and also...." She touched her throat, paused, fixed those saucer eyes on me, then mouthed an unmistakable word.

"Scimitar," I said, "like a dagger." The word felt thrust upon me, sucked from deep within me.

Cole shot a glance, and Marianne hastened on as if the word had not come up. "André tells me you wish to see mountains, Mrs. DeVere," she said, "and so you shall have them. But other ladies have no special ideas, and so the fabrics...Miss Haines, if you please."

Sabine spoke as if cued. "This was Mr. Asa Durling's idea," she said. "He remembered the House of Worth fabrics and talked to Mr. Cole. For their portraits, some ladies might rather have beautiful fabrics instead of animal skins."

"*Vraiment*, truly" Cole said. "And now, the presentation?"

Sabine reached for a fabric roll from the basket on the floor, looked around and began to unroll a velvety cloth while striding quickly toward Cole's easel.

"*Non, non*! You must stop!" Cole grabbed Sabine's elbow, spun her around, and snapped, "Come here, *ici*," at Marianne. Sabine Haines looked startled, Marianne chastened. Cole's face was white.

"We do it this way..."

Cole thrust the roll in Marianne's outstretched arms and pulled the fabric over her bony shoulder while she stood in place. Marianne turned her head away at his hearty, "*Voila*! We see it now!".

Sabine began to recite, "'The House of Worth presents azure and cerulean cut velvet in the Italian Renaissance styling that will impart a depth of field....'" She went on until Cole requested the next sample. Once again, a fabric roll was put in Marianne's arms and a swath draped over her shoulder as Sabine recited, "Here we have a silk brocade inspiration with feather garland motifs and a delicate trellis pattern of cream lace and silver threaded brilliants...."

Others followed until the artist declared himself satisfied and said the *négociation* between Miss Haines and Monsieur Durling could begin at once.

All the while, Marianne turned her head, eyes downcast. Sabine Haines blinked, seeming uneasy until Cole clapped his hands and said, "The hours of labor cease, and we now enjoy ourselves. So, Marianne...we rise."

He called us to the table where he worked the champagne cork while Marianne uncovered the tray to reveal a half-dozen bite-sized fruit tarts.

"For our little party," she said. "Tarts and champagne for the sweet tooth... André, if you please...."

The cork popped, and Sabine clapped her hands. "A nice surprise," she said. "My first party in Newport. And I came here only to work."

"'Work and play together,' my André's rule." Marianne sounded doleful. Her eyes looked tired. Cole poured the wine and handed glasses to me and Sabine, raising the third glass for a toast.

"But Marianne...a fourth glass? Another glass for you?" This was my first utterance, my first vocal sound since Marianne silently mouthed the word I had spoken aloud... spoke it twice.

"One mere sip for me," she said in haste. "The kitchen is my strict task master."

She raised her palm as if swearing an oath with sturdy fingers smeared a gray-brown. Or brown-gray. I could not guess what possible food would be that color.

She said, "And the kitchen is also my joy."

Cole declared the art of the portrait was his *maître* and *joie.* We toasted the art of portraits, sipped sweet champagne that cloyed my throat, and ate the tarts declared to be heavenly. Marianne touched André's glass to her lips but took no sip. The questions I had readied for Sabine Haines flew from my mind.

"And so, Mrs. DeVere," she said, "we will keep our appointment at the Travers Block salon within the hour." She narrowed her eyes. "That is, unless you are otherwise a busy lady."

"Otherwise, Miss Haines," I said, "I will take the liberty of rescheduling our appointment. I will be in touch very soon. We have much to discuss."

Chapter Thirty

A FAST TROT TOOK me straight to Drumcliffe. Roddy was out when I arrived, and Sands reminded me that Mr. DeVere was at the Reading Room.

Of course, surveillance for Chief Cherry.

"Sands," I asked, "did Mr. DeVere say when he expects to return?"

"He did not, ma'am. But we have had something of a busy morning."

The butler's "busy" was never positive.

I said, "How so?"

Sands drew himself up. "A newspaper photographer encroached on the garden, claiming the right to photograph the hydrangeas."

"Oh, yes," I said, "Mr. Bullard." Though I had neglected to inform the servants. "And he took pictures?"

"Certainly not. He was escorted off the property."

"Escorted...very well." The lady of the house in arrears again. Would I ever learn? "Sands," I said, "Please see that a telephone call is placed to *The Newport Daily News* office. Please inform Mr. Bullard that he is welcome to photograph the hydrangeas here...and Drumcliffe regrets the confusion."

The butler bowed without comment. No confusion on his part. He would have a footman make the call. Household rank was intact, with exceptions made for the French bulldog.

As for the Lady of the House? No quarter given for the Wild West woman who invaded this Knickerbocker bloodline, out of step in matters of decorum. The butler and housekeeper kept their own counsel about Madame's confusion.

Little did they know I would agree my middle name could be *Confusion.* The scene at the Catherine Street studio made me feel like a character in *Alice in Wonderland,* a book that made me queasy, off kilter. I would tell Roddy about this morning. Sabine Haines seemed both heavy handed and docile amid Cole and Marianne's give-and-take. The artist seemed boundlessly *taking,* while Marianne appeared to *give* without limits. She cooked, she laundered, she flattered. So terribly thin. Did she take stimulants? Did any of them think about Warren Eccles? Did Sabine? Did she feel remorse? Or did she bury him in the depths of her mind? Did Asa Durling help or hinder her?

Roddy was not home by 1:30 p.m. when I changed from the silk dress into a skirt and shirtwaist, relieved to shed the posing dress, the third lightweight dress consigning me to Cole's chair. Calista welcomed them for her travel to Greece this Fall. She would alter the shoulders and lower the hems. She was also welcome to my closet of Macy's fashions for her cousins in Athens.

I shuffled the morning mail and accepted the footman's offer of lunch. Roddy had not returned by 2:00, so I sat with Velvet on the loggia facing the sea, restless and befuddled as I picked at a salad and sipped mineral water. The dog begged with yearning eyes and short woofs. Roddy urged us not to feed her from our plates. I gave her pinches of cheese.

Deep in thoughts of the morning, replaying the scene, I shivered at Roddy's sudden soft touch. He had come quietly from behind my chair.

"Val, you can't be cold."

"I am off kilter," I said.

He looked closely at my face. "Feeling ill?"

"No, more like...like a morning of blurred photographs, all out of focus."

Roddy sat down, patted Velvet's head and fingered her collar, which gave him a minute to ponder my words.

"I'm not being cryptic, Roddy. I meant what I said. The morning at Cole's studio was...peculiar." Seeing my husband's fretful eyes, I wondered whether his past several hours were likewise skewed.

"Have you eaten?" I asked. The footman hovered at a discreet distance, ready with late lunch choices. In moments, cold lobster and ale were on the table between us. Roddy ate and sipped while I pushed radish slices across my plate.

"Your portrait sitting went ahead on schedule?" My husband asked as if testing the waters. "On schedule, Val, and then afterwards...?"

"There was no 'afterwards,' Roddy. I spent the morning posing, then Marianne brought tarts and huddled with André behind the easel. Then Sabine Haines arrived to show off Worth fabrics. It seems Asa Durling suggested the studio might purchase different patterns for portrait backgrounds."

"And you did not meet privately with Haines?" My husband's disappointment almost scolded.

"I couldn't, Roddy. Cole opened champagne to blend with Marianne's tarts and declared a time of enjoyment. I doubt the man is French. The whole scene felt off...just off. Marianne did not take one sip of champagne. And I noticed Cole switched hands from palette to brush, back and forth."

"Ambidextrous," Roddy said. "That's the word."

"I didn't notice it the other times," I said. "Then again, my mind was elsewhere. On purpose."

"But so far, you have not had one glimpse of the portrait?"

"Cole's ironclad rule forbids it, Roddy. One violation, and the portrait is canceled. I don't know how many additional hours are required in his studio. He's not paid by the sitting, is he?"

"Of course not." Roddy took a bite of lobster, said "no" to Velvet, then gave her a morsel. "Some rules," he said slowly, "are meant to be broken."

My husband's mood had changed. Was he giving me license to look at the portrait? Hinting that an early peek would not, in fact, cancel the work despite Cole's threat? The artist's income surely mattered. His expenses included two cottage rentals, and Marianne's marketing added up. Roddy had privately settled on my portrait outlay in Asa Durling's hotel suite, and I chose not to know the price of my face and shoulders in oil paint on canvas.

Ready to ask the meaning of my husband's words about broken rules, I held back while the footman approached about a dessert of chilled watermelon. Velvet sniffed hopefully at the footman's ankles, and we studied her glossy coat. Chalmers admitted that he and Bronson occasionally fed her a snack. Roddy and I declined watermelon but said yes to a sliver for Velvet, who eagerly followed the footman.

"Promiscuous dog," Roddy said.

"Fun," I replied.

Roddy's mood did not lift. His brow creased, and he squinted at the sea. I had yet to hear about his morning. The midafternoon sun was nearly blinding. I said, "Roddy, if you feel like describing your morning...." I shrugged. "Or let it rest."

In the silent moment, a seagull wheeled and glided out of sight. Roddy said, "We ought to look for property transactions in tomorrow's *Daily News.*" He spoke quietly.

"And what will we see?"

"A purchase by Battersby and Cowley."

"Those awful men on the *Conquest.*" I sipped the last of my water. Was Roddy's morning blurred too? "You heard this at the Reading Room?"

"I did."

"Why should we care?"

"It's the block of the Gill Street house fires," he said. "The investment block, the plan for the next Travers Block. The holdout owner has sold."

"You mean, the owner sold before his house was burned down? Or hers?"

"His." Roddy said. "A cobbler named Riley. Which is ironic because he bought a fire extinguisher."

"Roddy," I said, "I am losing your train of thought."

"Quite simply," my husband said slowly, "the man began to fear that his house was marked for destruction because of the neighboring house fires. He doubted the extinguisher could protect his house, so he agreed to sell. He remembers the woman who died in the fire...a vagrant, a wanderer."

"And you heard this at the Reading Room?"

"I sat on the veranda. The men came in for whiskies. They joked about the cobbler's extinguisher. Battersby holds stock in the Pyrene Company. He makes money if fires are extinguished—"

"—or if they burn to the ground?"

"On Gill Street, yes. The house will be razed. It's the lot they want."

"And got the whole block?"

Roddy nodded and sipped his ale.

"But no investigation will take place, will it? And that is what you heard for Chief Cherry?"

Roddy put his plate on the table. "Actually, no. I pieced together the property purchase. Then Cowley brought up his wife's birthday. He plans a surprise. A secret surprise."

"Aren't all surprises secrets?"

"No joking, Val. I heard names. Cowley said the gifts are under wraps and must stay under wraps."

"Like furs?"

"Like secrets. Cowley said two names...really, three. He said Millet and Dupré."

"The stolen paintings," My gasp was a whisper. "That man has the paintings. So, he bought them at a back door. Marco sold them before he came to Seabright."

Stone faced, Roddy said, "Doubtful, Val. Doubtful Marco sold them."

"What do you mean?"

"The third name," Roddy said. "The third name came with the third whiskey." My husband's fingers curled around the glass of ale. "The third name, Val, is...Cole."

Chapter Thirty-one

THE SUN BEAT LIKE hammered copper, and yet we sat in the loggia, speechless at first, then biting back the words that jabbed at reason and logic. Roddy stood by what he had heard, swearing his stakeout yielded the artist's name. Quite sure, he said over again, that he heard "Cole."

I tried "Marco" and "Gliano," but each time, Roddy said "Cole." Stubborn, I repeated the plasterer's name as if to keep intact what I thought I knew. Events as I understood them fractured each time my husband's tenor voice spoke that same name. Roddy held tight, but I floundered in a swamp of Who? What? Where? When?

"The paintings..." I said. "*Potato Planters* and...*Cows Across the Creek.*

"Almost, Val," Roddy said shortly. I believe the title is, *Cows Crossing a Ford.*

"Ford, creek...what's the difference?" My voice rose to a high pitch. The difference was André Cole in possession of two stolen paintings he sold to Randolph Cowley. The plasterer got his hands on *French Artillery*, but the other two paintings ended up with Cole.

By design or a fluke?

How did he get them?

Roddy had hours to settle into a likely scenario. "Cole obviously got them from the Cuveen Gallery," he said. "Both are small enough to conceal under a wrapping, and he had the advantage of artists who are seen at work in the open air. They carry frames and equipment outdoors, so Cole would not attract special attention. He could carry the wrapped paintings tucked under his arm, and no one would think twice about it."

"Or once," I said. Roddy wiped a handkerchief across his forehead. A fly swam in his half-drunk glass of ale, and a dark gray cloud smudged the horizon, possibly bringing one of the late afternoon thunderstorms that beset Newport. I suggested we go inside to a room without pictures on the wall, but the mezzanine was the only space without art in gilt frames. Roddy sat in a wing chair. I took the channel chair that Roddy's mother insisted belonged in my boudoir. Her insistence kept the chair right here.

"You will go to the police," I said.

"To Chief Cherry."

"In the morning," I said, "first thing?"

"That's my plan."

"And he will question Mr. Cowley?"

"Cowley, certainly," Roddy said.

"Receiving stolen goods," I said, "but will he be arrested?" The minute those words left my lips, the answer was plain as these walls, but I wanted to hear it from my husband. "Mr. Randolph Cowley will not face consequences, will he? A gentleman and member of the Reading Room need not be annoyed by law enforcement"

Roddy paused, then said, "Items sold door-to-door are a historical practice, Val. Think of peddlers. Your papa remembered whiskey peddlers."

"My papa told stories of the early mining days, Roddy. Nobody in the mining camps peddled art. Cowley knew he was buying stolen paintings. You heard him say 'under wraps.'"

Roddy tugged at his necktie. "Randolph Cowley is an acquaintance, not a friend. We possibly belong to the same club in the city, and I can check the membership book. But to your point, Val, it may be prudent for Chief Cherry not to press charges, especially if the paintings are surrendered to Cuveen. Cowley can claim he had no idea they were stolen."

My voice seemed to bounce off a wall when I almost shouted, "But the peddler was André Cole."

The mezzanine space grew silent. Roddy crossed his legs. For both of us, it took little effort to discuss Randolph Cowley, the bewhiskered man who bought contraband art and profited from the Gill Street fires. In this discussion, I could easily give rise to righteous anger, Roddy to lawyerly defense. My ire would meet my husband's rock-steady calm.

At base, however, we were both evasive. The core issue was André Cole.

How could it come to this—the portrait planned for my husband's study now tangled in thievery by the portrait painter? Thievery? The word itself sounded mild, akin to shoplifting or picking pockets. An evasive word steering wide of homicide.

"Roddy," I said, "the three stolen paintings coincided with Eccles stabbed and bleeding to death."

"We have thought so."

"Asa Durling advanced that idea. At least, he allowed it."

"He did, Val, and we did too. The plasterer was thought to be the killer. The police closed the case."

"But Marco was pushed off Cliff Walk, Roddy. I suspect Durling."

"Durling in league with your Miss Haines?"

"She's not *my* Miss Haines, Roddy. But the Arnold Constable saleswoman remembered the man tussling with Sabine Haines at Eccles's gallery had a white tuft of hair. That man could have been Asa Durling."

"Haines and Durling conspiring," Roddy said. "But the two paintings were sold by Cole."

Back to André Cole.

I said, "Suppose Cole joined with the others for theft. Suppose they are organized, Cole with Haines and Durling." I tried to lower my voice. "Asa Durling was Eccles's assistant for years...years of art dealing and forgery too. Theo told us about it."

I did not say aloud what surely crossed our minds, Theo Bulkeley's warning to keep clear of Warren Eccles. Too late, dear friend.

Roddy said, "You saw no sign of the paintings in the studio?"

"No. I doubt they were in the cabinet with the parrot, John the Baptist and the scimitar...." I shuddered. "Valuable paintings, Roddy, would not be stored with props. The risk of damage is too great."

"So, they would be kept in the other cottage? With Cole's lady friend?"

"On Cottage Street," I said. "The paintings could be hidden anywhere...under a bed."

I pictured bone-thin Marianne firing up the stove, stirring and kneading and chopping with her worker's hands. Would she pay attention to the paintings? What would she think?

Roddy uncrossed his legs and sat close to me. "Val, I will present this case to Chief Cherry in the morning. The police detectives must take over completely. The robbery is the reason to reopen the murder case. The police have the power to issue search warrants and make arrests. They can question suspects."

"How well I know."

"We both know, my dear. Our Tenth of July is a blistering memory." Roddy reached to take my hand. "Newport has treated you shamefully, Val. You have borne up against Society at its cruelest. Over the next winter, we will consider the Hamptons for our summers. Drumcliffe can be rented or sold. Perhaps a younger Vanderbilt would find it appealing. Or one of Mrs. Astor's daughters. For now, however...." Roddy held my hand tighter. "No matter how good an artist, Cole trafficked in stolen goods. He may be involved in Eccles's death. No more sitting for the portrait, Val."

My husband's sad eyes belied his firm words. The portrait meant so much to him. André Cole's luminous work at the Cuveen reception persuaded Roddy that my image would come to life in a frame on the wall of his study. For him, the portrait was something of a fixed idea. In my darkest thoughts, it occurred that Roddy might fear my passing from a mishap or the fevers that swept whole regions of the country and took a terrible toll. My portrait would be a memory.

"Roddy," I said, "here's an idea. Suppose I go to Catherine Street one more time and ask about the portrait? Suppose I insist on seeing the canvas, seeing it on the spot despite Cole's protests. You said some rules ought to be broken."

I said "'meant to be.'"

"Better," I said, "more like destined. So, it is destined that I have a look. It may be best if the portrait is not quite finished. Remember the pictures in Chicago at the Palmer House Hotel...the Impressionists? Maybe portrait art is changing for the new century. I will be a twentieth-century woman."

My husband's reluctance was plain to see. He tapped his boot heel and bit his lip. His wedding band pressed against my fingers as he gripped my hand. He did not forbid me with a *no*, and neither did I hear a *yes*. We left it cloudy. I would think just how cloudy when the first crack of afternoon thunder followed the lightning flash that put us within bare walls with nothing more to say for ourselves.

Chapter Thirty-two

SHORTLY AFTER 10:30 A.M. the next morning, I tied Shamrock at the granite hitching post on Catherine Street and took a deep breath. I had narrowly avoided two eager young women directly in my path as I drove to the studio. Since mid-July, the Fall River ferry brought day-tourists desperate for the reward. They have poked the bushes and pried up rocks like children on an egg hunt. They have crushed shrubbery and damaged garden ornaments. Newport's relief would come with the fast-approaching announcement of paintings found and returned to Joseph Cuveen.

My relief would come with today's final portrait sitting and a surprise visit to Miss Haines at the Travers Block. Roddy sent a message to Asa Durling to announce my appearance at Cole's studio by mid-morning. The day began early over a fast breakfast. Roddy would go directly to Market Square. We spoke only of scheduling. The real substance lay below, unexplored.

Calista laid out a lovely dress of silk faille with motifs of apple blossoms, but I chose a twill skirt with a jacket and shirtwaist. My maid advised the ensemble was for women in the business world. I said I felt like business today and asked her to fasten my Cartier watch on its neck chain. The skirt pocket was deep enough for a handful of silver dollars, which I carried whenever clothing permitted. The dollars were favorites. They reminded me of Papa.

I fingered the pocketed coins before raising the door knocker at Catherine Street, only to have the door opened before I knocked.

"Madame DeVere, *bienvenue*."

"Mr. Cole, good morning."

No beret this morning, and his rumpled smock looked slept in. Cole's moustache drooped, and a razor had not touched his cheeks. The whites of his eyes flared red. "You are in *precipitation* this morning, Madame?"

"You mean haste, Mr. Cole? No, but I am impatient. I will sit this morning for the final time. I need to know the state of my portrait, how close to completion."

"Ah, Madame...."

Too many *Ah Madames*. I marched to the draped easel, ready to snatch at the covering.

"*Non, non*...I forbid you." He leapt between me and the easel, almost catlike. Fair enough, I would go to the chair. "One last time," I said. He doubtless knew from Asa Durling of my impatience. I repeated, "Last time."

"*Certainement.*" He stepped behind the easel, plucked off the drapery and reached for the palette and a brush.

I sat down and waited. Not one brush stroke followed.

Cole pointed the brush at me, a silent order to unbutton. I had complied before, but the head-and-shoulders pose seemed needless by now. This moment felt like a contest, even rivalry. I loosened the top shirtwaist button.

Cole jabbed a finger at me, and I pulled my Cartier watch from the jacket folds and held it up to show my issue, time.

The face-off went on, neither of us yielding. What was at stake? Two more loosened buttons, and he would go to work. Did it matter? Not in the least for me, but the police would soon question Cole about the theft because Roddy was at the police station. What's more, Cole was probably feeling flush with cash from paintings sold to Randolph Cowley. He might be summoned to Market Square or simply declare *fini* and walk away, omitting details of my portrait, such the pupils of my eyes. Or an ear.

I thought of Roddy, tucked my watch away, and loosened the second and third buttons.

Cole went to work. "*C'est mieux comme ça,* Madame. It is better."

"Better," I echoed, sitting six feet in front of a thief, possibly an accessory to murder. Was this "better" for Marianne? I had not glanced at the corner table to see what might lie there. Had she baked bread before dawn? Croissants? Perhaps they had coffee together in the Cottage Street cottage before

André was summoned here on short notice. Asa Durling probably warned him the DeVeres had turned peevish.

What did Marianne think of her criminal lover? All that cooking, plus letting her arms prop up Sabine Haines's fabrics. Marianne's hard-at-work hands were stained a tawny brown-gray that day, and I could not guess anything edible in that color. Nothing enticing came to mind. A sauce? Gravy? Both washed off easily. Marianne's fingers were stained.

Stained like...paint.

My mind played a trick, a color game with paint. A dead-end thought...or might it be an opening? My portrait would call for greens and dull gold for hazel eyes and "dishwater" blonde hair. I had not asked Cole about accessories such as jewels or ribbons. I had requested a background of Rocky Mountains.

Mountains in tones of brown with shades of shadowy gray. Like the color on Marianne's fingers. Could it be? Could it possibly be?

My thoughts swam.

"Madame DeVere...you are perhaps *se sentir mal*... not well?

"No, no," I said. "Perfectly well." Unthinking, I had touched my palm to my heart. That must not happen twice.

Cole dabbed his brush at the palette, and I thought of *The Counting House* in the crate at Drumcliffe, said to be in the "School of Rembrandt." The "School" meant the artist had imitators or apprentices in his studio. Overseen by the master, the apprentices painted details like small animals or shells.

Could André Cole have an apprentice? Could the Rockies in my portrait be Marianne's assignment?

Knowing that self-absorption distorted everything, I still toyed at guesswork. Who else was André Cole painting this summer? We knew of cancelled commissions but not active ones, and social gossip had not spread the word. Asa Durling insisted on privacy for the artist and his clients.

Suppose Marianne painted details on the portraits. The brown-gray tone could work for a gentleman's coat or a lady's fur tippet. Who else sat in this chair hour after hour? If I asked him, would Cole erupt? If I asked about Marianne, would he accuse me of belittling his work? Diluting it?

A sharp rap at the door stopped all musing. Cole bristled, muttered, "Mon Dieu" and flicked his brush. The rapping grew harder, then faster, but Cole stayed fixed at the easel until the rapping shifted to a windowpane. Palette and brush thrust aside, he opened the door a few inches. Whoever was rapping pushed it wider.

Wide enough for the person in the chair to glimpse a dark blue tunic, belt, badge, and helmet. Wide enough, that is, to outline a policeman, the very officer who took notes in the Market Square interrogation room, then came to Drumcliffe with the chief. Wide enough, in sum, for the policeman at the door to become Officer Seavers.

He nodded at Cole and ignored me. Or did not see me. The artist rubbed his hands together as if to wash them.

"*Excusez moi*, Madame...*pour le moment.*" Dragging his feet, Cole slowly moved toward the policeman who called him outside. He shut the door behind him, but first flung the cloth over the easel.

Was the artist being summoned to headquarters for questioning? Handcuffed on the sidewalk and led away? I heard no voices, no English, no French. All quiet.

Alone, I sat like a trained animal, then woke up and stood up. What did these long tedious hours produce? I jumped down, crossed the tarpaulin, yanked off that infernal cloth, and faced the canvas....

And heard an ear-splitting, thunderous, "How dare you? You dare!"

The door flung open and slammed shut. Cole hulked, his mouth open. No Seavers here now. Cole bolted the door.

"Where is my portrait?" I shouted.

"How dare you?"

"There is nothing here! Nothing! Where is my portrait?"

He grabbed the cloth and hung it over a canvas that was dashed with streaks and spots.

I ripped off the cloth. "This is nothing. Nothing at all. Where is my portrait? Where?"

Spittle burst from his lips. "She told you," he hissed. "You saw her. She told you."

"Told me what?"

"Don't lie. She told you. Say it, she told you."

Not a French syllable.

"You met her someplace...the market. She told you... confessed."

I backed away.

"Say it!" He spat and smacked his lips. His fists clenched and unclenched. "Say it!"

We stood in place, Cole on the tarpaulin, me beside the chair. Minutes ago, I sat here while he held a brush and palette. Now...now the world gyrated. I gripped the chair arm. Focus...focus on Marianne, so nimble with brush and palette, so close to my face...my earrings that first day, my face, my lips. And the photographs. Marianne all along. It was...is Marianne.

The raging artist before me, no artist.

I heard laughter. Bitter, choking laughter...my own voice, my laughter. "My portrait..." I said at last. "Marianne...on Cottage Street. The studio is Cottage Street. Isn't it?" I laughed again. "Isn't it?"

I would pass over deceit, embrace the truth in this second's thought. "Cottage Street," I said again. "All right...the portrait is...is."

He panted, eyes blanked, eyes piercing.

"The portrait," I said. "Just get it. Marianne has it. Get it."

But he glared, deaf to my words. His hands clenched again. "She told you, didn't she...stabbed me."

"No, no," I said. "Nobody was stabbed, except...." I shut my mouth before the name burst out. Cole's fingers gripped as if with a brush...no, a knife.

"Stabbed in the back...me." He snarled like a beast.

I said, "You need not...."

Not what? Not guess the gallery manager had found out who painted the portraits? Found out and died?

Murdered.

Not by Haines. Not Sabine.

"Cole..." I whispered. "You...Cole. You killed Warren Eccles."

A cracking laugh, and calm descended at that moment. Eyes narrowed, Cole's fingers drummed lightly on the smock. He looked left and right, then stepped to each window to lower the blinds, eyes on me every second. A floorboard creaked. At the window by the table, he reached for the cord and pulled. The blind stuck. He jerked it once, twice....

Slow motion would edge me to the door, but he beat me, catlike again. His flint-black eyes focused but also carried him far away, glassy and beaming.

Insane eyes. A madman's eyes.

Shove him...I could shove and turn the bolt. I would have seconds.

One split second.

Until his hand struck like a snake to clamp my neck, squeeze and spin me against the door. Banged against the door...a ragdoll. A breathless ragdoll. His face mashed against mine, whiskers and licorice, my left side pinned, right arm flailing. I struck out, and he laughed. My free right arm beat against his smock, his back. He laughed.

My free hand gouged fabric, then felt metal, the silver dollars. Useless. Silly. One bare breath when he eased the clamp, then tight again. Crazed, he played with me. Too few pocket dollars to buy breath...to buy life. Hand in pocket, I gagged when my fingernails bit the edges of the useless coins.

Bit at the edges until one dollar slipped between my first and second fingers, then my thumb and forefinger. Then dollars between all fingers, like brass knuckles. Silver knuckles, each dollar punched out like a half-moon clenched tight in my fingers.

One punch...from skirt pocket to Cole's jaw. Clouds blurred my eyes...I felt faint, but his clamp eased enough for a last breath. I held it back, freed my hand from the pocket, squeezed my fingers, then drove at his face.

The soft squish, the unearthly shriek and rank smell chased me over the smock into the daylight. The open Catherine Street doorway echoed with a man screaming, but I took the reins and leaped onto the pony cart. Shamrock knew the way, the reins barely needed in my bleeding fingers.

Chapter Thirty-three

FORTY STEPS, RODDY TOLD me. I could count them but took his word for the wooden staircase leading from Cliff Walk to the foaming surf below. Newport's servants gathered at Forty Steps in their free time, but Roddy suggested we view it during our seaside stroll this morning of the third of August. Less than a mile from the start of Cliff Walk, the steep steps featured sturdy handrails, which my husband pointed out to remind me that dangerous places need safeguards.

In no mood for allegory, I tightened my angora cloak, took Roddy's arm, and nudged us forward. We decided to leave Velvet in the cool cottage, lest she overheat on this long walk. Cotton gloves hid the gauze bandage on my knuckles. The Drumcliffe household and stable thought I had badly scraped my hand. Ointment sufficed. No need for the doctor. The new Bayer aspirin pills helped.

Today's sun shone over fleecy clouds in a deep blue sky, and we agreed that Cliff Walk gave us privacy in public, unlike the Casino or Bailey's Beach. I needed a break from the countless half-hearted apologies for any "misunderstanding" that might have occurred this month. The misunderstanding, it was implied, lay entirely with me. No one in Society ever meant me ill. How could I entertain such a thought? Banish the thought. Theo's picnic was tomorrow afternoon, and I must be in good spirits. Behind my smiles no one would see gritted teeth, as I hoped for Roddy's sake.

And mine.

My husband nodded to a stocky man who passed by us. "That's Gus Meunchinger, Val."

"The hotel man?"

Roddy nodded again. "I'd guess he's avoiding the press. Good luck to him."

For the past week, reporters replaced day-tourists on the Fall River line. They ferreted every new detail, once *The Newport Daily News* printed the story of André Cole's impersonation and set newswires humming in every city, town, and hamlet from here to the Mississippi River. Market Square had become the reporters' hive, and the Meunchinger Hotel their nightly lair, though the Cuveen suite was shut down, no trace of artwork to be seen. Asa Durling was said to be with relatives in Boston, his whereabouts a matter for Joseph Cuveen and the police.

"Maybe we'll see Chief Cherry on Cliff walk too," I said in a feeble quip. "He needs time out from the press,"

"He needs...." My husband paused as seagulls cried. "Chief Ronald Cherry needs to toe the line between crime and Society."

"Not crime *in* Society...?"

Roddy did not take my bait. Randolph Cowley had willingly surrendered the stolen paintings with the excuse of innocence and ignorance. He pledged a handsome sum to the police charity and could expect a note of appreciation from Cuveen, as would the police for the return of *French Artillery in Snowy Winter.*

We walked in silence past an overlook, and I braced myself as we neared Ochre Point. Would I turn my face away from the place where Marco Gliano was pushed to his death? Or would I look?

Roddy drew me close. "Val, we agreed to this walk. We called it healthy."

"In the abstract," I said.

"But the police will reopen the case. That's what you wanted."

"Of course I did...I do."

So far, the name of Eccles's killer was my accusation and Chief Cherry's secret, first relayed from me to Roddy when Shamrock brought me to Drumcliffe. For the second time that awful day, Roddy spoke to the chief. He learned that Officer Seavers was sent to Catherine Street to request the artist appear at headquarters for a meeting with the chief. Roddy told the chief of Cole's rage when I exposed his fakery. He added my certainty that the make-believe artist fatally stabbed Warren Eccles. The chief asked why, then heard my husband say the terrified artist must have panicked, fearing the exposure would ruin his profitable masquerade.

"I want the trial now," I said. "I want André Cole convicted of both murders."

At this, my hand throbbed. The smashing impact bruised it badly, and healing would take a while. The memory would subside...Roddy said eventually.

"And Cassie had the premonition of danger," I said. "You cannot dismiss her visions, Roddy."

The Hazard's Point crab roast had bewildered my friend, but her intuition gave me a near-at-hand warning. The saints and the queen, I realized far too late, were a Saint Catherine and Russia's Catherine the Great, visions that warned me to beware the street where Cole operated his fraud. Danger struck there, though my friend's visions always transcended mundane calendars and addresses. Roddy said the so-called messages were useless. I said our thinking was too narrow-gauged.

"The second murder," I repeated, looking down at the rocks and surf below Ochre Point. "We are standing where Cole pushed Marco," I said, "afraid the plasterer knew too much. He invited Marco here to kill him."

Roddy and I guessed that Cole saw the young plasterer around Travers Block shortly after Eccles's murder. We believe he gave *French Artillery* to Marco and suggested he sell it and keep the money. The painting was too big to handle easily, so he gave it away, then worried about how much Marco knew, what he might have witnessed.

"We are at the exact place where André Cole committed premeditated murder," I said, having learned the term from my lawyer husband.

"Cole? You mean Alvin Coliski," Roddy replied. The reporters had done their job tracing the beginnings of the New York confidence man who convinced the talented young woman artist that her future was best pledged to him. The *Herald* and *World* exposed the paint salesman who prowled the Art Students League on 16th Street and convinced Mary Ann Comber of his vast knowledge of colors. She was poor, the daughter of a waiter, and he wined and dined her, then rented lodgings they shared in the city. Their French landlady came in handy for Coliski's scheme. Miss Comber honed her special skill for luminescent complexions, and the paint salesman saw his future in her talent. Eventually, her paintings would be signed *M. A. Comber*, he promised her. For the time being, she would be Marianne to his André Cole.

We knew this much from New York newspapers ferried to Newport. The rest seemed obvious when Roddy and I tallied artists' signatures on Drumcliffe's gilt-framed canvases. Rosa Bonheur was the outlier among men, and men commanded sizable sums for portraits.

"She will be a witness at his trial," Roddy said. "Whether she believes he killed Eccles or not, she can testify to the fraud."

"And to the murder weapon," I added. The personal objects Marianne had named from the parrot to animal skins also included a dagger which I assumed to be a grisly accessory, like the head of John the Baptist. "That jeweled dagger, Roddy...."

By instinct, my fingers curled at the word, and pain shot up my arm from my hand...the hand that held the murder weapon. I winced, took short breaths, and stood still for moments until I could say, "The dagger killed Warren Eccles, Roddy. The accessory became a lethal weapon."

Quietly we glanced together at Ochre Court, the baronial cottage at the Point, then moved along. "It defies logic," my husband said, "that the woman would allow herself to become that man's serf. Then again, logic is not the point."

"All too true, my dear. But for us, it comes down to my portrait."

We had avoided the topic thus far. The nearly finished canvas was now at Drumcliffe, having been delivered by the police who first served a search warrant at the Catherine Street studio, only to find the artist raving about a woman who blinded his eye with silver dollars. When he blurted Cottage Street, the police served a second warrant, expecting to find the female assailant. Instead, they interrupted a thin woman with a palette and brush at an easel. Tearfully, she begged the police to take the unsigned, unfinished portrait from the easel and drive it to Drumcliffe, which they did.

Wherever Sands or Mrs. Thwaite suggested the portrait be placed in the following days, I found it jarring to see myself. The Rocky Mountains took shape in the background, but one shoulder disappeared into a cloud of white paint, and my earlobes had no earrings. "My portrait..." I said as gulls wheeled and the surf broke on rocks below. "We could have it finished. My earrings...."

Roddy shook his head. "I love it...love it as is. We'll have it framed."

"Framed..." I said. "But one request, Roddy."

"Anything, my dear." He looked sweetly indulgent.

"Just this...no gilt frame."

Roddy put his arm around my shoulders as we neared The Breakers, the monumental Vanderbilt cottage by the sea. He leaned to whisper softly in my ear, "Believe this, Valentine DeVere...a beautiful woman needs no gilt frame."

For once, I did not argue, did not contradict, but let his words bathe me in warmth at this hour in the summer of 1899.

AUTHOR'S NOTE: FACT TO FICTION

Historical fiction commits an author to the lives and times of an era deserving readers' precious hours. In its pages, the past speaks to the present with color, purpose, and accuracy. Above all, readers must be able to rely on authenticity as the author brokers the past to the present.

After my many classroom and library years in decades branded by Mark Twain's novel *The Gilded Age,* it was high time to delve into mystery crime fiction! I had published *What Would Mrs. Astor Do: The Essential Guide to the Manners and Mores of the Gilded Age.* Following came *Gilded Age Cocktails: History, Lore, and Recipes from America's Gilded Age.* (It would be no coincidence that a main character in my new fiction series would a maestro of the bar.)

The Val and Roddy DeVere Gilded Age Series got its start in Newport, 1898, when the couple find themselves sleuthing to save a threatened friend's life. The western silver heiress and her New York Knickerbocker gentleman husband and lover become detectives who are later asked to solve dreadful crimes over the next several seasons (book by book in the series). From their Fifth Avenue mansion in Gotham, they venture to the Lower East Side and Hells Kitchen, then to Palm Beach, Chicago, and the Hudson River Valley before returning to Newport for the 1899 summer season, when the prospect of a delightful seaside summer turns deadly.

Readers' curiosity about characters and places leads me to add this postscript. *Death in a Gilded Frame* reprises the "odd couple" Valentine Mackle DeVere and Roderick Windham DeVere who are based closely on actual historical persons whom I have revealed to live audiences, including book clubs.

Readers of *Death in a Gilded Frame* will find the art connoisseur Joseph Cuveen shadowing the historic Joseph Duveen and Felix Vanderbilt's yacht *Conquest* bearing striking resemblance to Frederick Vanderbilt's *Conqueror*. Characters presented from documented sources include Alva Smith Vanderbilt Belmont (Mrs. Oliver H.P. Belmont), Mamie Fish (Mrs. Stuyvesant Fish), Florence Jaffrey Hurst Harriman (Mrs. J. Borden Harriman, known to friends as Daisy), Elizabeth Drexel Lehr, and Harry Lehr.

The scenes of a ladies' luncheon and a dinner party take place in 1899 Newport in two actual cottages, Belcourt and Crossways, while other locations include the Travers Block, Cliff Walk, the Meunchinger Hotel and cottages. As the DeVeres sojourn to New York City, readers find events occurring in the United Charities Building, the Arnold Constable Department Store, and the Waldorf-Astoria Hotel during a well-documented heat wave.

May you and yours time travel safely into summer, 1899.

Cheers,

Cecelia Tichi

ABOUT THE AUTHOR

Cecelia Tichi is a native of Pittsburgh, the steel city of the Gilded Age, and is an award-winning teacher and author of numerous books focused on American culture and literature. Her most recent titles: *What Would Mrs. Astor Do? The Essential Guide to the Manners and Mores of the Gilded Age* was followed by *Cocktails of the Gilded Age: History, Lore, and Recipes of America's Golden Age* and the sequel, *Jazz Age Cocktails: History, Lore, and Recipes from the Roaring Twenties*. The "Val and Roddy DeVere" mystery series premiers with *A Gilded Death*.

www.ingramcontent.com/pod-product-compliance
Lightning Source LLC
Chambersburg PA
CBHW021338150726
47989CB00005B/2029